A COLOUR OF BLUE

A COLOUR OF BLUE

GREG CARY

Also by Greg Cary

An Absence of Certainty
A Fascinating Investigation

First Published in 2025 by Echo Books

Echo Books is an imprint of Superscript Publishing Pty Ltd,
ABN 76 644 812 395
PO Box 669, Woodend, Victoria, 3442
www.echobooks.com.au

ISBN: 978-1-923441-99-6 (paperback)
ISBN: 978-1-923441-21-7 (ePub)

"Blue is the colour closest to truth"
– Steven Tyler

For Joan and Ian

Fighting injustice can demand a price;
They were prepared to pay it.

Author's Note

This book was written in real-time from July 16 to Christmas Day, 2024.

All commentary on current events was written on the day it occurred.

1

Tuesday, July 16, 2024

Lennox Head

Curiosity is one of the most compelling human qualities and is probably what led Dan Shaw into journalism. He had spent a lot of time asking the eternal questions: who, what, where, how, and ... why. He would often have reason to pose them in the days and weeks ahead.

Shaw owned and edited the *Lennox Chronicle*, the local newspaper serving Lennox Head and Byron Bay in northern N.S.W. He ran it with Shannon Leary, his closest friend and confidante. For complex reasons related to their pasts, the relationship was one that a father and daughter might enjoy, or wish they did.

Their partnership goes back a decade, and their friendship only marginally less. Together and separately, Shannon and Danny have been through a lot – enough to make you curious about all kinds of things. Today, he was curious about Americans.

Shaw was sitting in his Williams St home in Lennox Head sipping coffee and reading reports of the assassination attempt two days earlier on Donald Trump, the former president and current candidate. Shannon was on the way with croissants from The Bakery, and they would then take the twenty-minute drive north to Byron Bay to meet Jim Nicholas.

Along with many millions of his supporters, the intended victim had determined (or his advisers convinced him so) that his survival was the result of divine intervention. Extraordinary lapses by the Secret Service will take some explaining. Even after the bullet whizzed by, nicking Trump's right ear, his head remained stubbornly in sight of the second one that never came. The security detail was hapless to do anything about it, and two couldn't even re-holster their guns.

Trump had turned to the right a fraction of a second before the assassin's bullet arrived, reminiscent of French President Charles De Gaulle lowering his to pin a medal on a soldier in Frederick Forsyth's *The Day of the Jackal*. Perhaps that's where God learned the move.

Shaw's immediate question was why their Deity, who had so quickly reached down to divert the bullet aimed at Trump, did not take the trouble to save the decorated fire-fighter, Corey Comperatore, sitting directly behind the target. That, though, was a philosophical step not many wanted to take.

But, whatever you think of the larger-than-life politician, he was a curious choice for Godly intervention. As much, however, as his opponents seek to define him as unique in character failures, even a modest knowledge of the American political landscape and its moral wasteland would confirm that he was by no means alone.

Believing in God's intervention in our daily lives would also prompt some to wonder why He didn't tap Edward J. Smith on the shoulder as he navigated the *Titanic* too close to an iceberg on April 15, 1912, or warn the passengers on the Hindenburg that sailing was a far better option than flying in a balloon filled with inflammable gases – except, that is, on the *Titanic*.

Yes, curious. Such a good word. The search for knowledge has driven human invention and progress down the ages: the desire to know what's over the horizon, the quest to discover something that you have a hunch exists without the proof that it does.

Of course, the search for answers can lead to unintended consequences, as the legendary cat of cliche fame learned. But was it curiosity that led to its demise, or the poorly considered possibilities of where that curiosity might lead?

Dan Shaw received a report yesterday of a body briefly sighted at the bottom of the cliffs where the Cape Byron Lighthouse stood. He contacted local police, who showed little interest. He then rang another friend, Jim Nicholas, whom they would meet at the lighthouse soon. His journalistic juices were flowing, and questions were forming. So was his curiosity.

He was about to learn why the cat landed in so much trouble.

2

Tuesday, July 16

Cape Byron Lighthouse

J im Nicholas always liked Cat.

'Morning Has Broken', introduced with the sweet piano riff by Rick Wakeman, played softly on his internal soundtrack as the first rays of this day's sunlight rose cautiously over the horizon east of the lighthouse. Dan and Shannon would join him soon, and together they would take a closer look around the area and the rocks below.

Jim remembered music as Dustin Hoffman did aeroplanes in *Rain Man* ("QANTAS never crashed"), and friends often referred to the music that only he could hear as Jim's Jukebox. It played unprompted and led him down many interesting byways, and sometimes did more than that. Last year, it signalled a clue that resolved a murder, so when it played, he listened.

'Morning Has Broken' was one of Cat Stevens' many hits before he converted to Islam and became Yusuf Islam. The lyrics, written as a Christian hymn in 1931, spoke of praising the sunrise and welcoming every new day as a miracle.

Cat's story is fascinating. A much-loved singer/songwriter, Cat/Yusuf created international controversy when he publicly condoned the Iranian Ayatollah's order (fatwa) that author Salman Rushdie should be murdered for what he wrote about the Prophet Mohammed in his book *Satanic Verses*.

At Kingston University in London in 1989, Stevens was asked about the fatwa on Rushdie and replied, 'He must be killed … if someone demeans the Prophet, he must die.' He made similar comments subsequently but later said he was joking. It's doubtful Salman saw the humour. Cat tweeted his sadness when Rushdie was actually stabbed in 2022. Sometimes, you need to be careful what you wish for. In fairness, though, the singer wasn't the only one struggling with Islam.

After the attacks in London in 2005 that killed fifty-two people, Prime Minister Tony Blair launched a twelve-point plan to combat Islamic extremism. The plan went largely unimplemented, as did similar promises by every PM since, including those made by Theresa May in 2015, after an Islamist killed seven on London Bridge, which came shortly after a bomb exploded by an Islamist murdered twenty-two in Manchester Arena. In the last decade, there have been Islamist attacks across Europe in Brussels, Paris, London, Mannheim, Strasbourg, Reading, Nice, Marseille, Vienna, Oslo, Arras and Solingen in Germany.

In 2021, Islamic extremists forced a teacher into hiding after she showed students a caricature of the prophet Muhammad. Islam doesn't tolerate anyone mocking their Prophet, as the cartoonists at the satirical French magazine *Charlie Hebdo* learned in Paris in January, 2015 when eleven of their staff were murdered by angry Muslims. 'Je suis Charlie' became a worldwide statement of solidarity condemning the attack and the ideology that provoked it.

Not the religion itself but the interpretation favoured by zealots. And there are an awful lot of zealots. Violent fundamentalism has no place in societies based on religious and press freedoms, but they are the very freedoms that radical Islam rejects: a dilemma that will play out well into the future. Cat was correct in pointing out that there are tracts of the Bible that also preach harsh punishments, and was fond of quoting Leviticus 24:16, which says, '*Whoever utters the name of the Lord in a curse shall be put to death ... the whole community shall stone that person.'*

To the objective observer, the significant difference is that people around the world weren't currently being killed by Christians, who had long ago sought to reconcile some of the absurdities in their own religion. Others would say they still have a fair way to go.

In the meantime, many radio stations stopped playing Cat's music, and some wanted to burn his albums. They were sadly ignorant of events in Berlin in May, 1933 when the Nazis did the same thing to books. If you're going down that road, we'd be listening to few singers, and the art galleries might soon be empty.

Bruce Springsteen was right: admire the art, not the artist.

*

It was interesting how this beautiful sunrise evoked memories of a particular song, leading Jim to these instant reflections. How far Yusuf had travelled from the innocent Cat days and his breakthrough album *Tea For The Tillerman*, on which one of the tracks, 'On The Road To Find Out', explored his search for meaning. It concluded that *the answer lay within,* so we should *pick up a good book now.*

As much as Jim loved the song, it struck him then – and still does – that this was a massive contradiction. If the answer lies within, and the investigator thought Cat was right about that, then what purpose does a good book serve?

Rushdie would probably agree.

Also true is that if you search long enough, you'll likely find *something,* even if it's not what you want. How many people have been willingly led to disaster by charlatans who profess to have answers to unknowable universal questions? And why the desperate need to know? One of the wisest philosophers once said, '*Life is a journey to be enjoyed, not a mystery to be solved.*'

His name was Winnie The Pooh.

*

Cat says his comments about Rushdie had been distorted, but that's hard to reconcile with what you can hear him say. At other times, he was critical of the Jewish faith, and also saw value in amputation for theft and stoning for adultery – a sure way to thin the ranks of his contemporaries in the entertainment world. How had the folksy balladeer become a strident advocate of religious murder? A religion of peace, no less.

He wasn't alone, of course. There are now 4.5 million Muslims in England (out of a population of 69 million), a quarter of whom wanted Rushdie killed. In England? The home of the Magna Carta, Shakespeare, Churchill and the generation he led that saved Britain from the same fascism the fatwa represented. Somewhere, if you listen closely, you will hear people turning in graves.

Years later, when travelling in the U.S., Cat/Yusuf talked conveniently about the First Amendment and the right to free speech, momentarily putting to one side his religion's practice of killing people for exercising theirs.

Je suis Charlie!

Absolute free speech doesn't exist anywhere – and never has – but it's pretty clear that Cat's 'Peace Train' has travelled a long distance from its original station and, somewhere along the way, had become seriously derailed.

*

The music only Jim could hear worked its usual strange dance. Unprompted, it would regularly play tunes relevant to the occasion – even if he didn't always know why, as was the case in the search for 'Big Ed' Bradley's murderer. Curiously, that turned out to be Dan Shaw.

As the lead detective on that fascinating investigation, Nicholas ultimately decided that sending Shaw to prison would serve no purpose other than to punish a good man and the community he served. So, he lost the evidence.

In truth, he didn't so much lose it – a golf ball with a unique marking – as launch it into the morning sun with a sweetly hit seven-iron off the point at Boulder Beach, a thirty-minute drive to the south of where he now stood. He could just now begin to see the headland faintly in the distance.

Perhaps you will take exception to calling a murderer a good man, but you would do so without knowing the man, his victim and his motivation. It's also true that otherwise decent people have regularly committed murder down the years and been praised for it.

Jim's not a detective anymore – that would've been untenable – but he stayed in touch with Dan (Danny to many), and they have become friends.

These days, Jim Nicholas is studying defamation law and working part-time with Peter Grace, one of the country's leading libel lawyers, who also played a key role in that case. Jim married Alexandra Burns six months ago in a simple ceremony at Noosa Heads. Sunset. Four guests: Dan, Shannon, Peter and his partner Cassie. They walked down the hill afterwards and enjoyed dinner at Sails restaurant. Alexandra (Alex or AB) remains the respected and successful Program Director of the Talk Radio Network (TRN), part of the nation's largest media conglomerate.

Today, Jim is here because Dan rang him yesterday, and he flew up last night. Tourists reported seeing a body on the rocks below, but if there was a body, it's not there anymore.

Now, that really is curious.

3

Tuesday, July 16

Cape Byron Lighthouse

Shannon and Danny joined Jim shortly after eight.

They met next to the lighthouse that stood guard to the most easterly part of the nation's coast and had given guidance and protection to seafarers since 1901. It did the same these days for tourists from around the globe. Perhaps where they come from there are better views, but that's unlikely.

Machu Picchu in Peru would go close, and Kiwis might vote for the Bay of Islands or the walks around Queenstown, but of the places they'd seen (including the grandeur of the Rocky Mountains), this would do.

360 degrees of ocean, beaches, mountains and … the rocks below. A drop of 139 metres, further than that from the Golden Gate Bridge to the waters of San Francisco Bay. There isn't much chance of surviving if you fall (deliberately or otherwise), but sometimes people do. Most regret the attempt.

Talk to Dave, the Visitor Services Assistant here, and, in the laconic way common amongst locals, he'll tell you of the young bloke who drove up Lighthouse Rd a couple of years earlier, parked his car, paid the fee, calmly walked to the fence, climbed it and jumped. He landed on a grassy patch just before the steep drop, broke his leg, and was rescued before he could try again. Let's hope things improved for him, but did you hear that? He paid his parking fee first!

A family of six drove down the hill in the 1960s when there was no rail and went straight over the edge. Three survived.

In those days, Byron Bay was a small town, and the area around the lighthouse a farm. The assistant's cottage – still here next to the information office – is empty now. They tell stories of the phone in the cottage ringing in the middle of the night, even after it was disconnected. Ghosts? Why not? Cynics can always rationalise things that defy easy explanation, but Elbert Hubbard saw it this way: *the supernatural is only the natural that is not yet understood.*

*

There were horse stables here then, and goats roamed the cliffs. Like Peter Bailey, the last lighthouse keeper to live in it, they left in the 80s.

Peter enjoyed a stunning view, as it must've been from the ocean when Lieutenant James Cook sailed past and made anchorage here in 1770. Cook named the Cape after Vice Admiral John Byron, who circumnavigated the world and was the grandfather of Lord Byron. The younger Byron would see a lot of poetry in the place, but not so much the massacre of aboriginals in the 1850s in nearby Suffolk Park to the south, just twenty years after European settlement.

Much has changed. The Mabo decision of 1992 led to Native Title claims for the Bundjalung of Byron Bay – the Arakwal People – over areas of vacant Crown Land that were of great importance to them and in danger of being lost to development and natural impact. Scare campaigns were run during the Mabo debate, but like most scare campaigns, they were largely baseless.

The Prime Minister, Paul Keating, argued the case and convinced a largely sceptical public. Keating was a brave (some said crazy) leader who was kept waiting for many years for the top job as he and his predecessor, Bob Hawke, changed the political and economic landscape of the country. He was one of our best and made the current bunch look like pygmies. They can't find a cause they genuinely believe in, and when they do (as with the proposed Voice to Parliament), they make a total hash of it. Hawke and Keating – and, after them, John Howard – knew that to represent your people, you must first understand them.

More recently, the waters here were bloodied by the whale trade, which began in Byron Bay in July, 1958 and lasted until October, 1962. By then, the number of humpbacks in the southern oceans had decreased to about 5,000. This year, in the space of just two generations, 35,000 will pass by, as four of them are doing now. For all its failures, there remains something wonderful about the human race.

This morning, the whales were secure in the knowledge that the only shots fired were from cameras aimed in their direction. Tourists clapped and cheered, and children looked in awe at the graceful creatures that, not so long ago, had been hunted and killed.

Japan, Norway and Iceland still slaughter them. When challenged, they argue that whale hunting is part of their culture and that whales are no more advanced than cows, which the West has no trouble killing by the millions. There's a degree of logic to that, save for the fact that cows have never been threatened with extinction, and should their farming cease, there would soon be a lot fewer cows. Still, it made you wonder what we might be eating two hundred years from now.

One thing is certain: soon, the only place you'll find harpoons is in a museum.

*

Danny, Shannon and Jim spent a couple of hours discussing what, if anything, might've happened here. They stood where the German visitors, Ursula and Sandra, were standing when they saw what they thought was a body on the rocks below.

They looked around and talked to all who worked here but ultimately came up empty-handed. Jim would linger a little longer to get a sense of possibilities before driving down to Lennox Head, where they would meet for lunch. He was staying, as he did during last year's investigation, at the Lennox Apartments, which adjoined the Hotel and allowed a superb view of the ocean on the other side of the road.

Shannon and Danny drove back to their office in Lennox, where Shaw planned to write a brief story outlining what they had to this point, which was not much. No one had seen a body except for the two tourists who had first rung the police and, after they'd shown no interest, tried the local newspaper. That's where they found Shaw.

It's strange how things work. If Sandra and Ursula had not been at that particular place at that precise time, and had they not made the decision to ring Dan Shaw, and had his journalistic curiosity not kicked in, most of what follows would never have happened.

4

Tuesday, July 16

Lennox Head

This is the brief article Dan Shaw wrote after returning to his office, under the headline:

A DEATH IN BYRON ?

Ursula Bauer rang me at 1:45 p.m. yesterday to report a body she and her sister Sandra say they saw at the base of the cliffs below the Cape Byron Lighthouse.

They are visiting from Nuremberg (or, as they said in German, Nürnberg), an enchanting city in Bavaria that carries the historical burden of being home to the early Hitler rallies. The site at which they were held is now a quiet relic on the edge of the city, but the ideas expressed there resonate still in the dark recesses of the internet and in minds made foggy by hate and antisemitism. Nuremberg also hosts the Court where the worst of the Nazi leaders met justice. There's symmetry in that.

I told Ursula I would see her by the lighthouse at 2:30, which I did. The attractive sisters, in their late 30s, explained that they had taken the lighthouse walk yesterday morning up the steep path from Wategos Beach, carrying only water. No cameras. 'We prefer to see things,' Ursula told me with a winning smile. 'Brain much better camera than phone, ja?' Ja, indeed, but it would've been nice to have evidence of something that only they saw. Which, according to their story, was more than they'd planned on.

The ladies claim to have seen a body when they looked straight down at the rocks at 11:29. They had just checked their watches to ensure they would return to the beach on time for a planned lunch with friends at midday.

They told me, as they pointed, 'We saw down there, the korper ... the, the body.' Their English, save for a few elusive words, was excellent, and the phrasing – as with many for whom English was their second language – just a little awkward, which made it even more charming.

They called the police, who asked if the body was still there. It wasn't. Ursula and Sandra say it was gone when they returned from running to tell others near the lighthouse what they had seen. So, they saw it at 11:29, and it was gone by 11:31 at the latest. That's a small window, but why would they make it all up? They are confident, professional women, and there was nothing to gain.

The constable who answered the phone said police would keep an eye on things, which wouldn't happen. He immediately dismissed it as a prank. There had been a spate of recent robberies, which was his priority. Visitors, after all, must feel safe.

Police in the Northern Rivers have a chequered history with missing bodies. Theo Hayez, Bronwyn Winfield and Marion Barter are just three of the more celebrated cases. Each became famous after their disappearance and presumed deaths, courtesy of quality journalism and podcasts by David Murray (Theo – *The Lighthouse*), Hedley Thomas (Bronwyn) and Alison Sandy (Marion – *The Lady Vanishes*). They all showed more genuine interest, persistence, and creativity in each case than the police.

Bronwyn and Marion were almost certainly murdered, whilst the manner of Theo's death remains a mystery. The young Belgian was last seen approaching the base of the cliffs on the southern side of the headland at Cosy Corner, Tallow Beach.

More than forty years ago, police accepted Chris Dawson's rehearsed line, demonstrably ridiculous even then, that his wife Lynette disappeared of her own volition. Thomas made it look stupid (and worse) in his podcast Teacher's Pet. The mistake was to believe that, until proven otherwise, she simply went missing of her own accord. As a result, crucial evidence and time were lost. That was also true in the Barter and Winfield cases, where police failed to take seriously information that might have led to early arrests.

We will make inquiries and keep you updated on any progress we make. In that endeavour, we will be assisted by former Senior Detective Jim Nicholas, with whom I have enjoyed a productive relationship for some time.

If you have any further information, please contact me at *The Chronicle*.

– Dan Shaw, Editor

*

What Shaw didn't write was that his 'productive' relationship with Jim Nicholas began the previous year when the detective was investigating him for the murder of Ed Bradley, a shock-jock whose words at a vulnerable time in her life led to the death of his daughter Rachel. He did it, of course, and Jim knew he had. The detective also knew that Shaw was happy to pay the price, but decided there should be no price to pay.

Friendships have been built on much less.

5

Wednesday, July 17

Lennox Head

The phone rang as Dan Shaw sat in his Lennox Head office above The Bakery, hoping the story he had written the previous day might elicit a reaction.

"Simon," the voice on the other end said, "it's Mark Taylor."

Mark's greeting was a humorous reference to Shaw's likeness to fellow Lennox Head local, Simon Baker, who'd become an international star in *The Mentalist*. Shaw often wished he possessed the character's intuitive skills but realised that, in real life, you usually need longer than an hour to solve the mystery. Baker remained popular in the area, and they frequently shared a wave and a laugh.

Taylor lived in Brisbane and was recognised as one of the great photographers of his generation, which was about a generation older than Shaw's. He carried his seven decades well, and a smile was never far away. Life for professional photographers changed dramatically – and not for the better – with the introduction of smartphones that could produce quality shots, even if they lacked the artistry and creativity of the pros.

Who could've guessed when his career began that he would outlive film? What else might soon disappear that, for now, we imagine will always be around, or do we understand now that it's all impermanent? Mark still did freelance work, and *The Chronicle* ran his breathtaking photos of the Northern Rivers to the extent the budget allowed.

But money wasn't his priority; it was the work. The creation of something unique and enduring. Robert Frost wrote a few lines that summed it up:

Only where love and need are one, and work is play for mortal stakes,
is the deed ever really done for heaven's and the future's sakes.

Mortal Stakes is the poem, and Robert B. Parker wrote a book by the same name. It's worth reading.

*

"Good to hear from you, mate. What's happening?" Shaw said.

"I read your piece about the disappearing body."

"And?" He had his interest.

"I was in Byron yesterday. Thought I could help."

Mark then explained his presence in the area. A couple of friends, mining engineer Gregor Carr and respected horse trainer Brian Wakefield, were riding their motorbikes down for the day and wanted a record of their adventure.

Mark was an experienced rider and cherished his bikes, particularly BMW's GS/A models, for their manoeuvrability, ease of parking, and comfort on longer trips. He loved it all: the scenery, the wind, the smells, the connection with the road, and the oneness with the machine.

Cue Jack Nicholson, Peter Fonda, and Dennis Hopper in *Easy Rider*, the violent ending of which was a grim reflection on society's occasional ignorance of what the bikes and those who ride them represent. Or, perhaps it wasn't ignorance, but hatred of freedom and those who know how to celebrate it.

*

Mark told Dan something interesting. A few years back in Japan, researchers studied aging with twenty older men who had all ridden motorcycles in their youth but had long ago stopped riding. They were split into two groups. One continued with their daily lives, while the other was reintroduced to their motorbikes. They were given refresher training and then went on weekend rides through the Japanese countryside. They were also encouraged to use their bikes for everyday tasks, like going to the shops.

After three months, they all retook cognitive tests, with the non-riders showing no change. Meanwhile, the riders improved mental function and were generally happier.

It says something important, and not just about riding bikes.

*

Dan was keen to hear more about how Taylor could help.

"Well, I took photos at sunrise ... and more later in the morning," he added teasingly. "Some from the lighthouse and various perspectives to the east, north and south. And others from lower down the road with the focus on the lighthouse and the ocean below."

"OK," Danny said, "but what does that have to do with a body that was either there or wasn't?"

"A good question," Taylor said, "but first, let me ask you a better one. Have you ever heard of The Rule Of Thirds?"

He hadn't, but was about to.

*

"It's one of the elementary rules of artistic composition," Mark began. "Photographers, artists and film directors all use it. You place the main subject matter one-third of the way into the image. That becomes the main focus and then draws the eye to the other two-thirds."

Shaw had no idea where this was headed, but the photographer was warming up, and his friends had learnt down the years that, on such occasions, it was best just to let him talk.

"I had a variety of lenses and cameras and took hundreds of images. When I moved away from the lighthouse, I switched to a 300mm telephoto lens and began taking 'postcard' pictures of the area, using the long lens's compressing effect to change the images' perspective. You keeping up?" he asked with a laugh, knowing full well Shaw was doing his best but still had little idea of the destination.

"Well, last night," he continued, in the manner of the superb storyteller he was, "when I got home to Brisbane, I downloaded the photos onto my MacBook Pro and sorted them using Aperture. I tagged my favourites and rated them with 1, 2 or 3 stars. The ones around midday weren't up to scratch, so I set them aside for another look the next morning. It was the end of a long day, so I had a Corona and went to bed."

"That's it?" Danny asked with just a hint of exasperation.

"Not quite," he replied with some genuine laughter. "I'm getting to the Rule Of Thirds."

*

Taylor then explained why he always shot RAW files with his cameras. He said they contain all the data captured by the camera sensor, resulting in higher image quality. Shaw asked how that worked.

"There's no compression, mate," he answered, obviously keen to share some of the lessons of his lifetime's passion. "So you retain all the details. RAW files provide greater flexibility in post-processing."

Shaw didn't understand all these details, but his hunch was that they were leading to something interesting. So, after another signal that he was keeping up, Taylor continued.

"You can adjust exposure, white balance, contrast and other settings with minimal loss of quality. RAW files also have a wider dynamic range, meaning they can capture much more detail in the shadows compared to JPEG files that amateurs use. The image data is captured straight from the camera's sensor. No in-camera processing, so none of the image data is lost."

The journalist was doing some processing of his own, but the significance of what he hoped Mark was saying just hit him.

"In the shadows?" he asked speculatively, instantly thinking of the German tourists, Ursula and Sandra.

"So you have been keeping up," Taylor said, slightly surprised.

Dan could picture him smiling at the other end as he went on. "I was doing a final edit on the images in my workroom and decided to have one more look at the shots I took with the telephoto lens. I always do a final check before I delete them. Something caught my eye when I looked at the extended shadow detail in the two-thirds of the shot."

Shaw waited, patience dwindling and controlled excitement taking its place. "What did you find?"

"Lying between the rocks, way below the lighthouse in the part of the picture that I had in shadow, was a body."

Thoughts were swirling, but he managed, "That's incredible."

"It is Danny, although it's happened to me before and occurs in all our lives – the Rule Of Thirds. While we're focusing on the object of our attention, all manner of things can be happening in the background. They've done a lot of research on it. I'll send you a JPEG. Wanna know something else?"

He said nothing, knowing that Mark would quickly replace the silence.

"Blowing it up even more, I could see it was a man."

As a movie buff, Shaw thought briefly of *Blow Up*, directed by Michelangelo Antonioni. The main character, based on the famed 1960s photographer David Bailey, accidentally captured a murder.

There was one thing Shaw needed to confirm. "Can you tell me exactly when you took that shot?"

"I can," he replied, "let me just check." After a brief pause, as he looked at the metadata, he responded, "It was at exactly 11:29 and 45 seconds."

"Wanna know something else?" Taylor asked, enjoying himself. "He was wearing a clerical collar."

A priest's body on the rocks beneath the Cape Byron Lighthouse? A hundred questions started to form, all pointing to a story the *Lennox Chronicle* would be happy to pursue before Mark again interrupted Shaw's quiet musings.

"Oh," he said, "just one more thing. There was blood on his cheek that looked to have come from a small hole from where it flowed. The priest had been shot in the left temple."

"Didn't have a prayer."

Mark put a full stop to his discovery with a simple, "Amen."

6

Wednesday, July 17

Lennox Head

Dan called Jim to share what the photographer had said, and they agreed to meet near the surf club in an hour. Shaw sounded confident that the tourists were credible, and Taylor's photo – and the time he took it – seemed to confirm their story.

The JPEG proof should arrive in his inbox by the time he returned, and then they would know more. As they walked along the winter seashore, heading north from Lennox Head towards Byron Bay, Jim told Danny that he could give him as much time as he needed, not knowing when he said it that it would be longer than planned. Shaw appreciated it.

If Taylor's photo supported the tourists' sighting, Nicholas would begin by checking missing persons. Jim's former partner, Detective Cassandra (Cassie) Miller, had relocated to Sydney, where her relationship with Peter Grace was going the way of her career. Forward. There would be much she wouldn't tell him, but some she could. Cassie knew he wouldn't abuse those limits or her trust.

Last year, she was Jim's junior partner in the investigation that brought them to Lennox Head and Dan Shaw. Jim kept her at arm's length from his decision not to pursue Shaw. She knew what he had done, though, and he respected that she allowed him to do as he did. Nicholas would not have done it if he thought it would end what was going to be a sparkling career. She also knew it would be his last decision as a police officer.

If the photograph was decent enough to be published, that would save time, although a few practical and ethical decisions also needed to be made. Finding missing bodies can be challenging, and sometimes, they don't want to be found at all.

*

Police can often be hampered by investigative inertia, but we can cut them some slack regarding missing persons. In Australia, they receive more than 38,000 reports each year. Most turn up within a short period, but approximately 2,600 have been missing for more than three months at any given time. The vast majority disappear deliberately either to escape problems or start a new life.

It's a fascinating scenario, and many have explored it at one point or another – not necessarily to do it, but to think about what it would be like to begin afresh. The accumulated burden, the layers of life, suddenly lifted with a new name and environment. Would things work out differently? Not always.

What was known in this case is that the body Ursula and Sandra saw, and that Mark Taylor accidentally photographed, was in good shape (save for the possible bullet wound to the temple), which meant it went into the water recently. The questions remain: where and, more importantly, why?

It was a reasonable assumption that one answer might lead to the other.

*

Any photographic evidence would be a massive boost because the prospects were high that the body would never be seen again. This was true of most who went missing at sea. The currents are stronger than people think, and a body that enters the water in one place will quickly be far away.

Take the serial fraudster, Ponzi scheme operator Melissa Caddick. She vanished the day after ASIC agents and Australian Federal Police officers raided her home in affluent Dover Heights in Sydney, believing she had misappropriated nearly $30 million from investors, including family and friends. She was seen on November 12, 2020, near the cliffs not far from her residence.

Three months later, a shoe carrying a decomposed foot was discovered washed up on Bournda Beach, on the south coast of NSW. That's 500 kilometres from where she was last seen. DNA tests confirmed it was her foot, and the timing matched the tidal and drift patterns modelled by the Marine Police.

It surprised Nicholas at the time that investigators were puzzled by how her foot had become separated from her leg. Sharks were considered a possibility, but they should research the work of Gail Anderson, a forensic entomologist at Simon Frazer University in Canada.

Anderson dropped pigs into the water at different oxygen and temperature levels and chronicled what attacked their bodies at various times. Bigger creatures pierced the skin first, and then lobsters and crabs made a home – nature at work.

Her conclusions helped solve mysteries such as the 'floating feet' found wearing running shoes that were washing up along the West Coast of Canada and the U.S. in recent years. 'In fact,' she says, 'it's normal for ocean scavengers to gnaw off feet, and the running shoes simply make the body parts float.'

By now, Melissa's footless body would have long passed Tasmania on an icy ride south.

Her victims would be shedding few tears, and she won't be needing either the shoe or the foot on which it once comfortably sat any time soon.

7

Wednesday, July 17

Lennox Head

The JPEG Taylor promised to send was there when Shaw returned to the office. It confirmed what the German tourists reported seeing and what he'd accidentally photographed, although there didn't look to be much accidental about the wound to the left side of the priest's head.

There was much to consider, and the order to proceed was important.

A check of missing persons would confirm whether the body was indeed a priest, and not somebody dressed as one. An odd choice, if true, in light of the countless allegations against churchmen.

Jim would also contact Cassie Miller. Dan didn't know her well but was impressed with how she'd conducted herself last year in the investigation into … .him. She was bright, pleasant and understated. That her secret passion was the TV show about well-intentioned serial killer *Dexter* came as a bonus.

Shaw and Shannon would discuss the best way forward for *The Chronicle*. She was his best friend, partner in the business, and much-loved member of the Lennox community. When the swell was big, her surfing exploits created as much interest as her book reviews, one of the paper's most anticipated features.

The photo raised several questions: Should they publish it, and if so, in what context? They would also need Taylor's permission, which he was not guaranteed to give. He was no friend of the police and had little interest in whether the case was solved, or not.

Even if he agreed, they couldn't publish it before trying to identify who he was. To do otherwise would be grossly unfair to those close to him, and there were practical issues as well. Publishing photos in newspapers comes with unique challenges: when using a printing machine like a Heidelberg offset printer, ink is applied to paper, but the 'dot' of ink tends to spread.

The extent of the spread depends mainly on the quality of the paper. In an art book, for instance, the pages are coated to prevent excessive spreading, thus preserving fine details. Newspapers, however, are printed on cheaper paper, where the ink tends to spread. As a result, shadow details can become obscured on newsprint, making them difficult to see. And in this case, the shadows were important.

Also true is that, whilst Shaw had a photo of a body with what looked like a bullet wound to the head, that didn't necessarily make it so. Absent the body itself, proving murder was going to be difficult, and identifying the murderer harder still. But that wasn't *The Chronicle*'s job. The paper's role was to cover the investigation, make inquiries, and report on those.

Initially, they had to learn more about the victim, which meant finding out who he was. Police would no doubt be doing the same, but what they did was not Shaw's priority. There was a newspaper to run and a community to serve. More than that, he felt a responsibility to the two German tourists, Ursula and Sandra, without whom the priest's presumed demise might have remained an enduring mystery.

There are some who would later wish that had been the case.

*

Jim's mentor Bruce Mac, a former Assistant Police Commissioner in Queensland who now lives on Bribie Island just north of Brisbane, instilled in him the notion that momentum creates momentum – kinetic energy – and had put it like this:

'Clarity isn't some mystical revelation that strikes you out of nowhere. It's a byproduct of taking action; when you move forward, your subconscious mind starts unravelling the puzzle, connecting the dots, and bringing ideas to the surface. Action fuels clarity.'

Clarity, at this time of initial confusion, sounded like an excellent idea.

8

Thursday, July 18

Lennox Head

J im Nicholas provided some the following day. Responding to Shaw's questions, the former senior detective confirmed that a body typically floats to the surface after three or four days, which would then expose it to more than sharks, lobsters and crabs. Waves would inflict damage, and sea birds would sense a smorgasbord.

Jim went further. "Given that the body in the photo was recognisable and the prevailing current strong," he told Danny, "it's safe to assume it entered the water in the last week at the latest and travelled, at most, 200 kilometres."

That helped narrow it a bit. With Brisbane 164 kilometres to the north of Byron Bay and Grafton 163 km to the south, it was information enough for the next article he would write for The *Lennox Chronicle*. First, there was breakfast with Shannon.

*

She enjoyed her daily ritual at the delightful Williams St Cafe (avocado on toast for a change). The creative process – and where artists and writers draw their inspiration – is a mysterious business. You can visit Monet's extraordinary garden in search of answers or walk through the unremarkable rooms where Dickens or Hemingway wrote, but they will tell you nothing. Except for one thing: they felt comfortable there. At a time when both the nature and pace of change were faster than ever, providing a place where the world stands still is no small thing.

This place did it for Shannon Leary, a natural beauty who rejected makeup and still caused some passing by to think they were looking at her closest friend from high school, Margot Robbie. Part of her charm was that she would never describe herself or judge others in those terms. Dressed comfortably in fawn baggy shorts and a loose-fitting dark blue Quicksilver T-shirt, over which her sun-bleached hair flowed messily, she was prepared less for red carpets and more for the vast, blue ocean in which she spent as much time as possible.

Set across the road from Seven Mile Beach on the corner of Williams St and Pacific Parade, the café's atmosphere was casual. The benches and tables were wooden, and the staff the opposite – relaxed and friendly. People won't line up here as they do to visit the haunts of Ernest and Charles, but it's doubtful those legends would have liked the idea anyway.

It was a two-minute walk from Danny's house, and he would arrive soon. At his recommendation, Shannon had been reading John D. MacDonald, intending to write a review of his work – specifically his series based on private detective Travis McGee – in an upcoming edition of *The Chronicle*.

Shaw was confident she would one day write good books. To that end, he wanted her to read great authors, including Richard Ford and James Lee Burke. It says something about the publishing industry and the dependence authors have on them that Burke's first book – *The Lost Get Back Boogie* – was rejected one hundred and eleven times before a smaller independent picked it up. It was nominated for a Pulitzer Prize and launched the career of one of the best. How is it possible that so many whose job it was couldn't recognise his transcendent talent? J.K. Rowling's *Harry Potter* was turned down at least a dozen times, and it would be good to know how those publishers feel as sales of *Harry* edge towards 700 million.

*

Happily, Shannon's reviews were welcomed by a growing audience, to the extent that she is often invited to interview visiting authors at The Book Room, an integral member of the village. She'd finished her piece just a few minutes ago, between her habitual first and second coffees (very hot, regardless of the time of year):

It might be that you've never heard of John D. MacDonald, and if you like crime fiction, that would be a pity.

His character, Travis McGee, is the spiritual godfather of Harry Bosch, Jesse Stone, Jack Reacher, Spenser and every other knight errant fighting the good fight against the worst of human behaviour. MacDonald, in turn, acknowledges his debt to Raymond Chandler and Dashiell Hammett.

The content easily crosses narrow borders of time and place. He's the favourite writer of Dean Koontz and many others, including Carl Hiaasen, whose humorous and insightful takes on environmental vandalism in Florida pay homage to MacDonald, who was doing the same fifty years ago.

The author regularly goes 'off script' for a meditation on (then) modern life, with much of the social commentary increasingly relevant. An example: In 'The Lonely Silver Rain', he discusses the negative impact of television, which was relatively new at the time, and worries about where it might lead society. He was ahead of Paddy Chayefsky's prescient Network, *but he surely could not have imagined the narcissism that is now such a prominent and corrosive part of mainstream entertainment. The same debate now focuses on social media.*

Some of MacDonald's attitudes are criticised for being out of date, but he wrote, as all writers do, in his time, and it's enlightening (and amusing) to see how things have changed – often for the better, but not always. There is no need to tear down statues; it's better to understand why they exist.

There is way too much of this retrospective moralising. Whose statue will be next to fall? And what, I wonder, are the sins we are blithely committing that will earn the censure of wiser future generations? No doubt there are many.

Like some unexpected artefact on an archaeological dig, the discovery of authors often forgotten – or consigned to another time – is a reminder of what was, and the impact they had on what is.

It's no small irony that the plaque the local council created where McGee moored his fictional boat in Fort Lauderdale, Florida, was removed so that two large towers could be built on the marina. John D. MacDonald might've laughed, but Travis McGee would've hunted down the despoilers and done them severe damage.

Both Dan Shaw and Jim Nicholas had much in common with Travis McGee.

9

Friday, July 19

Lennox Head

The *Lennox Chronicle* came out every Saturday, enough to keep Danny, Shannon, and a couple of part-time contributors busy. On Friday morning, just four days after the presumed sighting, Shaw wrote an editorial that he hoped would have a wider reach than his immediate market. That happens often.

City newspapers keep an eye on breaking stories in smaller markets and often take 'ownership' of them. Shaw had been around long enough to recognise there were sometimes advantages to the arrangement. This is some of what was printed in the Saturday morning edition:

'Earlier this week, I reported that a body believed to be dressed in clerical clothing was sighted by visiting German tourists on the rocks below the Cape Byron Lighthouse. Initial investigations by The Chronicle *tend to support their claims, and we have begun inquiries into his identity. We will now check all Missing Persons lists, confining our search area to communities between Brisbane and Grafton.'*

Danny made no mention of how they knew any of this. Instead, he was keen to get the ball rolling. Lee Child used to start each Jack Reacher story with a blank sheet of paper and a single sentence, after which the action would then unfold. Six months later, he'd put the final full stop. As of now, six months looked a long way off; Christmas was in five.

*

Danny's wish for broader coverage was granted on the Saturday afternoon when the Editor of the *Sunday Telegraph*, Lorraine Dylan, rang to let him know she'd read his editorial and that her paper, which boasted the nation's highest circulation, would be devoting a few paragraphs to the story the next day. After pausing briefly, she asked if he would care to write them.

"I'd love to," Danny replied in a nanosecond, hardly containing his genuine excitement to be back on the pages where his byline was a guarantee of a story worth reading and in which he had – under a series of pseudonyms (he was, after all, a murderer) – orchestrated a public discussion on the nature and ethics of revenge and free-speech the previous year.

A body that might well be that of a missing priest at one of the country's most famous landmarks was compelling fare for a weekend audience keen to break the shackles of the daily media staples. And surely a priest would be missed on Sunday?

Shaw and Dylan met years earlier as young journalists making their way in a competitive and exciting trade. Both had seen and experienced the massive upheavals in the business they loved, and while there was a place for mourning what used to be, if you spent too much time doing that, you'd soon be reading the paper instead of writing it.

During Dan's glory years as the *Tele*'s ace crime reporter, Lorraine was breaking stories in Canberra as the head of their political division. They stayed in touch and spoke regularly, sometimes sharing stories and often just laughing at the odd turns their careers had taken.

Lorraine knew nothing of the previous year's events but would probably have laughed even harder if she had.

10

Sunday, July 21

St Vincent's Parish, The Gap

A t 8:30 a.m. in the small sacristy of the church where he had spent the last twenty-five years of his life, Father Ralph was reading the *Sunday Mail*, the weekend edition of Brisbane's only daily newspaper and stablemate of Sydney's *Telegraph*. News Ltd owned both and increasingly shared stories. There were many reasons for that, some financial and others just common sense.

The newspaper industry, like all traditional media, was under pressure. Most of the revenue streams of previous decades were gone, as was a loyal readership that once accessed its news mostly from daily newspapers. With evolving technologies, news was now available twenty-four hours a day and was often known to people long before the paperboy arrived each morning.

There's not much use yelling *read all about it* when you already had. Except the paperboy, who used to make his rounds in the morning and afternoon, was also virtually extinct. These days, you took your chances that the paper – now wrapped in annoying plastic wrap and thrown by a driver in a hurry – would land somewhere in the vicinity of your house. A rare occurrence.

The need to reduce costs meant staff cuts, and journalists weren't immune. Indeed, their ranks had been savaged. As a result, media organisations were increasingly networking their talent. Opinion writers, for example, can easily fashion content that appeals to people in various places; likewise sports specialists, who were often the best writers on the paper. Sadly, many of the great ones

– Patrick Smith, Mike Colman and, long ago, Mike Gibson – are gone now.

*

Father Ralph was the popular and respected priest at St Vincent's in The Gap, a leafy, middle-class suburb in Brisbane's west. His congregation comprised a mixed demographic, and nothing delighted him more than to sometimes see three generations of the same family in attendance on Sunday mornings. Nothing, that is, except the occasional par he would make when playing his beloved golf at nearby Keperra or Ashgrove, where he would endeavour not to be heard uttering too many profanities.

He wasn't a great player, but you didn't need to be to enjoy the game. Every round was a fresh challenge, and amidst the regular disasters, there were occasional jewels, and redemption was always close at hand. Not unlike the religion that had been part of his life since he attended Sunday School at age six. That was sixty-four years ago. Like anyone fortunate enough to compile three score years and ten, he gave thanks daily and wondered at how those years disappeared. Willie Nelson had it right: *ain't it funny how time slips away.*

Religion, he knew, confronted numerous challenges (many self-inflicted), and one of his was to ensure he made their weekly visits worthwhile. The service would begin at ten precisely, but as was his habit, he was relaxing with a cup of tea, giving thought to any changes in his planned homily.

He always read the tabloids to ensure he stayed current and could relate to the younger attendees. After all, his message was timeless and transcended age, trends and eras. That was the central dilemma confronting all faiths. Earlier in the week, he'd read of a footballer *forgiven* by his club after yet another transgression. That would be his theme, and he would talk to his assistant, Father Jack, about it when he arrived.

At 8:45, he was pursuing that thought when he saw the brief story in the paper about a priest presumed to be missing. He didn't think too much about it and, after finishing his tea, went about the ritual of his preparation; it was something he enjoyed and celebrated.

At 9:25, he went outside to chat informally with parishioners as they arrived. Father Jack would be here soon to join him and help prepare for the post-service tea and biscuits. In fact, he should've been there by now. His assistant usually arrived reliably before 9:15 and had done so for many years. Father Ralph spoke amiably and with genuine interest to the congregants about myriad subjects – from politics to music and books – but when his phone alarm signalled it was 9:57, he excused himself to go inside, don his vestments and begin the service.

One question bothered him: Where was Father Jack?

*

At 10:14 Father Ralph began his sermon on the importance of forgiveness. He included plenty of biblical quotes and real-life anecdotes to support his argument, and most in the congregation went away inspired to turn the other cheek and forgive those who had caused them grief. Short of stature, he was long on wisdom. But when the whole story about the missing priest was known some months later, Father Ralph's choice of this particular subject on this day would have been considered a remarkable coincidence – if you believe in coincidence, that is.

Sitting in a pew near the back of the church was a woman in her mid-60s of medium height and above-average looks. Her hair, which she wore loose and didn't quite reach her shoulders, was grey and her eyes a colour of blue you might see on the Barrier Reef.

Her name was Katherine and she didn't agree with a word Father Ralph said. In her younger years she had been a very beautiful woman – and still was. The French anthropologist Claude Levi Strauss said that age *removes the confusion, possible only in youth, between physical and moral beauty.*

Katherine possessed both, but a sense of sadness in her peaceful demeanour suggested that life had not always been as kind as the priest to whom she now listened. Father Ralph completed his homily by apologising for Father Jack's absence and explained that he had another, unavoidable, commitment.

Katherine smiled and forgave him that small lie.

11

Sunday, July 21

St Vincent's, The Gap

By 5 p.m. that same day, Father Ralph was beginning to get worried. Nothing had been heard of Father Jack since the night before, when he'd watched the Rugby League with his sister, Anna. He left in a positive frame of mind after successfully backing the Broncos, who beat Newcastle convincingly. It was known that he enjoyed a small bet.

His mobile went unanswered, and his car wasn't outside his small apartment in Lang Parade, Auchenflower. A fifteen-minute drive from The Gap, the inner-city suburb was next door to Milton and only a short walk from Suncorp Stadium. Veterans still called it Lang Park, the spiritual home of the game in Queensland and the site of many of their famous victories. A statue of Wally Lewis greets fans these days, but not many years before, "The King" thrilled packed houses with his unique genius.

Father Ralph called the Wesley Hospital, just three minutes from Merryfield's unit. Situated on Coronation Drive, the primary gateway to the City along the Brisbane River, it's where he would've been taken in case of an emergency. But Father Jack wasn't there, or at any of the other hospitals. That was good news on one level, but the story in the morning paper about a missing priest was now sending alarm signals.

At 8 p.m., having still heard nothing, Father Ralph picked up the paper and saw, under the story, a contact for its author. Journalists giving their email addresses was a recent innovation. Potential contacts were everywhere, the thinking went, so why make it hard for them to get in touch? Which is precisely what Father Ralph did. He opened his iPad and sent a brief note to:

DanShaw@gmail.com

*

At 8:04 Dan again checked his inbox for feedback on his story. He'd received a few letters, but most just wanted to say g'day and seemed unlikely to lead anywhere.

He was sitting with Shannon in his Williams St home at Lennox Head.

They'd enjoyed a takeaway seafood dinner from the consistently excellent Fishy Fishy in the village and were now planning stories for next Saturday's edition of *The Chronicle*. Shannon's book review would get a run, as would her continuing series on the various methods they were trialling to mitigate the shark menace ahead of the upcoming summer, including the use of drones.

None of them were a match for those creating havoc in Ukraine, but they might advance the cause of protecting local surfers. Their range was limited, and Danny remained unconvinced, but Shannon was coming around.

"This might be interesting," he said, reading the email that awaited him. Shannon looked his way, feet tucked underneath her on his couch.

"Dear Mr Shaw," it began (he hadn't been called that in a while), "I'm the priest in residence at St Vincent's Catholic Church in The Gap, Brisbane. My assistant, Father Jack Merryfield, didn't turn up for this morning's service. That is extremely out of character for him. In fact, nobody has heard from him since last night. I am undoubtedly premature in contacting you, but your story disturbed me. Could you please give me a ring in the morning?" He then provided the number and wished Dan a good night.

"Father Jack Merryfield," Shannon said. "It might be that the body now has a name."

Danny's journalistic antenna was spinning. "It just might," he said.

He went to bed, looking forward to the new day and the possibilities it would bring – as he did every night.

12

Monday, July 22

Lennox Head

The sun rose at 6:51, but Danny beat it by over an hour. After a 45-minute walk on the beach, during which he gave thought to his meeting with Father Ralph, he made himself a breakfast of steak and eggs and was sipping his second coffee (strong, no milk) whilst browsing *The Telegraph* for any sign of a follow-up to the previous day's story. He would talk with the editor, Lorraine Dylan, later, but before that he needed to call St Vincent's. Father Ralph answered after one ring, suggesting he was also up early awaiting the call.

Shaw liked the priest immediately and could hear the empathy and concern in his voice. Their conversation was off the record for now, which meant Shaw couldn't use any of what they would say to each other in any article. That would quickly change when Father Ralph noted the journalist's manner and professionalism. Instead, he asked only that the information be on background and that nothing be attributed to him. Yet.

The journalist was happy to oblige. He didn't need quotes about the missing priest, just a sense of who he was. Which, to the extent he could, Father Ralph was happy to provide.

Interestingly, as he spoke, Father Ralph began to realise how limited, beyond the superficial, his knowledge was of the man he had worked alongside for the last fifteen years. Perhaps that is true for most of us. They were never friends – their differences and interests being far too incompatible for that – but they'd been a good team, or so he thought. What, then, *did* he know about Father Jack Merryfield?

He knew he was seventy-five and enjoyed music, including many of the folk and rock acts of his teenage years. He knew he spent much time with his only sibling, his sister Anna, and took regular walks around Mt Coot-tha, Brisbane's highest spot and home to its television stations. At 6.31 kilometres from start to finish, it kept him fitter than most.

He was neither short nor tall, fat nor thin, handsome or not. His looks were such that he would always be the character actor rather than the star. The type who could camouflage himself in any scene and shop in happy anonymity at the supermarket on the weekend. The only distinguishing feature was a small mole on the left side of his chin, which added to – rather than detracted from – his appearance.

As a young man, he attempted, with only minimal success, to style himself like singer/songwriter James Taylor, whilst in his later years, he occasionally looked worryingly like the architect of the Holocaust, Adolf Eichmann. Although, without his uniform and borrowed authority, most would've thought even Eichmann just a disgruntled second-tier public servant. A character actor, never the star. The passing years and how we spend them make their mark.

Father Jack liked sports, mainly cricket and horse racing, in which he'd had a long interest and was known to have the occasional small bet. He knew the Bible well enough to get by, but there was no obvious evidence of biblical scholarship or even curiosity. He was a priest and knew what a priest must know, and that seemed to be the limit of his knowledge and interest. This man came with a somewhat clouded past, performed his duties, and was liked well enough by the congregation. Beyond that, Father Ralph knew little, but that was enough if he was honest (and he tried to be).

Merryfield was transferred to Brisbane after some unpleasant allegations concerning a teenage girl at his previous parish. That was not unusual in the Church at the time (although problems with young boys were far more common), and Father Ralph was encouraged to give him another chance.

'Encouraged' was a euphemism, for *you have no choice in the matter*. If a Cardinal could be seen walking to court with the worst of pedophiles, as George Pell did for Gerald Ridsdale ('to support him'), and if a Pope could employ serial molesters like Theodore McCarrick, then who was he to do differently? Ridsdale is believed by police to have abused more than five hundred children, but given the notorious under-reporting of abuse, that number could be well in excess of a thousand. Pell and Ridsdale lived together for a time in the 70s, and the Royal Commission found Pell knew about his offending, something the late Cardinal denied.

Two Bishops of Ballarat – Mulkearns and O'Collins – also knew but did nothing.

John Paul 2, a Saint, refused to believe the allegations against McCarrick, the corollary of which was that he refused to believe the accusers. The second John Paul appointed McCarrick as Archbishop of Washington despite receiving detailed allegations of his previous behaviour from the Cardinal of New York. Amongst other things, McCarrick was accused of soliciting sex from minors *during* confession.

The Spectator newspaper in the U.K. covered McCarrick – and the Church's response to him – closely. 'Many bishops and two popes,' they wrote, 'were warned about McCarrick, though the Vatican has kept all the most sensitive details secret. We know that in 2016, America's foremost authority on clerical sex abuse, the late Richard Sipe, wrote to Bishop Robert McElroy of San Diego, with whom he had previously discussed the matter, telling him that he had interviewed twelve seminarians and priests who attest to propositions, harassment or sex with McCarrick. Bishop McElroy chose to disbelieve Sipe and said he was not to be trusted.'

So, what happened? The Pope made both McCarrick and McElroy cardinals. You can't make it up.

*

Father Ralph avoided details of the claims against Merryfield and tried to remain focused on his flock. He agreed with one of his favourite writers, Morris West, who said it was best to *tend your own garden*. And Father Ralph's had flourished.

The Church's garden, meantime, was seriously overgrown with metaphorical weeds that should've been culled long ago. Any farmer will tell you this: if you leave the lantana long enough, it will trap everyone and everything. Churches of all persuasions had long placed reputation and survival above decency, justice, and, yes, Christianity. They continue to pay a considerable price in every way, although their victims pay a bigger one. But like Pope John Paul 1, whom Father Ralph so admired, he was content to do good where he could and provide pastoral, moral and spiritual guidance to those seeking it.

The first John Paul, Albino Luciani, was also a kind and gentle man. Danny once read a book titled In God's Name and interviewed its author, David Yallop, who contended that Luciani's death after only thirty-three days in office might not have been as natural as the official version suggested.

Yallop thought the new pope was murdered because of his stated intention to clean up the Vatican Bank, which was doing serious business with the mafia, as well as the corrupt, breakaway freemason group P2 that was doing its best to take over Italy. The head of the bank was an American Archbishop, Paul Marcinkus.

Not many of those who had been paying attention to the Vatican's recent decades of lies and cover-up would be surprised if a pope was, in fact, murdered. And, if a Pope, why not a humble priest?

*

Father Ralph promised to send a photo in the next few minutes, after which Danny thanked the priest for his time and promised to stay in touch. He then went straight to his file and the expanded, more defined photo of the body taken by photographer Mark Taylor. A few minutes later, he laid it alongside the one sent by the priest.

Although not in perfect focus, and with the length of the body difficult to accurately assess as it lay on the rocks below the Cape Byron Lighthouse, it was easy enough to compare Father Ralph's photo (which reflected the description he'd given) with what he was now observing in more detail:

A man who is neither short nor tall, fat nor thin, handsome or not. His looks were such that he would always be the character actor rather than the star. The type who could camouflage himself in any scene and shop in happy anonymity at the supermarket on the weekend. The newish hole in his left temple did him no favours. A closer inspection would also detect a small mole on his chin that added to – rather than detracted from – his appearance. Historians might notice more than a passing resemblance to Adolf Eichmann, the architect of the Holocaust.

Father Jack, a man who prized his looks and fitness, would no doubt be unimpressed with the comparison.

13

Monday, July 22

TRN Sydney

Jim Nicholas was up in time to take the earliest available Virgin flight from Coolangatta to Sydney. The headwinds were strong, and the flight, at one hour and twenty-three minutes, was longer than usual.

Which he appreciated, because chance saw him seated next to Queensland's most decorated detective, John 'Bluey' O'Gorman. Bluey's legend straddled both sides of the border, and his deeds were spoken of with immense respect. Nicholas was usually happy to pass the time with a book or his music, but opportunities like this weren't to be ignored, so he introduced himself and the two swapped stories for the duration of the flight.

Whilst O'Gorman's reputation spun on acts of daring and heroism, he took most pride in defending the majority of decent coppers during the Fitzgerald Inquiry into corruption and, later, in organising the farewells of colleagues slain in the line of duty – something he did for the last fifteen years of his career.

One of them involved the funeral of much loved Senior Sergeant Perry Irwin from Caboolture Police Station, who was murdered by a twenty-one-year-old drug addict in August 2003. Make sense of that if you can. There were nearly 3,500 police in the guard of honour at the church on Anzac Avenue, Rothwell, near Redcliffe. Those there will never forget it, nor the man they came to honour.

After landing, Jim wished Bluey well, grabbed his overnight bag, and headed for the long-term car park. On the way, he turned on his phone just in time to receive a call from Danny, who sounded excited. *The Chronicle*'s editor outlined the conversation with Father Ralph and his comparison of the photos so that Jim could quickly share his excitement.

"When are you back?" Danny asked.

"Tomorrow," he replied, "First, I have to visit my wife." The former detective liked the sound of those words, *my wife.*

Alex virtually launched herself from her chair as *her husband* (she liked those words, too) made an unplanned and unexpected visit to her office 45 minutes later. Not long ago, the trip from Mascot to the city centre would've taken twenty minutes tops. She was expecting him on the weekend, but from Jim's perspective, she didn't seem to mind the change of plans. In fact, after locking the door, they kissed for several minutes. Soon, they did more than that.

Hey, they hadn't seen each other for a week!

*

Afterwards, as they sat quietly (and far more chastely) on the couch in her office, Jim began updating her on the investigation. As was usually the case when she was working on radio strategy – and occasionally doing other things – music was playing from the speaker above her desk. Although she was the Program Director of TRN, the nation's largest and most dominant Talk network, the music from their sister station made for easier concentration. Right now, it was Hall and Oates singing 'Rich Girl', a great song that played regularly on Jim's Jukebox, his internal soundtrack.

Released in 1977, it hit number one in the U.S. and reached as high as six in Australia. Although brief at only two minutes and 23 seconds, it was still 46 seconds longer than the shortest song to reach number one, Maurice White and the Zodiacs' 'Stay' at 1:37. The Beatles' 'From Me To You' clocked in at 1:56, a long way from their 'Hey Jude' at 7:11.

In the meantime, the Fab Four's legacy endures and grows. They were a unique band made great because of the synergy of the distinct personalities and extraordinary talent of the individuals who comprised it. It was their differences that made them so formidable. For a long time, Jim thought Paul McCartney was seriously underestimated – in all ways. He'd heard a story years back.

When John Lennon left his wife, Cynthia, in 1966 after falling in love with Yoko Ono, he knew Cynthia would have to raise their son, Julian, then just five years old. He later regretted that he gave her only a small allowance to do it, as he did much else. That brings him credit.

After a few years, Cynthia was just about broke and decided to sell the love letters and drawings John had given her when they were teenagers in love. She is said to have been heartbroken to part with these keepsakes, but desperation breeds this kind of thing. The buyer of the memorabilia? Paul McCartney, who paid a considerable amount to keep other bidders at bay.

A few days later, Cynthia received all the letters and drawings back in the mail. They were neatly framed and came with a note:

Never sell your memories. Love, Paul McCartney
Classy.

*

It is somewhat baffling why Jim remembered all this, but occasionally, it helped. He pays attention to hunches, instincts, and intuition.

His internal jukebox played music from all eras. Most people revisit the songs they listened to in their formative teenage years: a reminder and time machine to places, smells, and experiences. He did that, too, but he also listened to many of the songs his father loved from the Vietnam era and after. His dad served and lost friends in that war and was never the same after it, just like most who were sent on that fruitless and thankless mission. The music they shared was a generational link and a quiet tribute.

*

One of the reasons 'Rich Girl' resonates is that it was initially thought to be about the kidnapped newspaper heiress Patricia Hearst, a case Jim studied closely for his detective exams as it related to coercive control and Stockholm syndrome. Daryl Hall later said it was about a former boyfriend of his then-girlfriend, but thought 'Rich *Boy*' would never have worked. He's probably right. Besides, the Hearst story is much better.

Patty was seized from her apartment on February 4, 1974, by a group of militant terrorists calling themselves the Symbionese Liberation Army. She was held hostage, kept for weeks in a cupboard and raped by the group's leader. Brainwashed, she eventually took part in a bank robbery carrying a machine gun before being captured and sentenced to seven years imprisonment.

It was a highly controversial case, with her defence based on the premise that were it not for being kidnapped, she would never have even contemplated robbing a bank or carrying a machine gun. It speaks to how circumstance and environment shape us all and how everything goes out the window when free will is denied. Responding to public pressure, President Jimmy Carter commuted the sentence after twenty-two months, and Bill Clinton pardoned Patty on his last day in office.

Jim would never have charged her, but as was evidenced in his investigation of Dan Shaw the previous year, he had form in that area.

*

Progress was being made in their investigation – humble and incremental, but that's the nature of all progress. The need for a wheel long preceded its invention. Father Jack Merryfield was in all likelihood dead, and the next step would be to determine how long the line might be of people who wanted him that way. You only needed a line of one.

TRN's popular morning announcer, Adam Christopher, picked up the story that day from *The Telegraph*'s coverage after being referred to it by his program director who, as Adam knew, had a source very close to the case: former detective Jim Nicholas, her husband.

Dan wanted as much publicity as possible for the story, so welcomed TRN's involvement. He understood the nature of media and how symbiotic its different branches could be. They fed off each other in particular ways, and an irresistible momentum was created when harnessed. Adam was going to feature the investigation and ask questions. He wanted to meet Nicholas later for more background, which he would be delighted to provide. The Beatles weren't the only ones who understood synergy.

In a bizarre twist, Shaw was the journalist writing the stories for *The Tele* and *Courier-Mail*. His early coverage demonstrated that he'd lost none of the reporting skills that had made him a legendary crime reporter in Sydney for many years.

That was before the death of his daughter Rachel ten years ago and his move to the Northern Rivers. It was nearly a year since he'd killed the men he held responsible, one of whom was Adam's predecessor on the networked morning program, Edward 'Big Ed' Bradley.

The Tele covered that investigation extensively, and circulation rose dramatically at the time. The journalist with all the scoops last year was Steve Anderson, an old friend of Jim's from their Bondi

Surf Club days. Dan's return to *The Tele* was only made possible because Anderson was in the United States covering the last months of their presidential election campaign.

A crime writer covering American politics? Who would've thought?

14

Monday, July 22

TRN Sydney

Alexandra Burns and Jim Nicholas joined Adam Christopher in his office shortly after he finished his program at midday. Jim had met him on several occasions during last year's investigation. Christopher was never really considered a suspect, although Nicholas briefly permitted him to consider himself a person of interest for a few days so that he could share the moment with friends.

Christopher loathed Bradley, having regularly been on the receiving end of Big Ed's bullying and threats. His homosexuality also left him open to Bradley's unique brand of viciousness. Bradley was an all-purpose hater, particularly of those who stood in the way of something he wanted. In Adam's case, that was the morning program, which he grudgingly deserted several years earlier after none-too-subtle threats from Bradley to expose his sexuality if he didn't. Christopher's primary concern at the time was not for himself but that it would also have outed his partner, Nguyen, taking from him the agency to make a decision in his own time. In all our lives, that's important.

Not that Christopher minded philosophically. Those who knew him best had always known he was gay, but he considered it none of anyone's business, and there is no doubt that it could have hampered his career on a reasonably conservative radio station. That, too, was changing.

Listeners had accepted many gay broadcasters down the years (as they had Prime Ministers) without the slightest idea they were, in fact, gay. Like most homosexuals (and most heterosexuals, for that matter), he didn't celebrate his orientation, nor did he deny it. He and his family and friends simply accepted it as part of who he was.

At 175 cm (5'9"), Adam wasn't a big man – Michael Jackson, Rory McIlroy, and Hitler were the same height – but he possessed a deceptively rich voice which, when combined with an ironic sense of humour, natural intelligence, and a deep interest in many diverse subjects, made him a natural for the business he was in and the shift he was now doing. Thanks to the premature and permanent departure of Big Ed.

As he made clear to Nicholas the previous year, it would've been hypocritical of him to mourn the loss of Bradley when he was the happy beneficiary of the show he left behind, a hefty pay rise and the freedom he now enjoyed. The search for Bradley's killer was now consigned to the back burner, and little was spoken of it. Nor would it. Only four people knew definitively who killed Bradley, and two of them were the detectives on the case. And, like Big Ed, they would remain forever silent.

*

After initially dipping, Christopher's ratings levelled out only a couple of points less than Bradley's at his peak, and Adam was bringing in new listeners, many of whom were alienated by Big Ed's bullying and controversial style, which attracted as many libel actions as it did sponsors. Adam liked Alexandra's programming mantra, learned from a Brisbane mentor: *to be interesting, you must first be interested.* And Adam was – in all kinds of things.

Listeners liked that more than the hectoring that was now a regular part of the media landscape, just as they liked his intellectual consistency and even-handedness. He was more libertarian than conservative, and the audience embraced his unpredictable, but always well-argued, opinions. They appreciated, too, how he accommodated all views, even dissenting ones.

Particularly dissenting ones, because in disagreement both sides could be argued in good faith. Unlike X (formerly Twitter) and other social media sites, he rejected rudeness and ugly commentary, which made him a rare species in the partisan and polarised media world. Even more, he always let callers have the final say, a concept Ed Bradley would've found most peculiar.

Adam dismissed X owner Elon Musk's idea of total free speech entirely and pointed to Musk's often inflammatory and incorrect statements as proof. Likewise, Adam had no time for the censorious hypocrisy of Mark Zuckerberg's Facebook. Mark was no benevolent dictator and had let his creation become a manipulated (and manipulative) political plaything.

The world was increasingly in the grip of technological geniuses whose skills, knowledge, and wisdom often extended no further than their inventions. Most were only minimally interested in the responsibilities or unintended consequences that accompanied them. They were very strange men, but history is often forged by such people.

*

Adam read about the missing priest in Sunday's paper and was immediately drawn to the mystery, and knew his listeners would be, too. In the media the skill is often in recognising a story's potential at its birth and taking your audience on the journey.

By establishing your interest and intention early on (and by doing all the research necessary to sound credible), you also increased the odds of people who knew more about the case getting in touch and providing breakthroughs and exclusives.

In this case, the *Lennox Chronicle* would fashion information for its local market, and *The Tele* would tell the wider story. The city tabloid, published every day and not once a week, would prevail. Jim's loyalty was to Dan Shaw, who had already permitted him to answer any questions Adam asked, leaving him well ahead of his radio and TV rivals. The one exception was there would be no mention of Taylor's photo; that was Mark's prerogative to share, and he didn't seem keen.

The broadcaster appreciated and accepted the arrangement. As did his Program Director, Alexandra Burns (alternatively Alex and AB to friends), who would bridge the occasionally blurred line between her relationship with Jim (his wife) and her responsibility to TRN.

The remarkable fact is that had Dan Shaw not murdered Ed Bradley, she would never have met Jim Nicholas, and neither they nor Adam Christopher would be sitting together in this room. It follows that, but for that sequence of events, as well as two German tourists and a Brisbane photographer being where they were at a single moment in time, Father Jack Merryfield's story might never have been told.

His body unseen, and the crime, if that's what it was, forever unsolved.

15

Sunday, July 28

The Gap, Brisbane

Father Ralph paid more attention than usual to the newspapers that week. He was hoping for an update from Dan Shaw but heard nothing. He liked Shaw and trusted he would honour his promise to keep him informed when there was something to report. Shaw and Jim Nicholas, in the meantime, spent several days planning next moves.

Adam Christopher was also awaiting more information on which to base follow-up broadcasts. He kept the story alive for listeners each day by reporting that there was no news (which, in its way, *was* news), but they would be the first to know when something broke. He filled the vacuum by exploring the number of people who went missing every year. There were many reasons, but it turns out that sometimes the grass really is greener elsewhere.

Father Ralph told his congregation that morning he had no idea where Father Jack was or what caused his absence. He led them in prayer for his well-being and safe return before moving on to his sermon – today, on gambling.

There were political moves afoot to ban gambling advertising, which Father Ralph supported.

"*1 Timothy 6:10* is clear," he said in his homily. "*For the love of money is a root of all kinds of evil.*" This verse is often used to caution against pursuing wealth through activities like gambling, where the primary motivation is monetary gain. What Father Ralph would make of the activities of the Vatican Bank and the gang of thieves they dealt with is anyone's guess.

He was aware his assistant was a small punter but knew the associated dangers when things spiralled out of control. As a result of the chemical response to stimuli, people become addicted to all kinds of things, including religion.

Like the tobacco companies that preceded them decades earlier, gambling agencies attached themselves like barnacles to the most popular pastimes. Also like barnacles, the gambling industry was given a stable place to thrive, a free ride and access to plenty of sustenance. Not a bad deal.

And, like the tobacco industry (but unlike barnacles), the gambling industry lied through its teeth. With media companies losing revenue in every direction and governments in need of taxation streams, gambling advertising is now present everywhere. And, as with any addict, the media was denouncing any prospective ban on the basis it would ruin them. That's akin to the drug peddler claiming financial distress if customers stopped using their product. The irony was rich.

Children who previously rated their team's chances as good or bad were now encouraged to see them as a $2.50 or $10 chance. You could bet on presidential races, beauty pageants and every sport around the world twenty-four hours a day. Who knows when you might get lucky on Race Six at Happy Valley in Hong Kong or, if you're in an adventurous frame of mind, Race Seven at Charlottelund in Denmark. Either drunk or sober, you could gamble from the sanctuary of your lounge room and, between races, listen to advertising telling you where next to bet.

With a straight face, they would also ask you to be careful not to bet too much. Oh, and if you've just lost the money for the rent or mortgage, here's a helpline. If you asked nicely, they would probably give you a price for the sun rising the next day. Or Father Jack being here for next Sunday's service, about which Father Ralph sounded more confident than at least one of his congregants thought wise.

Her name was Katherine, and she smiled inwardly while outwardly looking serene and concerned at Father Ralph's words. She liked and respected him enormously, but as ever, didn't agree with a word he said. All life was a gamble (hadn't God set it up that way?), and to deny that was to deny the reality we all faced, including the billions-to-one chance of any of us being here in the first place.

She also thought the biblical quote citing 'a love of money' was trite and had caused untold misery. It is not to love money to appreciate that having enough of it to live a pleasant life is not a stupid or sinful thing to do. Indeed, living a responsible life should include having enough to get by and being able to assist those in need. Sometimes, she believed, we too readily accept these clichés. It's the same with 'money doesn't buy happiness.' Of itself, that's true, but money is only a means of exchange, and it allows you to buy many things that actually *do* bring happiness, and just as importantly, help to avoid *un*happiness.

*

Katherine had attended St Vincent's for fifteen years, from when she learned Father Jack was the curate or assistant priest. Father Ralph always enjoyed her calm presence, even if their conversations were limited to polite greetings and small talk, in which she showed no particular interest outside courtesy. She came to church for a reason, and he was pleased to be able to play a role, regardless of what it might be.

As she did every week, Katherine arrived at 9:59 precisely and left immediately after the service. She didn't live at The Gap, however, and there was a long way to drive. Having timed it many times, Katherine knew it would take two hours and twenty-eight minutes to drive the 174.7 kilometres to her home at Wategos Beach in northern NSW.

Just below the Cape Byron Lighthouse.

16

Friday, August 2

Shelly Beach Ballina

Another week passed with little new information. No body had washed ashore anywhere, and beyond the reasonably sketchy background about Father Jack Merryfield, they were still light on leads. Dan Shaw rang Father Ralph and told him they had reason to believe his assistant was dead but, absent a body, that couldn't be confirmed. It might be wise, he suggested, to continue with his prayers. Why he would do that, however, escaped Shaw. God would surely know the priest was dead (if it was him), in which case prayers weren't going to do much good.

Nor could Dan tell Father Ralph what led him to that conclusion. The priest volunteered to speak with Merryfield's sister and would know best what to say to his congregation, although Shaw did advise caution. Jim Nicholas committed to driving to Brisbane the following Sunday to speak with the priest and the parishioners, who had come to know Father Jack well.

Or so they thought.

*

Dan would also write further pieces for *The Chronicle* and *The Telegraph*, but he needed to be creative with so little to add. Pondering all this, he sat on the bench next to the memorial for Tadashi Nakahara about a hundred metres up the walking/cycling path from the surf club at Shelly Beach, Ballina. Behind him was the Cafe (more a spacious restaurant), which he would visit for breakfast soon.

Tadashi was forty-one, a popular local enjoying a quick surf when, at 10 a.m. on February 9, 2015, he was fatally mauled. 25% of shark attack victims die of their injuries, and Tadashi was one of the unlucky minority. But there was more than good and bad luck involved. The randomness of his death, a man Shaw didn't know, raised questions for which he had no answers. How do those who think that God choreographs everything explain events like this? A divinely inspired shark attack?

Shaw comes to this place often to contemplate, and heaven knows (a Freudian slip?) he had plenty to think about.

Ironically, he'd read yesterday that this year marked the 50th anniversary of the release of the movie *Jaws*. Younger than him by two years, he could remember the first time he saw it, and few films since have impacted so much.

Directed by Steven Spielberg, it was based on the book by Peter Benchley, who died at sixty-five regretting that sharks (and the fear they generate) were the central memory of the film. A journalist and speechwriter for President Lyndon Johnson, Benchley created Amity in his novel, a fictional town on Long Island, New York, whose economy was driven by summer tourism – tourists who liked to swim in the ocean.

In the introduction to a later edition of the book, the author wrote that he 'had no interest in writing a one-note horror story: shark eats people.' Instead, Mrs Benchley says, her husband set out to write a story 'about how people cope with a danger that they cannot control.'

It was a question that inspired Spielberg in his debut feature, *Duel*, in 1971. A motorist is followed, seemingly for no reason, by a truck. A malevolent force pursuing and ultimately killing. Not unlike the shark.

*

There are different attitudes to fear. President Franklin D. Roosevelt famously said, in the depths of the Depression in the 1930s, '*You have nothing to fear but fear itself*.' It's a great line, but does it make sense?

At the time, people were losing their jobs and homes and jumping from tall buildings in large numbers. They were struggling to put food on the table and saw no future for themselves or their families – enough to instil fear in anyone.

His point, though, was that fear makes things worse because you start thinking negatively and acting from that perspective. People needed courage and optimism, not despair and negativity. But fear? That's real and can be both positive and negative – it depends on your fear.

If you're in the trenches in war, you know fear.

If someone suddenly confronts you with a knife, you know fear.

If a loved one is seriously ill, you know fear.

Fear has helped the human race progress. In evolutionary terms, it makes us less likely to take ridiculous risks (I will NOT feed that dinosaur) and has driven most of our greatest inventions. Fear has its place and can keep you alive, but *irrational* fear is the danger. There's a big difference.

This line of thought prompted Danny to think of a good friend, Cam, now living in Portugal, who'd told him: 'All of us know fear, mate. Anyone who isn't scared at some point in their lives is either a psychopath or an outright liar. What we do with that fear is entirely up to us. Some people freeze, and others either run forward or away. Individual circumstances dictate what response we should apply, and our training or personal abilities then kick in. We know that all of these fears can be overcome, especially the irrational ones. Fear is an emotion; danger is real. When we allow our emotions to take over, we lose control. And then you're done.'

Cam liked the story of the American Western legend Tom Horn. He was the cowboy and bounty hunter responsible for capturing the mighty Indian leader, Geronimo. Steve McQueen played him in a 1980 movie. Tom would be surprised to learn, or perhaps not, that these days there are statues of Geronimo, but none of him. Tom once said, 'Fear's been good to me.'

That was just before they hung him.

*

In one of their more entertaining conversations since the investigation of the previous year, Danny asked Jim Nicholas how he came to suspect him of being Big Ed Bradley's killer. Jim, then the lead detective but now a close friend, talked with him about instinct.

Sure, there was the investigation into defamation and who might (and, importantly, might *not*) have taken legal action after one of Big Ed's many tirades. There was, too, the discovery of what happened to Rachel, but much was driven by hunches and the occasional tune that popped up on his internal jukebox. In that case, it had been the Beatles' Penny Lane and the electrifying piccolo trumpet cameo one minute and six seconds in.

As Jim's mentor, former Assistant Police Commissioner Bruce Mac had told him: 'Trust your instincts. They're based on all you've ever known.'

Fair enough, but why are these thoughts about fear now being generated by a brief reflection on the fiftieth anniversary of *Jaws*? Two possibilities jumped out. Was Father Jack Merryfield living in fear? If the stories of his past were true, the reasons could be many, or was someone fearful of Father Jack? Interesting, but who would be afraid of a priest? Danny would think more about that. One thing is sure: Father Jack wasn't taken by a shark.

Not before he died, anyway.

17

Monday, August 5

TRN Sydney

Adam Christopher opened his program at 9:05 that morning by promoting an interview with Dan Shaw on the case of the missing priest. That would be coming up at 9:25. Alex would be thrilled with the precise forward promotion. Now, like a good chess player, he needed to navigate the moves that would get him there.

First, he would check in with TRN's U.S. correspondent about polling on the presidential race that showed the new Democrat candidate was now level-pegging with her Republican opponent. Many on the left (and some on the right) were fearful that the former president, Donald Trump, would win the Presidency in November and once again take occupancy of the White House.

History is often best understood, to the extent it ever can be, from a safe distance somewhere in the future, and Trump will undoubtedly be discussed and analysed as long as people do such things. Not just the man himself, but the country that elected the man. Those on the left loathe him, and many conservatives share their passion. Amongst his many and varied qualities, however, Trump possesses the ability to extract hypocrisy from his opponents much as Dracula did with blood.

Andrew Sullivan, one of America's more interesting conservative writers, is a good example. He says the former president is 'a moron', and there will be plenty who share that view. But, in Andrew's case, glass houses and stones come to mind.

Along with many of his neo-con colleagues, he strongly supported George W. Bush's incursion into Iraq, in which more than a million – mostly innocent – people subsequently died. Andrew, to his credit, says he will never forgive himself, but it's not his own forgiveness he should be seeking.

He thought the U.S. could (and should) impose democracy on a place where power has always depended more on religious and clan affiliations, and that Saddam was so bad that removing him was a moral good. But, using that logic, you'd be invading a lot of countries, many of them far less critical strategically than Iraq.

Years later, he admitted becoming 'enamoured of his own morality'. President Bush and those pushing for an invasion wrapped themselves in the protective cloak of Iraq possessing Weapons of Mass Destruction, but you could only believe that if you were ideologically inclined to *want* to believe it. The facts never supported it. Yes, the word 'moron' covers a lot of territory.

*

On his way to victory in 2016, Trump virtually took over the Republican Party, and on his way out, a few of his supporters attempted to take over the Capitol. Trump's election – and what followed – was a direct consequence of failed U.S. policy, political ineptness, lies, and corruption going back as far as the assassination of John F. Kennedy.

That's when the distrust began. Before November 23, 1963, 75% of Americans trusted their government. Ten years later, after the charade of the Warren Commission report into his death, that number was down to 25%, and it has never recovered.

To understand Trump's rise and appeal, it's essential to recognise the profound disconnect between voters and their political leadership. None of what occurs today (or tomorrow) happens in isolation, and America's next few presidents will emerge directly as a result of the current period, just as Trump did.

In recent decades, their leaders consistently misled Americans on significant issues. That forged a massive divide between the leaders and the led; a chasm of distrust and cynicism. It is no small irony that many of those yelling loudest about Trump are the same people who made his election possible. Populists don't rise in a vacuum; there must be a reason. And, in America, there were plenty. Just one example:

On September 9, 2016, the Democrat candidate and front-runner, Hillary Clinton, used the term 'basket of deplorables' to describe half of Trump's supporters. She smiled as she described them as 'racist, sexist, homophobic, xenophobic and Islamophobic.' She thought it somehow clever to say this about a quarter of her fellow citizens, but then blamed sexism for why she lost. Many in the U.S. had a good idea of who was deplorable, and it wasn't them.

It was happening elsewhere, too. When German Chancellor Angela Merkel said in 2015, 'Wir schaffen das' (we can do this), she was responding to criticism of her decision to allow approximately one million refugees into Germany from the Syrian civil war. Mostly Muslims into a predominantly non-muslim country already struggling with cost-of-living pressures and housing shortages. What could possibly go wrong?

By Christmas that year, sexual assaults by the newcomers were reported in huge numbers, including a mob attack on young women outside the glorious cathedral in Cologne. Nine years later, non-citizens comprise 15% of the population but commit 41% of the crimes. It should surprise no one that 77% of Germans want the immigration policy changed.

Coming from East Germany, where she grew up behind the Berlin Wall, it was easy to appreciate Merkel's sentiment that walls must come down. But walls and fences also serve a purpose and

don't have to be evil. The Berlin Wall was about keeping people *in*
– not out.

And it's true around the world. Consistently telling people losing
their jobs that globalism is excellent and that unfettered immigration
that disrupts and divides their societies is good, and you don't need
to be George Washington to figure there will be a response. And
that it might not be pretty.

*

With that background in mind, Adam Christopher welcomed
Steve Anderson, who was reporting the election from the U.S. for
both *The Telegraph* and TRN.

"Three months to election day, Steve," Christopher began after
his introduction, "how's it looking?"

Anderson, better known these days as a crime reporter, went to
the U.S. at short notice to replace the esteemed Arnold Richards,
who was recovering slowly from a car accident. Anderson was deeply
interested in politics and knew the American scene well.

"Morning Adam. Yes, three months to go, and there are still a
few chapters in this story to write. A fortnight ago, having survived
an assassination attempt, Donald Trump looked an almost certain
winner against a president who was clearly in cognitive decline and
had performed terribly in their debate. But, with Biden choosing
not to run and his Vice President Kamala Harris now the candidate,
things have changed dramatically."

"Can she win?" the host asked.

"She most certainly can, Adam. Her candidacy has given the
Democrats a real boost, and there is now hope, whereas a fortnight
ago, there was none. And as Barack Obama proved in 2008, hope
is a compelling message. She has reinvigorated her party's base and
will attract some independent and swing voters. The extent to which

she succeeds in doing that could well decide the election."

Anderson went on to say, "Harris will attempt to position herself as the candidate of change at a time when many Americans are saying they want just that. But she's been there for the last three and a half years as the U.S. stumbled from disaster to disaster, so that could be a tough sell. Trump remains a formidable opponent, and as Hillary Clinton could probably tell you, they will underestimate him at their peril.

The debate on September 11 will be vital, and the Republicans are in danger of setting the bar way too low for her. Debates are often about perception, Nixon versus Kennedy being a stark example. At this point, she will only have to turn up to do better than many predict. Harris was a poor candidate in 2020 and dropped out quickly. Her supporters will be hoping for better things this time. She's begun well, but the race has a long way to go."

They talked a little longer, and then Christopher cut to an ad-break, after which he promised to speak with Dan Shaw, who would have the latest on the case of the missing priest.

*

Adam Christopher didn't know that the man he was about to introduce was why he now sat in Ed Bradley's old chair. That is because the chair and all other reminders of poor dead Ed were packed up quickly. Adam knew many reasons people wanted Bradley dead but would never know the real one. Neither that nor his predecessor's murder, however, caused him to lose any sleep.

In welcoming Shaw to his large networked audience throughout NSW and Queensland, Christopher highlighted his reputation as one of the great crime writers in newspaper history (which was true) and how, as the owner/editor of the *Lennox Chronicle*, he broke the story of the missing priest and his presumed death. His opening question asked Shaw how he became involved, and after his answer, Christopher followed up with, "How much have you learned so far?"

"Not as much as I would've liked Adam, but enough to develop some lines of inquiry. Police will no doubt be doing likewise. I believe I know the missing man's identity and that he was, in fact, a priest. We're pursuing leads, and I should be able to tell our listeners and readers more in days and weeks to come."

In the media's lexicon, this was a terrific 'tease'. First, outline the elements of the case, then point out some of what's to come – but not too much. What Christopher and Shaw were doing was developing an on-air relationship that would help drive the investigation.

Like the experiment with Pavlov's dog, conditioned to react to repeated stimuli, listeners would automatically think of this case and pay attention when they heard Dan's name and voice. They were also, step by step, seeking to bring their audience along on the journey. In radio, you never knew who was listening at any given time, or who might be prompted to ring in.

*

In a refurbished house in Pandanus Place, her home for the last twenty years and only a two-minute walk from Wategos Beach, one person was paying close attention. It was a woman in her mid-60s of medium height and above-average looks. Her hair, which she wore loose and didn't quite reach her shoulders, was grey, and her eyes were a colour of blue you might see on the Barrier Reef.

She was smiling.

18

Sunday, August 11

The Gap, Brisbane

The Gap is ten kilometres by road northwest of the Brisbane GPO and is named appropriately enough for its location in the valley between Mt Coot-tha and Enoggera Hill, which form part of the Taylor Range.

When you drive down Waterworks Rd and across Walton Bridge, it's as if you're entering your own village, albeit one that is now home to nearly 20,000 people. That's about the same population as Armidale, Maryborough, and Goulburn and twice that of Kingaroy, Casino, and Murwillumbah.

The suburb's popularity has grown in recent years with the low crime rate, leafy surrounds, and convenient access to exceptional schools proving a powerful magnet.

It wasn't as leafy, though, after the devastating storm of November 16, 2008. It hit just before 6 p.m. and, like Hannibal or the Wehrmacht arriving uninvited, reeked the same kind of havoc. Some called it a mini-tornado, but there is no such thing. Other amateur meteorologists said it was a small hurricane, but what you called it didn't matter much.

The storm lasted less than an hour, and the most devastating moments no more than a couple of minutes. At that time, palms blew parallel to the road, and noise like a train echoed around the streets with a distinct, accompanying whistle. Then came the whiteout. Nothing. Even the stoutest of hearts started beating harder and faster. Micro-burst down drafts caused the wind to come from all angles. That's when the trees snapped, windows imploded, and roofs flew.

Those who had seen The Gap earlier that afternoon awoke to a different place the following day. With a backdrop of chainsaws and shock, neighbours comforted the elderly and helped each other where they could. Then went about cleaning up. For anyone who loves their surroundings and suddenly sees them decimated, it was a heartbreaking sight.

Residents wondered, as they surveyed the enormity of the damage to houses and trees, whether the place would ever be the same. Today, you would never know there'd been a storm. Nature, like people, reinvents itself quickly. It gives, it takes; it endures.

The path of carnage was only the width of a few streets, and St Vincent's survived unscathed, with Father Ralph doing incredible work organising food drops and shelter for those who needed it.

This morning, in the last month of winter, the sun shone, and a high of 23 degrees was forecast. There would be no storms, and all was well in one of Brisbane's prettiest suburbs, save for growing concerns about a missing priest.

*

Jim Nicholas left Lennox Head in northern N.S.W early for the drive to Brisbane. He arrived at St Vincent's at 8:32, leaving plenty of time to speak with Father Ralph and parishioners before the service began promptly at ten. He would catch up with the priest again afterwards. Nicholas knew none of this local history but was keen to learn more about the priest who had been part of this peaceful middle-class suburb for many years.

Father Ralph welcomed him at the front door of the presbytery and invited him in for tea. The priest, whilst keen to hear the latest on the investigation, seemed resigned to the results not being good.

"He's dead, isn't he?" he asked Nicholas.

"In all likelihood, Father, but without proof, we simply can't be definitive. The German tourists saw the body too briefly to be certain, and it was more than a hundred meters down the cliff." Jim made no mention of a photo.

At 9:15, as people mingled ahead of the service, Nicholas took his leave and organised with Father Ralph to talk some more after he'd farewelled everyone at around 11:30.

The priest explained that the congregation comprised people from diverse professions: teachers, lawyers, the local bus driver, businesspeople, former military personnel, public servants, a well-respected physiotherapist, a pharmacist, and students. Others were retired and satisfyingly engaged with grandchildren and various interests and causes. Most were serious, if not passionate, about their religion, while some saw their Sunday visits as a social occasion.

Father Ralph welcomed them all with the same sincere greeting, hoping that casual visitors might find something here that made their appointment more permanent. He recognised loneliness as one of the worst aspects of modern society and thought that if he provided nothing else, he could offer company and something to think about. There are less productive ways to spend our time.

The first person Nicholas spoke with was a frail man who looked to be in his 80s. He was tall, stooped and walked with the assistance of a cane. His wife's arm guided him, and he was clearly not destined to be around much longer. In response to Jim's, "G'day mate, how are you?" the old bloke, Stan was his name, smiled and said, "I'm fine, thank you." And in the most profound of ways, he was. It said something good about Stan (and Father Ralph) that a man in his end days was on such good terms with the world and himself.

Stan and his wife Edna added little to the stored knowledge of

Father Jack Merryfield except to say they liked chatting with him about football and racing, subjects Father Ralph was happy to leave to his assistant. Stan saw no problem with a priest having a small bet but was often surprised at how deep his knowledge of thoroughbreds and Rugby League went.

Their granddaughter, Simone, thought Father Jack 'cool' and liked how he related to younger people.

This was the common refrain as Jim spoke with those preparing to enter the church. He spoke to nearly everyone, but nobody seemed to know much more than the mundane. It seems Father Jack liked it that way, and it occurred to Jim that perhaps he had *planned* it that way.

He learned that Libby, along with her husband Doug, one of the more popular members of the group, was not a fan of Father Jack's interest in horse racing. Her idealism was admired, as was her love of all creatures great and small. Libby considered racing a cruel business and had told Father Jack as much. His reply – 'But, Libby, they love to run' – angered her even more. 'Yes,' she'd told him, 'they love to run ... around the paddock, stop under a tree, take a nap, and then run some more. When they feel like it, and without a whip in sight.' The priest responded by suggesting that without horse racing, there would be far fewer horses. To which, having heard the argument before, Libby replied, 'They said the same thing about slavery and African Americans.' Such was her passion that Father Jack, not always successfully, did his best to avoid her.

The other exception to all the positivity came from an esteemed former military man, Andy. Approaching seventy, he was a plain speaker who thought there was something, in his words, 'sus' about Merryfield. He tried too hard to be one thing, which, in Andy's experience, often meant you were another entirely. His wife, Jennifer (*please call me Jen*), with a joyous laugh reminiscent of novelist

Colleen McCullough's, said her husband could be a bit of a cynic, before adding, 'But he's usually right.'

*

Jim Nicholas took a seat in the back pew, across the aisle from a lady who arrived at precisely 9:59. The former detective didn't know that she had done just that for the last fifteen years – ever since Father Jack Merryfield joined the parish.

What struck him most were her eyes, the shade of blue you would find on the Barrier Reef. She answered his greeting with a pleasant nod, seemingly neither happy nor unhappy at his presence. Father Ralph was about to speak, so he would catch her later.

Today, as he told Nicholas he would, the priest spoke about loneliness. Why, he questioned, are people lonelier and more isolated than ever? We've never had access to so many ways of staying in touch, and yet people have rarely felt more disconnected from a world that is going increasingly faster.

Father Ralph talked about a report from the U.S. Surgeon General, who argued that loneliness and social isolation were a more meaningful threat to their national health than diabetes and smoking. Social isolation, the report said, increased the chances of premature death by 29% and was the equivalent of smoking fifteen cigarettes a day. Good luck, Jim thought, if you were isolated *and* smoked.

He said we are spending too much time on devices, which is not really 'connection' at all. Connection requires talking to people, looking at them, touching them, and hearing them. Social media was, in many ways, *anti*-social as it removed the necessity to interact in person.

"Human interaction is vital," Father Ralph said, adding that Jesus also spoke of loneliness. "In John 16:32, He says, *And yet I am not alone, for my Father is with me."* Then Father concluded, "Jesus is always with you, and that means you can never be lonely."

Katherine digested all of this and thought two things: that Father Ralph really was a kind and gentle man and, not for the first time, that she didn't agree with a word he said. Loneliness, she thought, was more mental than physical. She believed the problem with computers and online lives wasn't that they made people lonely but that they had removed the joy of *being* alone. She thought loneliness was only the residue of not being happy in your own company. That was the key to it.

Katherine had never been lonely. Alone, yes, but never lonely. And, bizarrely, she had Father Jack to 'thank' for that. Even in her darkest days, she had been accompanied by a burning hatred of the man who, when she was just fourteen, groomed and then molested her. For more than thirty-five years, she lost all trace of him until, fifteen years ago, a friend told her of his reappearance at St Vincent's Parish, The Gap. She hadn't missed a weekend of church since. He looked at her strangely at times, but if there was a hint of recognition, he never said anything. Nor had she.

Father Ralph's words kickstarted Jim's Jukebox, and Roy Orbison lamented that 'Only The Lonely' knew how he felt. It was the song that began it all for The Big O. After writing it, he offered the song to Elvis and the Everly Brothers. Fortunately for Roy, they declined; it's a familiar story.

In the meantime, Nicholas wanted to speak to the lady in the back pew, but that wasn't going to happen. She was gone.

*

Jim sat with Father Ralph in the presbytery after he farewelled his parishioners, encouraging them to seek out people they thought could use some company. Nicholas was curious about the woman he had wanted to speak with and asked Father if he knew much about her, to which he replied with a puzzled look: "You know, Jim, she's been coming here for many years, and I wouldn't have spoken more than a dozen sentences to her. She arrives at the last moment and leaves as soon as I finish. She's always pleasant, and I decided long ago that she liked what I was offering, and that was enough."

For reasons that would become clear, Jim's trusted instinct was buzzing, and he asked the priest where she lived. Father Ralph replied, "I haven't the faintest idea." Nicholas made a mental note to return the following week and stood to leave. As he did, Father Ralph placed a hand on the former detective's arm and asked him to sit back down.

"There's one thing I feel I should share, Jim. I'm breaking a confidence, but under the circumstances, I believe it's both necessary and right to do so." At that, he looked down momentarily as if doubting the correctness of the chosen course before lifting his eyes and saying it anyway.

"Father Jack was dying."

Surprised, and not trying to hide it, Jim immediately attempted to factor that revelation into what they knew so far. Experience told him that a calculation of possibilities drove most cases. "How do you know that, Father?"

"He told me more than a month ago, and asked that I hear his confession and give him final absolution. That was meant to happen this week. I guess," he said ruefully, "that won't be necessary now."

A reasonable guess, Jim thought, as another question came to mind: Who on earth would want to kill a dying priest?

19

Monday, August 12

Lennox Head

Several things were decided in the following twenty-four hours that would chart the next phase of the investigation. Jim rang Dan Shaw while driving home from Brisbane the previous day and agreed to meet with him and Shannon for breakfast at the Williams St Cafe. There was much to discuss.

When they gathered at 7:30, Nicholas told them about his visit to the church and his instinctive feelings about the lady who seemed to be in such a hurry to leave. He also informed them that the missing priest had organised for Father Ralph to hear his final confession this week to gain absolution for his sins, of which, they would soon learn, there were many.

He spoke more about Father Ralph, whom he liked immensely, and the somewhat shallow pool of information he'd gathered about Merryfield from congregants. Among them all, the words of former military man Andy echoed loudest: that Merryfield was 'sus'. Military men also know a lot about instinct; it keeps them alive.

Jim planned to return to St Vincent's the following Sunday to talk some more with the priest and, hopefully, the mysterious lady in the back pew. He kept it to himself but was also keen to hear what Father Ralph might be discussing. Jim hadn't been in a church for many years, but there was something about it he liked, not least the way Father Ralph explained things he'd previously dismissed. Jim had seen too much in his police years to believe in an interventionist or arbitrary God and thought even the idea of 'meaning' was a uniquely human concept. What other creature contemplates these things, and why is it necessary? Balanced against that, he acknowledged the possibility that human beings, having reached a higher level of consciousness, are predisposed – or 'programmed' – to do just that. They call it the God Gene.

*

When speaking with Alexandra he told her that he and Danny would visit the TRN studios in Sydney the following week to update Adam Christopher on their progress. The press coverage was sparse for now, but that would change quickly. He also told her he loved and missed her, both of which were true, although neither felt it necessary to spend every moment of every day together. They thought it better to enjoy their moments together and to anticipate them when apart.

Danny and Shannon, sipping their coffees, listened quietly and absorbed all Jim told them. When he looked to have finished, Shaw mentioned his visit to Tadashi's memorial the previous week and how it coincided with the 50th anniversary of the release of *Jaws*. He told them how the question of fear loomed large at the time, but he wasn't sure why.

In the meantime, Shannon was thinking about all they knew, and waiting for the answers to emerge. Forcing them never worked, so she began to list what they'd learned, and as she did, they all realised it was a lot more than just a few weeks back. Change happens step by step – and then all at once. Hemingway said something similar about bankruptcy. She started speaking in a stream-of-consciousness fashion, knowing the others would take it all in and add things where appropriate.

"Two German tourists believe they've seen a body on the rocks below the Cape Byron Lighthouse;

Mark Taylor's photo confirms it and indicates the person was probably murdered;

His photo suggests it could be a priest;

The articles in the *Chronicle* promote interest from the *Telegraph*;

Those articles attract the attention of TRN and Father Ralph;

His assistant, Father Jack Merryfield, was missing;

The missing priest was mostly liked, but despite being at the parish for fifteen years, not much was known about him other than that he enjoyed Rugby League and horse racing, on which he placed small bets;

Father Ralph was aware something unsavoury happened in his colleague's past but preferred not to know about it;

There is a mysterious woman who attends church every week about whom little is known;

And we now know Merryfield was dying.

Is that it, or have I missed something ?" she asked.

"We also know." Jim added, after thinking about it, "that he was going to make his final confession to Father Ralph this week."

*

They meditated on all of this for a few minutes, with Jim and Shannon also factoring in Danny's questioning of why he was thinking about fear, even before he knew Merryfield was dying. Three intelligent people who liked and trusted each other, none of them reluctant to say something the others might laugh at because they all knew that would never happen.

It was Shannon who uttered the sentences that would change their immediate future.

"Based on what we have so far, there are two choices: either someone from his past wasn't a great believer in forgiveness, or someone knew he was dying and was fearful of what he might confess."

20

Sunday, August 18

Brisbane

The alarm sounded at 5 a.m., and before driving north the investigator walked on Seven Mile Beach to confirm what he needed to address with Father Ralph. Jim never took the new day for granted and thanked the sun for giving it life. The sun rose today and will again tomorrow. Are you sure? Like breathing, there are some things it pays not to think too much about. They are so natural and separate from thought that thinking about them changes the nature of what you're thinking about.

The priest's declaration that Merryfield was dying added an unanticipated dimension to proceedings, but Shannon's working theory was worth pursuing: that a dying priest about to make his final confession could be dangerous, or that someone from his past – without knowledge of his impending demise – might have hurried things up a little.

Jim wasn't Catholic – and was content in his questioning agnosticism – but the idea of confession had always struck him as odd. Surely God knew both our actions and their motivation? More broadly, he felt that no religion possessed a mortgage on truth. Recognising the good they'd done was easy, rationalising the bad less so.

After arriving at 8:45, they were questions he put to Father Ralph when they'd settled into comfortable chairs in the presbytery for the pre-service ritual of biscuits and tea.

The priest answered in his usual self-deprecating way.

"Jim, I remember as a teenager when I first felt a calling to the Church, trying to make sense of evil. I was thinking of becoming an artist and gave myself the task of creating a piece of art under the title: *God is all powerful; God is all good; evil exists.*"

"How did it turn out?" Jim asked.

"Not well," Father Ralph laughed. "In fact, a mess. It led me to the biblical conclusion that God created human beings with free will, which meant they could choose between good and evil. And that evil exists when good is corrupted. It was a choice."

"But why would God do that?" Jim was asking questions out loud that he'd asked silently for a long time.

The priest smiled again before answering humbly, "Who knows, Jim? That would be to know the mind of God, and I'm prepared to have faith that things are ordered as they should be, even if we don't know all the answers. Sometimes, the questions are more important. There's a quote in Hebrews that says, '*Faith is the substance of things hoped for, the evidence of things not seen.*' So, in a way, you're suspending judgment on what you see and having faith that all is as it should be. I can understand that's a leap sometimes, particularly for a detective who deals in facts." He said it in a friendly, slightly teasing fashion.

Jim then guided Father Ralph into discussing Merryfield's impending final confession. "How does that work, and what's the aim?"

"Well, in the Sacrament of Penance – sometimes we call it reconciliation or confession – the dying person relates their sins to the priest, in this case, me, who then forgives them in God's name."

"With respect, that sounds a bit convenient, Father, particularly when the Church has had so many people committing dreadful sins for centuries. Are they all forgiven?"

"Are you sure you're still not a detective, Jim?" he grinned.

"You ask good questions, and I wish my answers were better, but our knowledge is limited because *we* are limited. But God is not limited, so it's a paradox without an answer, which comes back to faith. He points out that we are all redeemable if the person seeking forgiveness is genuinely remorseful and contrite. And only they and God know that."

"How, though," Jim pressed, "can you be contrite for sins you have committed over many years in the full knowledge that what you were doing was wrong and that you were destroying people's lives? If you were genuinely sorry for what you'd done, wouldn't you stop doing it?"

They travelled further down that road before, without being rude, the priest looked at his watch, signalled that it was time to meet his arriving congregants, and promised to pick up the conversation next time they talked. Unexpectedly, Jim looked forward to that chat. Father Ralph really was a kind and gentle man – wise as well.

*

Jim again sat in the back pew, awaiting the appearance of the person he wanted to talk to. She arrived at precisely 9:59 and nodded in his direction – neither happy nor unhappy to see him – with an enigmatic smile. The artist in Father Ralph could work with that.

In his homily, he picked up on the theme of choice: that everything we say and do is a choice and that we can't blame others for the ones we make. He explained how the brain becomes wired to certain behaviours and thoughts and that if we practice good habits, they will become our default positions.

He encouraged his parishioners to remember what he said in the week ahead: "When you're driving and get cranky, stop and ask yourself why, and remind yourself that you have a choice. Smile instead. If you feel yourself getting angry with someone, stop and ask why. And remind yourself that your response is a choice."

"Sometimes," he concluded, "I know that might sound difficult, but it's not. People often say, *but that's just how I am*. But that's not true either. *You are who you choose to be*. As our Holy Father, Pope Francis, said this week, always choose good over evil, and when confronted with a choice between evils, choose the lesser one."

On the last point, Katherine couldn't have disagreed with the Pope more. She consumed a lot of media, particularly as it related to the Catholic Church and the growing number of Royal Commissions and reports into the worldwide abuse of children by its priests, so she was aware of what Father Ralph left *un*said.

Pope Francis made those comments when asked during a visit to the United States who he would vote for in their upcoming election. Most who knew of his leftist leanings could hardly imagine him voting for Trump, but he answered with: 'They are both against life. One throws out migrants, and the other one kills babies. I can't decide; I'm not American. Choose the lesser of two evils.'

It was hardly the answer the questioner sought. If the preeminent religious figure in the world couldn't decide or make an ethical distinction, how could the average person? And what did his not being American have to do with anything? Should Catholics in all parts of the world not seek the Pope's guidance because he didn't share their nationality?

And why decide only on those issues? Biden, after all, was a practising Catholic who supported abortion as an electoral weapon, and Trump collected sins the way he did golf courses. Both also had strengths, even if their critics would be slow to concede it. How did Francis balance it from a religious or ethical perspective?

Katherine, not uniquely among those who had followed his career (including many Catholics), was often dismayed by the pontiff's statements and, when the time comes, his legacy will be mixed. The global warming advocate cited air conditioning as an example of the 'harmful habits of consumption' that will lead to mankind's self-destruction; others might see it as the kind of God-inspired invention that saves millions of lives every year and makes life more comfortable for all who can afford it.

In the early part of his papacy, Francis defended a man charged with punching someone on the basis that he would do the same if someone insulted *his* mother. A punch for an insult? This said little about his understanding that one punch can kill, and regularly does, and that we all – even popes – bear responsibility for our choices. Ask Father Ralph.

The Church, of course, has long known a thing or two about the lesser of two evils. In the lead-up to World War 2, although opposing National Socialism, it preferred the Nazis in Germany (where Catholics comprised 30% of the population) over the godless communism of Russia. Pope Pius, unlike many brave German Catholic priests who ended up in Dachau for their courage, did nothing at the time to protect the Jews. He preferred peace with Hitler, whose virulent antisemitism had been known since the publication of his best-selling book *Mein Kampf* in 1925. The Church's own antisemitism had been practised for two thousand years, so it was in an awkward position.

The lesser of two evils? After the war, the Church helped organise the ratlines that smuggled many of the worst war criminals to Argentina, the home of the current Pope, whose anti-Israel comments did not go unnoticed during their current conflict in Gaza.

Katherine also wondered about the ageing Pope's hypocrisy related to his criticism of the American (and some European) approach to illegal immigrants. In the Eternal City outside the papal walls, Italians paid scant attention to what he had to say on much at all, whilst Vatican City was one of the most secure areas in the world. It was only 49 hectares (121 acres) with a population of less than a thousand, but it would be unwise for even the poorest shepherd and his pregnant wife to try taking their donkey past the well-armed Swiss Guards in search of a place to sleep. The inn was full, and visitors weren't welcome.

*

As Father Ralph wished everyone a good week, Jim Nicholas looked to his right to meet the eyes of his fellow congregant in the back row. That wasn't going to happen; she was gone – again.

After mentally kicking himself, he quickly exited the church in time to see a blue Mazda 3 leaving the car park. It was 11:01 when, unprompted, Jim's Jukebox began playing the haunting opening chords of 'Every Breath You Take' by The Police. The fourth and fifth lines made clear why it was playing, as Sting sang that *every step you take I'll be watching you*. When the song was released and became a worldwide hit in 1983, many thought it was a love song. Not even close. These days, it would be identified as being about possessive love and stalking – dangerous stuff. Jim had no intention of stalking the lady in the blue Mazda, but he did plan to follow her.

*

Expecting that she lived nearby, Nicholas was somewhat surprised when, one hour and twenty-four minutes later, they'd travelled 99.6 kilometres and were arriving in Surfers Paradise. But the lady in the blue Mazda wasn't stopping just yet, and seventeen minutes later, they were cruising past Coolangatta on their way to the NSW border. Jim maintained a safe distance of about ten cars from the Mazda; his years of training as a detective made following an amateur without being noticed a pretty straightforward business. Besides, she would have no reason to believe she was being followed. Jim was thinking many things, not least that it was a long way to go to church. The obvious follow-up was: why was she?

Forty-two minutes later, the blue Mazda turned left off the highway at the Byron Bay exit and, after passing through the township, drove three minutes up Lighthouse Rd before turning left into winding Palm Valley Drive, which, in two minutes, took him down to Marine Pd along the beachfront at Wategos Beach. One street back from the beach – and parallel to it – was Pandanus Lane, and that's where the blue Mazda drove into the garage of a two-storey refurbished beach home with a balcony on the second floor that boasted a view to the ocean that many would kill for.

A poor choice of words, perhaps, given that only 1.5 kilometres up the hill was the lighthouse, which Jim believed was where, on the rocks below, Father Jack Merryfield was last seen. He parked in the narrow lane with no idea of where this was going but with faith that it was going somewhere. Faith? Now, that was interesting.

His watch showed 1:29. The drive had taken two hours and twenty-eight minutes exactly.

*

He sat in his car contemplating next steps and the consequences – intended or otherwise – of his choice. Father Ralph would be impressed! Jim reminded himself that some of his most successful investigations as a detective began with the premise that action created more action – set forces in motion and let them lead the way. So, what did he do? He walked across the road, approached the large door, and rang the bell.

It was a simple act, but if he hadn't done it, he would never have discovered the how and why of Father Jack's disappearance. Simple acts often assume an importance unimagined. The Butterfly Effect says that, in our deeply interconnected world, one small occurrence can influence a much larger complex system. It happens every day.

The door opened less than a minute later, and he was welcomed by a woman wearing an enigmatic smile and a comfortable kaftan, the hues of which mirrored the ocean below. She put out her hand and introduced herself with a hint of humour.

"Hello, my name is Katherine. Were you going to sit there all afternoon?" she asked, her smile wider now. "Please, come in, Jim. I'll make us some coffee, and we can talk."

Jim?

21

Monday, August 19

Byron Bay

"And then we talked," Jim Nicholas told Danny and Shannon when they met to discuss the previous day's events, right up until he was welcomed into Katherine's home. More accurately, the lady who'd previously said very little talked – a lot – but before he told them what was said, Shannon asked how she'd known his name.

Jim, looking sheepish, replied, "She followed me back to Lennox Head last week."

"Jim," Katherine told him, "I read the papers and knew you were working with Dan Shaw. I figured you'd be visiting the church where Merryfield worked." Trying not to rub it in, she added: "It wasn't hard; you had no reason to believe you were being followed."

At that, re-living his thoughts about following *her* that morning, he laughed, after which she asked, "Now, what would you like to know?"

"Everything."

*

She wasn't ready to do that and told Jim she would tell him in instalments – enough to provide Dan Shaw and Adam Christopher with plenty to write and talk about. And, no, she wouldn't be talking with police and didn't want her name used in any stories. "That would make things difficult," she said.

Instead, she wanted Jack Merryfield's story told as representative "of the others he abused." Jim noticed there was no mention of the word *Father*.

"Do you mind if I record our chats, Katherine?"

"I don't, Jim. Accuracy is important." She only insisted that the police never hear it, which was fair enough. The former detective was now working with Dan Shaw in an unofficial investigation and, in that capacity, was talking with a source who had every right to maintain confidentiality. He was in no position to share any of what he heard with Detective Cassie Miller, nor was solving the crime his responsibility, even if it was the aim. With that clear, he asked where she would like to start, to which Katherine replied, "At the beginning."

*

She was born to Dutch parents, who came to Australia after the war. They learned the language, worked hard, and, despite a difficult time finding work after their marriage in 1952, settled happily into a migrant camp in Brisbane. Katherine's brother and sister were born within the next five years, and she came along in 1959. Her parents were strict Catholics and attempted to live according to the dictates of their religion. That included no artificial contraception. Sex was primarily about procreation, and barriers to that were considered a grave sin.

After Katherine's birth, her mother suffered several miscarriages, one of which almost claimed her life. As a result, her father decided to defy that injunction so that he could both protect and love his wife – her mother. He continued praying, attending church every Sunday and living a good life. Several years later, her grandfather, a devout Catholic, announced he was coming to visit from the Netherlands, and her parents decided to confess their "sin" of using contraception to their local priest so that they could all take communion together during his stay.

Her father went into the confessional, quickly followed by raised voices and yelling. It continued outside as the priest refused them absolution. Her parents never returned to church, so her grandfather – she called him Opa – cut a lonely figure walking to Mass by himself.

At the same time, she said, Catholic clergy at every level all around the world were abusing children, ruining their lives and protecting colleagues who were doing the same. Those priests continued to say Mass, consecrate the host and attend confession, at which they were always forgiven. Jim now played the remainder of the recording, and Danny and Shannon heard Katherine say:

"My magnificent Opa returned to Holland and died shortly thereafter, convinced that his son and family were destined to spend eternity in hell. That's a shameful legacy from the Church he'd devoted his life to. When he arrived in Australia, he gave me a beautiful present: a small black box containing rosary beads. I haven't used them for many years, but they remain a special part of my life. They remind me of the grandfather I adored and would never see again, and of the incredible cruelty and hypocrisy of the Church."

She then spoke of her early days at Zillmere State School in a northern suburb of Brisbane. She loved it and absorbed everything. She took Communion in Year 5, and by the time she went to high school was playing the flute, violin, and piano. Her parents, for reasons of convenience, sent her to Sacred Heart at Sandgate. It was the kind of decision all parents make along the way, never knowing until later where the choice might lead. This one changed her life.

It was there that, when she was fourteen, she met Father Jack Merryfield, a young priest in his mid-twenties who also took an interest in music.

*

Jim wanted to talk longer but Katherine set the guidelines, and given the nature of what she was sharing, he was happy to play by her rules. She agreed to meet again the following Sunday and for as many Sundays as it took to tell her story.

The conversation ended when Jim Nicholas asked Katherine this question:

"Did you kill Merryfield?"

"You'll have to wait until the end of the story."

"Is he definitely dead?"

"Yes."

She said it immediately, firmly, and without the slightest hint of a smile.

22

Sunday, August 25

Byron Bay

Aweek later, Jim was waiting for Katherine at her Wategos Beach home when she arrived precisely two hours and twenty-eight minutes after leaving St Vincent's Parish, The Gap. She smiled when she saw him and said, "I missed you in church." It might have been the first time that sentence had been aimed in his direction.

His week had been busy and included a long phone conversation with Detective Cassie Miller, who, whilst making some progress of her own, fully respected Jim's inability to tell her more. But he did tell her – and the public would learn soon enough – that the body was, in fact, that of Father Jack Merryfield.

He couldn't tell her how he knew it definitively because that would mean involving photographer Taylor, but she knew he would never mislead her and proceeded on that basis. She also knew he would do all he could within his unique ethical boundaries to assist. Last year, after all, he'd let a killer go free with her implicit knowledge and consent. He told Miller where Merryfield had worked before his disappearance, which was also easy to determine. He mentioned none of this to Katherine, took her outstretched hand, and asked what Father Ralph talked about in his homily.

"Cats and dogs," she replied, amused. "He never ceases to amaze."

She was a serious woman with a serious story, but he liked how naturally and often she laughed. That raised this question: would she be laughing if she'd recently killed Merryfield?

"Give me five minutes," she said, "and I'll tell you more."

*

She walked down the steps, dressed comfortably for the twenty-minute walk around the path from the western end of the beach, near the famous Rae's on Wategos, to the Beach Cafe on the other side of First Point. She walked it every morning, which was at least part the reason she was in such good shape. It was a fine day, around 24 degrees, and surfers unprepared to wait for summer – or even spring – were doing their best on a small left-to-right break.

The path initially rose steeply, and they soon had a magnificent view of Wategos Bay below and the ever-present lighthouse behind them. She then went into more detail about Father Ralph's sermon.

"He was talking about what Pope Francis said in Indonesia this week. The Pope praised the Indonesians for having so many children and lamented that Europe wasn't even having enough to maintain its population. The Pope lost his patience and scolded a woman who asked him to bless her dog. 'Children are hungry,' he said, 'and you want me to bless your dog?'

Apparently, it didn't cross his mind that many were hungry *because* they had too many children. Father Ralph, who loved animals, nonetheless spoke of what God said our relationship with animals should be. He quoted Matthew 6: "*Look at the birds of the air; they do not sow or reap or store away in barns, and yet your heavenly Father feeds them. Are you not much more valuable than they?*"

Katherine, as was her habit, disagreed with every word he said but still thought him a kind and gentle man. She'd long ago decided that animals, with their natural curiosity, loyalty, consistency, enthusiasm, and capacity for love, were much more valuable than (most) human beings.

After arriving at the Beach Cafe, they were soon seated by the open window watching the whales making their way south. Awaiting the arrival of their meal – barramundi and salad – Katherine picked up her story unprompted. She didn't miss a beat, and the following sentence flowed seamlessly from her last one a week earlier.

*

"Father Jack was popular, and it was not hard to see why. He was the youngest of all the priests and appealed to our youthful idealism. He talked about the things we liked to discuss: music, the future, how to make the world a better place and what the Bible said about all this. It was as if he understood us, which he did. Groomers always do.

"He would often play songs in class and lead discussions about the lyrics. Bob Dylan's 'The Times They Are a-Changin'' was his favourite. Peter, Paul and Mary weren't far behind, and it occurred to us even then that he spoke a little too enthusiastically about the beautiful Mary Travers. Still, we figured, why can't a priest admire beauty as long he didn't act on it?"

*

The food arrived and they spoke of other things as they enjoyed it.

Of how she came to live here;

Of her career as a music teacher and how she still practised it several days a week;

Of his career (most of it anyway);

Of her late husband Isaac, a remarkable man.

Of his wife Alex, and her work in radio;

They spoke, too, of the curious way Jim and Alex had met and some of the details of the case that brought them together.

A case, he would learn later, that Katherine had followed closely.

*

Over coffee, she told Jim about Merryfield's admiration of children.

"He used a lot of Biblical quotes to make his point," she said as she reflected on it. "A Kingdom for David, a son of God for Mary. God was always choosing young people, he told us. And then he said something that would be carved forever into my fourteen-year-old heart: *God loves young people; never be afraid of being chosen.*"

Merryfield had made his choice and would act on it the following year. Jim paid the bill, and they walked back to Katherine's house. He gave her a brief hug and felt the need to say nothing. Only: "Next week?"

"See you then, Jim."

Katherine looked out at the sparkling blue of the ocean and found peace in its vastness. Today it was more cobalt, the colour Van Gogh likened to the divine.

23

Wednesday, August 28

TRN Studios Sydney

After speaking at length with Jim about his most recent chat with Katherine, Alex updated Adam Christopher, who was keen to name the late priest a paedophile. Before he did, the Program Director insisted he talk with TRN's defamation lawyer, Peter Grace, not only to make sure he was free to do so but also to be able to say, if legal action ensued, that he had taken all reasonable measures to ensure he could.

That would be vital for insurance protection and for arguing a Qualified Privilege defence if sued. Adam knew that Shaw was going to break the latest on the story in Sunday's paper and wanted to be ready the following morning. Likewise, Danny knew that Adam's coverage might open possibilities more widely amongst those who didn't necessarily read the papers.

This was what brought them all together at the TRN offices in Phillip St, Sydney, on that last Wednesday morning of August.

*

Qualified Privilege is one of the most common defences media outlets use when sued for defamation. To mount it, you must prove you've taken all necessary and possible steps to ensure that you are reporting factually and that the comments you are being sued for were based on that research.

That's why Network Ten's Qualified Privilege defence failed when Bruce Lehrmann sued them in the controversial case involving Brittany Higgins earlier in the year. The story they ran on the television show The Project was highly critical of Lehrmann but depended too heavily on information they'd secured from Higgins, much of which didn't stand up to intense scrutiny in the courtroom. Ten won, however, on their Truth defence. The impressive Justice Michael Lee didn't have much time for either Higgins or Lehrmann as reliable witnesses, but on the balance of probabilities, he sided with Higgins on her central claim that she was raped.

Christopher was confident that, based on what Shaw would write (which, for now, would rely almost entirely on what Katherine had told Jim), there would be enough information in the public arena to name Merryfield, but any potential danger might come from the link the story made with the Catholic Church. It has a stable of highly paid lawyers and is never reluctant to use them. As the investigation proceeded, they would learn more about how some of them earned their money.

*

They gathered in the conference room soon after Adam finished his show at midday. Sandwiches, water, and coffee were on the table in the middle.

Peter Grace was now widely considered among the country's elite defamation lawyers, a group that included Sue Chrysanthou and Dr Matthew Collins. They regularly appeared in high-profile cases, where watching their intellectual brilliance was not unlike admiring Roger Federer, Lionel Messi, or Simone Biles at the peak of their powers. Trained excellence became instinctive. Facts, like a favoured overhead smash, were saved for the precise moment they would do the most damage.

Last year, Peter Grace supplied the link that eventually resolved the case concerning the murder of Adam Christopher's predecessor, in which defamation and freedom of speech (and its abuse) figured prominently.

Like Elon Musk, Bradley thought unfettered free speech was good and that he was only doing what a healthy society required him to do. That was, of course, nonsense on many levels. His ugly words led directly to the death of Dan Shaw's daughter Rachel and, in a twist Ed Bradley could never have envisaged, his own as well.

*

Free speech and its limits were among the most contentious issues governments and media were confronting worldwide. On the one hand, major tech companies with global reach, like X and Facebook, were setting their own agendas, while on the other, countries and families were increasingly uncomfortable with the impact these 'freedoms' were having on their children, communities, and political life. Division was created and then exploited by algorithms developed to capitalise on the discord. Musk thinks that is somehow healthy.

There is no denying he's a genius and often uses his power productively, but it's equally true that Elon is a very peculiar and, in some ways, dangerous man. Just that week, American provocateur Tucker Carlson posted an interview on X with Darryl Cooper, who Carlson described as one of the best modern historians. The problem being that Cooper is also a Holocaust denier and antisemite who blames Winston Churchill for starting World War 2 – some historian. Musk initially said the interview was 'very interesting' and 'worth watching.' Neither is true; it was a lit match to rampant antisemitism.

Once a fine writer, iconoclast, and thinker, Carlson has 14 million followers on X and Musk 197 million, so that stuff is all out there awaiting an incurious and often impressionable public.

Young people unburdened by facts or study will presume it to be true. Surely you couldn't say it, they would reasonably think, if it weren't? By the time Carlson and Musk's Twitter feed was 'liked' and forwarded to their followers, more than a billion people viewed it. Well done, Elon; congratulations, Tucker.

Dani Dayan, chairman of Yad Vashem, the World Holocaust Remembrance Centre, responded with the unadorned truth: 'Tucker Carlson and his guest Darryl Cooper engaged in one of the most repugnant forms of Holocaust denial of recent years. These far-fetched conspiracy theories are not only dangerous and malevolent, they are antisemitic.'

None of this bothers rapper Kanye West, who busily keeps his 32 million followers up to date with his latest racist and antisemitic ravings. His grip on sanity is fragile, and there was a time when he would have been locked away for his own good. Kanye is living proof it wasn't such a bad policy.

Despite Musk's best efforts, there is no untrammelled right to free speech and he shouldn't act so surprised when countries like Brazil start banning X. Germany is making similar noises and others will follow. What right, the billionaire should ask himself, does he have to tell other countries what is best for them? The thing is, though, that people like him never ask those kinds of questions.

It was one of the reasons for their success.

*

Peter Grace was still celebrating the decision handed down by Supreme Court Judge Peter Applegarth the previous day. He was part of a team employed by News Ltd, the publisher of *The Australian* newspaper and the podcasts it produces, one of which was *Shandee's Story*. The podcast was the work of highly respected Hedley Thomas, whose previous work on *The Teacher's Pet* led to

Chris Dawson's conviction for the murder of his wife Lynette on January 8, 1982. Grace then provided some background.

Shandee's Story detailed the vicious stabbing murder of Shandee Blackburn, 23, in Mackay in February, 2013 as she walked the short distance from her work to home. Her former boyfriend, John Peros, was charged with her murder and found not guilty. A Coroner later concluded that he did, in fact, murder Shandee.

Grace explained that the different conclusions were mainly due to the coroner being able to hear *all* relevant evidence, much of which the jury couldn't access at the criminal trial. Different burdens of proof were also a factor, as was the monumental incompetence of the Queensland Forensic Laboratory.

This was discovered by the brave whistleblower Dr Kirsty Wright, whose extraordinary claims on the podcast, initially denied by the laboratory and the Queensland Government, turned out to be true.

The lab's maladministration, scientific irresponsibility and systemic failures related to DNA samples resulted in thousands of cases being reviewed. Some guilty people had no doubt walked free, whilst others (lacking available evidence to prove their innocence) were falsely imprisoned. Could bureaucratic incompetence get any worse? An official investigation followed, and the recommendations were scathing of the lab. As always, a government resisting controversy and lousy publicity was slow to act. Inertia and bureaucracy are on first-name terms.

In the Peros case, the lab found none of his DNA in his car, which was impossible. His DNA would be all over it, as all our DNA is in our cars and everywhere else we spend time. But, inexplicably, no one was curious enough to ask what was happening. It was easier that way. But how could they have found Shandee's if they hadn't found his? Grace then explained the nature of the case Peros was seeking to bring.

Hedley Thomas chronicled all of this superbly in the podcast, but Peros took action, claiming the thirteenth episode gravely defamed him and caused him 'serious harm.' Most wondered, as did the judge, how someone already called a murderer by a coroner could have his reputation damaged. It didn't help his cause that he didn't produce one person who thought less of him because of the podcast; anyone who listened to the evidence would have long ago formed an opinion.

All Peros achieved with his actions was to let even more people know about the case and refocus attention on what many believe to be a grave miscarriage of justice. Given the strict double jeopardy laws, he can't be re-tried for murder unless there is new, fresh, and compelling evidence. The kind of thing an adequately constituted and professionally run forensic laboratory might be able to provide.

*

As interesting as Grace's explanation was, they were keen to get down to business: Could Adam name Merryfield a paedophile, and if he did, how might the church respond? Dan Shaw would factor it all into his upcoming article as well. He had strong views on freedom of speech, as demonstrated the year before. He believed responsible speech was necessary in a democracy, but irresponsible speech was highly damaging. The balance lies, he believed, where my freedom *to* meets your freedom *from*. Peter Grace was in the business of sorting the one from the other, and his answer had several components.

"If we start," he began, "with the premise that Merryfield is dead, then you have no problems with him. The dead can't sue. Anyone who defames a deceased person is not liable under the Defamation Act of 2005 because the underlying principle asserts that, and I quote, *Dead people can feel no shame or humiliation.*"

A pity, Alex thought fleetingly. A large dose of humiliation would've been well deserved in this case, although it appears likely the priest suffered an even harsher penalty.

Grace went on to say that, as they'd anticipated, the only legal threat might come from the Church, which – by implication – could be held responsible for allowing Merryfield to maintain easy access to children.

"But if your witness, Katherine, is to be believed," he concluded, "there's only a remote chance of them taking action. Better a sullied dead priest than yet more negative publicity. I'd publish."

And on the following Sunday, that's precisely what they did.

24

Wednesday (evening) August 28

Coogee Beach

Jim resigned from the police force late the previous year after the conclusion of the investigation into murdered shock jock Edward 'Big Ed' Bradley. He had no qualms about how he conducted the case (and choreographed its ending) but knew he couldn't continue in that line of work. He had crossed boundaries that you can't uncross. If he did what he thought was right regarding Dan Shaw, then resignation was also the correct course of action.

He often thought what an odd turn of events it was that had it not been for Bradley, he would never have met Alexandra Burns. Myriad things, most of which we are unaware of, conspire to impact our lives. Alexandra became Alex and then AB after their first couple of interviews and dates, one of which led to dinner where they now sat – on a two-seater lounge in the three-bedroom house they shared in Vicar St Coogee.

The Salvador Dalí print, 'Young Woman at a Window' ('Jeune Filles à la Fenêtre'), hung in the same place and was a constant reminder of one of their earliest discussions. The oil-on-canvas painting, which Dalí completed at just twenty-one, is of his younger sister, Anna Maria, staring pensively out the window at the light blue ocean beyond. What is she thinking? It is a mystery without an answer and has travelled down the years and around the world. It was during that early conversation that Jim and Alex recognised they had never been able to speak of such things with anyone else – one of the aspects of love.

The music on the sound system was a reminder, too, that Van Morrison's 'Brown Eyed Girl' was playing that night. At the time, he wasn't sure of the colour of her eyes. Van was wrong: they were mostly green, about three shades lighter than emerald – chartreuse would be close. Regardless of colour, they were beautiful and reflected the soul of a young woman whose intelligence, curiosity, and decency had taken her to the top of one of the most competitive of industries.

She came to the Talk Radio Network after early success programming Sydney's top music station, but her skills proved instantly transferable. Bill Conrad, the head of Conrad International, now vested most responsibility for the daily running of his powerhouse TRN in her hands. Alex, still in her 30s, carried the responsibility lightly.

The broadcasters respected and liked her, the latter not being compulsory but undoubtedly handy.

She understood the nuances of broadcasting instinctively and the maths and science of it deeply. He recalled her ringing one of the younger announcers at two a.m. and saying: "Murray, it's Alex. You're sounding terrific. Just one thing: Never say 'Good morning *everyone*'. Everyone isn't listening – it's just me. You're talking to one person." The announcer must've thanked her, and she replied, "Cool. See ya soon."

Two things about that: the young bloke learned a valuable lesson about the psychology of what he was doing – how many people do you hear commit the same communication 'sin'? – and she had also let him know she was listening. It was one of her mantras: you never know who's listening. That was about to pay a heavy dividend related to the case of the missing priest.

*

After the lunchtime meeting, Jim caught up with Cassie Miller and touched on the current case. She appreciated that Jim would have more investigative freedom and mobility, so gave him a few contacts that might shed more light on Merryfield's past. They agreed to stay in touch.

When he let himself in the front door shortly after six, AB was emerging from a shower wearing one of his old T-shirts. It was dark green, XL, and featured a picture of David Bowie on the front celebrating his 2004 Australian tour. It ended just above her knees, and with her hair pulled back in a pigtail, she looked all of nineteen.

David's music was a constant in his life, and it regularly appeared on the jukebox only he could hear. They both loved Bowie and respected his ability to remain relevant and influential for five decades. Of how many artists can that be said? Interestingly, they admired him as well for the way he died. He was only sixty-nine, but consistent with how he lived his life and the personas he created, this was just another thing to be experienced. No huge deal, no press conferences, no tweets, no leaked newspaper stories, no desire for sympathy, no farewell tours, no weekly medical updates. He just checked out, and only those closest to him knew. Farewell, Ziggy; thanks, Major Tom.

In her days as a music announcer, Alex interviewed the respected music historian David Ward, whose words about Bowie resonated still:

'Bowie's genius was that he never ceased to evolve, and if he was inspired by the musical output of others, he always distinctly mutated it into his own. Until Blackstar, *his final LP, where he simply chose to reveal to the public his final and most honest and unadorned persona. Himself.'*

*

Over dinner (Chinese, excellent), Jim told AB about Katherine and hoped she would meet her soon. He also told her about Father Ralph, the kind and gentle man with whom Katherine never agreed. Perhaps she would meet him as well.

After they ate, it seemed appropriate to play some Bowie. First, it was 'Let's Dance', and they did. Then came 'Absolute Beginners' and the lines that said so much:

Long as you're still smiling
There's nothing more I need
I absolutely love you

The green of her eyes complemented the T-shirt perfectly. Hues of Green, he thought. Dalí would've liked that.

They danced some more, holding each other close, and he soon learned that Alex wore nothing under the T-shirt. Hey, he was a detective!

25

Sunday, September 1

Brisbane

Father Ralph enjoyed his Sunday ritual. He rose at 6:15 every week, which gave him plenty of time to make a hearty breakfast and read the paper to finalise his thoughts for the homily he would deliver during the service starting at ten.

As a courtesy, Jim Nicholas rang him several days earlier to tell him that the *Sunday Telegraph* would be running a story on Father Jack Merryfield that he and the congregation might find disturbing. He also advised him that Adam Christopher would now be pursuing the case of his missing associate on his networked radio show on TRN, which also broadcast into Brisbane. There was no predicting at this point where the chips would fall.

When Jim arrived a little earlier than the 8:45 they'd agreed upon, he found his new friend sitting alone in his study off the presbytery with his usual smile nowhere to be seen. Father Ralph looked understandably worried.

He'd read Dan Shaw's article and was still trying to come to terms with it. Shaw's piece was short, but so are most fuses. Of the 330 words he wrote, these were the 87 that rocked Father Ralph:

'We can confirm that the missing priest was Father Jack Merryfield and that he has been the Assistant Priest at St Vincent's in the Brisbane suburb The Gap for more than fifteen years. We have information that indicates he had been the subject of serious allegations involving juveniles in the past. He was defended at

the time by lawyers representing the archdiocese and was moved without his new associates and colleagues being informed of the reasons for his arrival.'

The article added sketchy background information and mentioned Merryfield's love of rugby league and his enjoyment of placing small bets on the horses.

"I'd heard the rumours, Jim," Father Ralph explained, "but had no idea of this alleged reality. How would I? Head office told me not to worry about it, and perhaps to my shame, after watching Father Jack closely for some time, I didn't. Do you think this has something to do with his disappearance?"

Jim replied honestly. "It's possible, Father, but I don't know for sure." Without telling him why, he added, "But I might soon."

*

Nicholas didn't believe Father Ralph had cause to be ashamed. He thought him a good man trapped inside a worldwide culture where the most grievous sins had been committed for decades (centuries?) and the guilty protected at the highest levels. The many decent priests did their best to protect those in their care and do what their calling demanded: preach the gospel, which Father Ralph would do in his sermon at 10:15.

Before the service began, he spoke casually with parishioners and promised to address any concerns. He then commenced his homily by talking honestly about the article many had already read. He told them, as he told Jim, that he had no idea what these allegations were about, but thought that was no excuse. He was, in fact, far more critical of himself than many in the congregation thought warranted. But that was his way; he was a kind and gentle man. Wise, too.

Jim watched Katherine intently as the priest spoke, just as she watched Father Ralph. More than anyone, she was keen to hear the answers to how much he knew and, being aware of the circumstances, believed him. As he often did, Father Ralph leveraged his personal crisis for a broader meditation on worry.

He mentioned Mark Twain's quote – *'I've lived through some terrible things in my life, some of which happened'* – and made the point that most of the things we worry about don't happen, and therefore, most of our worrying is a waste of time.

To underline his point, he quoted Matthew 6:34: *'Therefore do not be anxious about tomorrow, for tomorrow will be anxious for itself. Sufficient for the day is its own trouble.'*

And then Proverbs 3:5–6: *'Trust in the Lord with all your heart, and do not lean on your own understanding. In all your ways, acknowledge him, and he will make straight your paths.'*

It sounded to Jim as if the Lord had some work to do.

*

After making another fast getaway, Katherine waited for Jim outside. That was a first. She, too, had read the story that morning and was keen to progress it. "Follow me," he said smiling, knowing that's exactly what she'd done several weeks earlier. All the way back to Lennox Head.

Seven kilometres and twenty-three minutes later, after cutting through the backstreets of Bardon and Toowong, Jim drove into the University of Queensland grounds at St Lucia. Katherine was close behind.

Set on the banks of the Brisbane River, the University was established in 1909 to celebrate Queensland's separation from the colony of NSW. Most Queenslanders would agree that it was a good thing they separated; otherwise, there would be no State of Origin football!

When he worked in Brisbane, Jim often walked around here and stopped by Wordsmiths café and the bookstore. They strolled for a few minutes, and he talked with Katherine about the strange directions life could take, and how he was now doing the university course he'd rejected more than twenty years earlier. Thanks again to Big Ed.

The City Kat ferries made their way quietly up the river to the terminal before the Eleanor Schonell Bridge, which opened in December, 2006. The bridge links Dutton Park to the University and was the first in Australia designed exclusively for buses, bicycles, and pedestrians.

Because of that, it was criticised at the time, but the critics were wrong. It's a beautiful piece of engineering and diverts thousands of people from the main thoroughfares, Ipswich Rd and Coronation Drive, that served the precinct at either end. They also questioned the cost, but try building something like that now for $55 million.

In 1973, Prime Minister Gough Whitlam was widely pilloried for spending $1.3 million on Jackson Pollock's 1952 painting 'Blue Poles'. It now hangs in the National Gallery and is worth over $500 million. Sometimes, the critics just don't know.

Jim and Katherine made their way back via the rugby field, the home ground of the mighty Red Heavies. Since they were founded in 1911, the team has won 33 first-grade premierships, a feat not equalled by many other sports teams anywhere. The ground is surrounded by the athletic track, which many visiting countries used as a practice facility before the 2000 Sydney Olympics.

Knowledgeable observers on the Saturday afternoon before the Games began would've noticed a dark-skinned African woman run two consecutive sets of 800 metres (with only a brief rest in between) in a fraction over two minutes for each set. It was extraordinary. She was the Mozambique champion, Maria Mutola, and two weeks later she easily won the women's Gold Medal in 1:56:15.

*

After ordering sandwiches and coffee, they sat beside the tennis courts at Saint Lucy Cafe. Katherine picked up where she'd left off at Byron Bay.

"Merryfield had chosen me," she began. "It started subtly and simply enough. The small groups from music class would meet to practise and listen to the songs of the day. We would talk about movies, life and love. It occasionally felt uncomfortable in ways I wouldn't understand until much later. Why would I have cause to?

The priest, whom we all loved, also seemed to love us, but soon he culled the pack even more. Like a cowboy cutting a cow from the pack for sport, our group – those who spent the most time with him – was reduced to three and, not long after, to one: me. He spoke of our strong bond and how no one must interfere with it. Not friends, not family. That can be a powerful message to a teenage girl dealing with emotions and feelings not previously experienced. In the eyes of someone I respected, I was special. I was loved."

She paused then, as much to be sure Jim understood her words rather than any reluctance on her part to express them. She had long ago come to terms with all that had happened and was convinced that she would not be here to tell the story if she hadn't. Which continued:

"One afternoon after school, I was in his apartment, a habit that had begun towards the end of that year. There were no alarm bells, and I felt extremely fortunate. He played Bob Dylan and mentioned the singer's lyrics that *love is all there is; it makes the world go round. Love and only love, it can't be denied.*"

Jim's Jukebox played Dylan often enough that he was now

tempted, inappropriately, into a few bars of 'Forever Young', one of Bobby's sweetest songs. For Merryfield and all the others, that was the obsession: youth and innocence, lust and selfishness. Dylan's song was about an ageless spirit.

Jim also had a serious problem with this lyric. Even on its surface, it was patently absurd. Love no more made the world go round than hate, envy and greed. As for being the *only* thing, that is also nonsense. There were plenty of reasons to enjoy and experience life without the word *love* ever being mentioned, and there was danger in saying such things. If love is all there is, then what do you have if you don't have love? Nothing. That's a bad idea when spoken to anyone, let alone a teenage girl.

Sensing Jim processing what she was saying, Katherine gave him a little time before adding:

"He then told me three things that changed it all. That he loved me, that he was dying, and that before he did, he wanted to make love to me. I had just turned fifteen."

Jim paid the bill, and as they walked back to their cars, it wasn't music Jim heard, but the words written by Joseph Conrad in his book *Heart of Darkness* and spoken by Marlon Brando's character, Colonel Kurtz, in *Apocalypse Now*.

The horror, the horror.

26

Wednesday, September 4

TRN Sydney

Alexandra was sitting in her office reading the media section in The Australian newspaper, where one of their writers was commenting on the ratings of the TRN afternoon program hosted by the network's only prime-time female presenter, Sonia Wilkes.

Sonia was bright, pleasant, and clearly on the rise, which appeared to be reason enough for someone to undermine her. Talk radio was not new territory for women, and many had achieved great success in the Sydney and Brisbane markets as far back as the 1950s, 60s, and 70s.

The refrain would often be heard that women weren't good at talk radio, and that neither men nor women wanted to listen to them. Arguing that women were no good at something (so, therefore, didn't deserve the opportunity to disprove it) was one of the barriers destroyed by the feminist movement – and common sense.

When Alex read the story on Sonia, which was appallingly incorrect and unfair, she was tossing up whether to laugh or get angry – something she rarely did, except on questions of fairness and abuse. The offending article said, in part, that *'station management at TRN is concerned with the dramatic fall in the afternoon show's ratings and that they were now reluctant to offer a new contract to host Sonia Wilkes, the station's lowest-rating performer.'*

It's usually best not to spotlight these things because doing so only adds attention to what would otherwise be forgotten in the relentless nature of the news cycle, but imagine if you were Sonia and read that.

Balancing it all, Alex felt that her loyalty and responsibility to her announcer, who would feel terrible and understandably insecure, was not to let this damaging misinformation remain unchallenged. She also wanted to demonstrate that she wouldn't stand for the station or its staff being the victims of this kind of journalistic bullying. They say you should never pick a fight with someone who buys ink by the barrel, but those kinds of odds didn't deter Alex.

The journalist had plainly been leaked the information by someone with an agenda and hadn't bothered checking information that was both wrong and could be highly damaging to the individual in question.

Alex believed that one of her most important responsibilities was to protect her announcers, just as it should be for any responsible employer or manager. Too often, it's not. She knew intimately the daily pressures of putting a radio program together and the frequently negative and nasty feedback to which announcers were now subjected on social media. So, instead of getting angry, she emailed a brief letter to the editor.

'Dear Editor,

Just a quick note regarding your story on our afternoon program's ratings. Your 'journalist' suggested that the number of listeners had fallen dramatically, and it was now the fourth-ranked program on the station. You further said that TRN was reconsidering the host's position. Several points:

• The program didn't lose *any* listeners. The slight decrease in its ratings (.03%) is within the margin of error and was caused not by any loss of listeners but by a slight reduction in TSL. Time Spent Listening is one of the components that determines the overall figure. Your correspondent should've known that, or checked with me.

• Likewise, he should have known that the afternoon program on Talk stations almost always has a lower overall audience than Breakfast, Mornings, and Drive because of the smaller potential audience and the ebb and flow of listenership throughout the day. Sonia's figures are, in fact, much stronger relative to those shows than her counterparts on other Talk stations in Sydney and Melbourne. She turns radio theory on its head. Your correspondent should've known that, or checked with me.

The article claimed that TRN management is concerned about Sonia's ratings and that she might not be offered a contract extension. I am the Network Program Manager, and I couldn't be more delighted with her – so much so that Sonia signed a new contract extension yesterday. Had your correspondent checked with me, he would've known that.

As a longtime reader of your newspaper, I was surprised at how sloppy and nasty this reporting was. It occurred to me that if you were so lazily wrong on a subject I know about, what should I make of areas where I trust your reporting to be accurate?

Alexandra Burns, Program Director TRN.'

She pushed send.

Alex forwarded her note to TRN's defamation lawyer, Peter Grace, requesting that he demand the letter be published in full, or defamation action would proceed. The case would be a no-brainer: there is no doubt the article was wrong – perhaps maliciously so – and that it had damaged Sonia. Alex also asked Peter to insist that the quotation marks around the word 'journalist' remain. She then cheerfully went about her work.

*

At 10.05 Alex settled back with her mid-morning coffee to listen to thirty minutes of Adam Christopher. It was a half-hour he usually reserved for callers unless there was breaking news. She always enjoyed how he handled them and that he remained open to any advice she offered.

Like all on TRN, Adam's program was networked around NSW and Queensland, so it reflected what Australians were thinking at any given time. The first caller was Chelsea from Bondi.

"I just wanted to thank you, Adam, for how you and the *Telegraph* are covering this business with the missing priest. Any day we can highlight what these bastards did and the damage they inflicted is a good day. I hope you can tell us exactly what he did and how he got away with it for so long."

Adam had been talking enough about the case off the back of Dan Shaw's story to arouse interest. At this point, he knew no more than Shaw had written but planned to do as Chelsea suggested. The caller went on,

"As a victim of abuse, I have no idea how anyone can do it, let alone a priest."

Adam asked her how she managed to deal with it, and she replied,

"I found a place for it and moved on. I was damaged and would never be what I otherwise would have been, but I'm alive and have a life to live. Not everyone gets that opportunity. I was not going to let my abuser have the final say in my life. He'd had enough say already."

Adam, whose empathy was one of his strongest qualities, asked Chelsea,

"Do you mind me asking what happened to him?"

"No, I don't," she said. "The answer is, nothing happened. I was young and had no idea how to deal with it. My father was gone, and my mother was busy raising my brother and me. I didn't want to bother her. At the time, I didn't know what to do. Like most abused children, I carried it with me. Abusers are fully aware that's what most victims do, and prey on it."

Adam knew it was a common refrain, thanked her for her call, and promised to stay on the case of Father Jack. His listeners would never know that he had also been a victim but decided early on that, despite it being literally true, he would never use that word to describe himself. It was one of the reasons for his empathy: he tried to understand other views and was slow to judge. You rarely know all of what others have been through. His predecessor, Ed Bradley, would never have let such a thought get in the way of inflicting his daily cruelties. In the end, of course, it resulted in his death.

Adam thought Taylor Swift's song had a point.

Karma's gonna track you down; Step by step from town to town.

Big Ed should've listened more to Taylor; Father Jack, too, perhaps.

Alex liked how Adam handled both the caller and the issue and made a note to tell him so later. She also knew that Jim and Dan Shaw were hard at work on the case, and there would be more to come. Soon.

27

Wednesday, September 4

Byron Bay

As Alex was running the daily affairs of the Talk Radio Network, her husband Jim Nicholas had returned to the headland where this all began fifty days earlier. Progress can often seem limited until you look back and see how far you've travelled. He parked down the hill on Wategos Beach, but this time he didn't go and see Katherine. Instead, he took the walk from the beach up to the lighthouse. He was in no rush and reached the top in seventeen minutes.

On the way, he passed a young couple excitedly taking selfies, not thinking for a moment (why would they?) that what they were doing was not even contemplated until recently.

Jim was only in his forties but sometimes felt the world had passed him by. He took comfort from the notion that there were probably people in their twenties who felt the same way. Such was the pace of change.

Much was being gained with technology, but some things were being lost, including a sense of wonder. Jim sometimes pondered what might now cause someone under twenty to say, 'Wow.'

That's what people said in 1967 when Dr Christiaan Barnard performed the first heart transplant on Louis Washkansky in Cape Town, South Africa. Louis lived for eighteen days, but Susan Burkhart received hers forty-one years ago and is still going strong. Wow.

It's what they said when Roger Bannister broke the four-minute mile in 1954 and when Edmund Hillary climbed Mt. Everest in 1953. Both were deemed impossible – until they were done. Wow. It's what they said in 1956 when TV was introduced in Australia, and when Neil Armstrong walked on the moon in 1969. It's the same response the printing press would've evoked six hundred years ago, and any of the great inventions along the way. But now?

U.F.O.s could land tomorrow and might rate three paragraphs on page five. Teenagers would read about it on their phones, and the reaction would be, 'But do they have Instagram?'

The same teenagers have already booked the minor procedure a few years from now that will implant a chip into their brains, allowing instant access to Wi-Fi, the Internet, and knowledge of all that has ever happened. What then? They won't just think they know everything; they will!

For the first time in human history, everything is possible; therefore, nothing comes as a surprise. Most things we take for granted were considered impossible until not long ago, but nothing now is unimaginable, which makes future inventions even more likely. Where will it stop? It won't.

*

A strong, cold wind was swirling around the lighthouse precinct as Jim looked over the fence and down to where Father Jack Merryfield was last seen 139 metres below. At 9:15 a.m., it was 14 degrees, but felt about eight. Earlier that morning, he read an interesting explanation for two recent days of cooler spring weather.

It came as no surprise that local Greens were saying, with a certainty that a quick study of their qualifications couldn't support, that it was all because of climate change. Few would doubt that the climate was changing, and even Jim was aware that the planet could survive, at best, for only another ten years. They'd been telling him so for the last forty.

The 'expert' was saying something about cooler fronts bringing warmer weather, but with warmer oceans, there were fewer cold fronts. It turns out they're linked to the Southern Annular Mode (SAM). When SAM is negative, the cold fronts extend further north. When SAM is positive, they head south towards Antarctica. The higher pressure anomalies are likely related to an overall warmer climate compared to previous decades.

To Jim, it felt like a southerly change, so he wore a jumper.

*

His growing respect for Katherine was starting to resemble the previous year when he allowed Danny to go free because he understood what he'd done, and at one level, agreed with it. But did she kill the priest?

Given what she'd already told him, there was compelling motivation, and she lived just down the hill from where the body was last seen – seventeen minutes away. That's some coincidence, and Occam's Razor is often correct: the simplest explanation is usually the best.

First asserted by William of Ockham in the 14th Century, the theory removes the tendency to identify complexities that don't exist.

Jim's mentor Bruce Mac, the former Assistant Police Commissioner in Queensland, had given him the layman's version years earlier: 'Mate, if you hear hoofbeats, think horses, not zebras.' Bruce was a wise man, and they remained good friends. He knew as much about music as he did detective work and when stuck during an investigation, would look in the mirror and start singing the Waylon Jennings/Willie Nelson lyric,

I know what you're thinking and I don't think you're thinking at all.

So, what should Jim be thinking now?

His habit over the years was to return to the scene of crimes he was working on, although for different reasons than criminals who did the same. Unlike the murderer or pyromaniac who might want to re-live their deeds – either for sexual gratification or from a sense of triumph – Jim didn't know if this was the actual scene of the crime or only where the body ended up.

That's where Occam's Razor kicked in. Katherine lives down the hill. She had every right to want Merryfield dead, and he'd ended up on the rocks below the cliff. Could hoofbeats make any more noise?

Jim, as tutored by Mac, would also cross-examine himself. *Let's say she did do it; how on earth did a woman in her mid-60s kill a man and get him over the fence?* He liked questions because they presumed answers, even if not initially apparent. The question commenced the search.

He wanted to fully understand the physical and psychological geography of this place and take it all in. Possibilities would then emerge. He measured distances and contemplated where the German tourists Ursula and Sandra were standing when they spotted the body and where, from further down the hill, photographer Mark Taylor took the telling photo.

Confirmation bias was always a problem for detectives, and Jim constantly checked his reasoning, realising that what made perfect sense yesterday wasn't always so evident today.

Bruce Mac often reminded him to be aware of his limitations and to ask this question: What aren't you seeing? 'Stupid' behaviour can frequently result from a failure to do just that and has a scientific name: the Dunning-Kruger effect. It describes a psychological phenomenon involving a tendency of capable individuals to over-estimate their level of intelligence or competence. They may, at the same time, misjudge the expertise or competence of others.

Interestingly, people inclined to exaggerate their knowledge are often attracted to others in politics and the media who do the same. The former Assistant Commissioner frequently reminded him of a book he'd read, which suggested an absence of certainty was no bad thing. Voters don't seem to agree, which is one of the reasons we end up with the politicians we do.

Jim was uncertain, and the question of the body was playing on his mind: Did it come from somewhere else, as initially thought, or had it been here all along, wedged between rocks and unsighted under a high tide?

He took his jumper off; things were warming up.

28

Sunday, September 8

Lennox Head

In the three weeks since Jim followed Katherine back to Wategos Beach (a week after she had followed him back to Lennox Head!), Dan had pursued the story more holistically relative to the timeline. This would help put Katherine's experience into a broader context.

If she was abused around 1973/74 and was now in her mid-60s, that left a lot of blank space regarding the missing priest. And, if Merryfield was seventy-five at the time of his disappearance and arrived at St Vincent's fifteen years earlier, that meant a gap of about thirty-six years unaccounted for. His mission these last few weeks was to fill in some of those blanks.

Before leaving *The Telegraph* ten years earlier, Dan Shaw was the paper's ace crime reporter. He was trusted by police, lawyers, and a few judges as well. His credibility lent him access because they knew he would be fair, even if that fairness wasn't always to their immediate advantage.

They could trust Shaw to give them an objective hearing when it mattered. And, unlike many of his colleagues, he didn't sensationalise and never played for cheap headlines. He made sure the stories carried their own weight.

The question of fairness had figured prominently in events of the previous year when he decided to kill Big Ed Bradley, who he blamed directly for the suicide death of his daughter Rachel nine years before that. Big Ed's words after Rachel's rape, at a time of immense vulnerability, had been the catalyst to the tragedy. Bradley impugned her character and virtually blamed her (and, by implication, him) for what she'd endured.

Her actual rapist, Jack Phillips, died shortly after Bradley as the result of what police determined was an accident in the surf at Maroubra Beach, a carefully choreographed 'accident'. One witness thought she had seen another man in the surf near the victim but couldn't be sure, and although never confirmed, she had been correct. Dan felt neither regret nor guilt at his actions and slept soundly that night – and every night since.

*

Dan believed Katherine's story had to be told on two levels: the general issue of abuse and her personal experience, which would reflect that of many thousands of others. Three weeks of hard work and conversations with former (and still active) police, professors of religion, lawyers and victims' organisations led to his first major story on the case. With Peter Grace's advice regarding defamation ringing in his ears, and confident he'd met all the investigative criteria, he began the story that broke that morning under this headline:

THE MISSING PRIEST
by Dan Shaw

This masthead is now in a position to confirm that the missing priest at the centre of recent speculation, Father Jack Merryfield, was a serial paedophile who, for fifty years, was moved from parish to parish as the Church sought to protect its reputation and limit any legal jeopardy and liability.

We don't suggest that the individual churches – or the priests in charge of them – knew of his crimes, but the hierarchy most certainly did. The Catholic Church was not alone, of course, in the epidemic of abuse. The Anglican Archbishop of Brisbane, Peter Hollingworth, let a paedophile priest who had abused five boys remain in the ministry for financial and reputational reasons. His comments related to a later case in Toowoomba, which saw him resign as Governor-General, again reflected his lack of understanding of the nature of abuse and a total absence of empathy for the victims.

Hollingworth did a lot of fine work but was always less than honest about what had happened on his watch. In 2002, he wrote a letter to the Queen saying he was the victim of an orchestrated 'tall poppy campaign' when he knew full well why he was in trouble. He admitted as much later when he said he'd been 'ill-equipped' to deal with the issue and relied on the advice of lawyers and insurers. An Archbishop relying on lawyers and insurers over victims? He had been perfectly equipped, save for the desire to do anything.

Sadly, even a woman as admirable as the late Queen and her son (now the King) saw Hollingworth and the Church as the victims. Troy Bramston disclosed in The Australian newspaper that the Queen's Private Secretary had earlier written to Hollingworth expressing 'much sympathy' for the situation in which he found himself. He won't be surprised to learn that the victims of the church over which he presided didn't share it.

The enormity of the Catholic Church's crimes still defies comprehension, as does the fact that so few went to prison. Independent Commissions in Spain and France reported recently that the number of victims in each country was over 200,000. And that's only since 1950. Given the reluctance of many victims to come forward, that is a very conservative figure. And it didn't stop with archbishops.

According to Nicole Silver, a professor of religious history at the University of Sydney, 'This went all the way to the top. Referring to a case in 2018 involving Bishop Juan Barros in Chile, Pope Francis accused the victims of slander, saying Barros would never do such things. But he did, and it wasn't an isolated case. Bishop Gustavo Zanchetta, one of the Pope's earliest appointments, was eventually sentenced to four-and-a-half years for his horrendous assaults on Argentinian seminarians, but only after the Pope appointed him to oversee the Vatican treasury.'

Two months later, Francis apologised for his *grave error*, but if the head of any reputable business said that kind of thing these days, they would be sacked. And have been. It was not dissimilar to what, rightly, had cost Hollingworth his job.

Francis's predecessor, Pope Benedict XVI, wrote from retirement in 2019 that the sexual revolution in the 1960s had deemed paedophilia *allowed and appropriate*, which came as a surprise to those who were around at that time, particularly victims of the abuse. Attitudes in the sixties had done no such thing, except in the minds of paedophiles.

Benedict also failed to act against four priests accused of child sexual abuse when he was the Archbishop of Munich. He denied the allegations but stood down as pontiff in 2013. Two of those cases concerned abuse committed during his tenure, and in both instances, the alleged perpetrators remained active in pastoral care. This was the crux of the issue with Father Jack Merryfield.

According to well-placed sources with knowledge of Merryfield's history, he was moved from a parish in Brisbane in 1974, and subsequently from parishes in different parts of Queensland in 1982, 1991, 2001, and 2009. Legal action was threatened in every instance before the Church intervened and settled the complaints. *Settled* is a nice way of saying they rejected the claims, threatened to ruin the complainants financially, and then aggressively attacked them in court after they had already been abused.

Although we have learned relatively little about Father Jack Merryfield, we know that in his latter years he was liked and performed good work, but that seems to have been true throughout his career. Either he was an otherwise good man who committed terrible crimes, or his superficial decency was a disguise for something inexcusably different: a very bad wolf in sheep's clothing.

Merryfield and most of the others went unpunished because the Church considered these crimes 'moral failures'. Dr. Silver believes an understanding of the history of that proposition is essential. 'The Catholic Church', she told me, 'works under Canon Law, which it argues must be obeyed above all else. Canons (laws or principles) 489, 490, and 491 deal with priests' sins of *moral failure*. Popes, Bishops, Archbishops, and Cardinals since 1922 have followed these laws, but it wasn't always the case.

Before then, the Church was strict in punishing abusers. In fact, during the Spanish Inquisition (1570–1630), many clergy were executed for what were viewed as dreadful crimes. And in the 17th and 18th centuries, a virtual zero-tolerance policy existed.

The cultural shift began in 1842 when, under Pope Gregory XV, the Church became reluctant to surrender priests to secular authorities. In 1866, there was more change. At that point, there was not only a reluctance to hand priests over but even a refusal to dismiss them for the most vile behaviour. By the early 20th century, Pope Pius X abandoned the practice of delivering rogue priests to the proper authorities. The Catholic Church had become a law unto itself.'

So, they have known about the abuse of children but deliberately protected the abusers as a matter of Church policy. It was a system ascribed to God when it was very much the making of men more concerned with their organisation's corruption becoming public and impacting their credibility than doing something to eliminate the abuse. It had nothing to do with God. In response to widespread international outrage, Pope Francis rescinded the laws verbally in 2020 (he had no choice) so that, in theory, confession in these cases is no longer sacrosanct.

At the Royal Commission into the Institutionalised Response to Abuse, the esteemed Royal Commissioner Peter McLellan concluded: 'I cannot comprehend how any person, much less one with training in theology, could consider the rape of a child a moral failure but not a crime.' He went on to say, 'This statement by leaders of the Catholic Church marks out the corruption of the church within Australia, and ... in many other parts of the world.' And further on, 'Rather than ensure offenders were subject to the criminal law, ineffectual attempts at treatment were undertaken by the Church.'

Many will reasonably ask if it was a simple coincidence that this approach was so geographically universal, or was it the result of something more deliberate? About Father Jack, we know that he supported the Brisbane Broncos rugby league team and enjoyed the lifetime habit of making small bets on the races.

Our tip is that the sins of the Father might well have caught up with him.

29

Sunday, September 8 (afternoon)

Byron Bay

Jim Nicholas was waiting for Katherine outside her Wategos Beach home when she pulled in two hours and twenty-eight minutes after leaving Father Ralph and her fellow parishioners at The Gap. Following Shaw's story that morning in *The Sunday Telegraph* and its Brisbane stablemate, *The Sunday Mail*, there would be much for them to discuss.

As they walked around the cliff to the Beach Cafe, Katherine told him how it had unfolded earlier at St Vincent's. To Father Ralph's credit, he said he would stay behind until he had answered every question about the article and its allegations.

It was clear to everyone that Father Ralph was distraught and, rightly or wrongly, was taking some measure of personal responsibility for what was now known about his assistant. He even offered to resign if that's what they thought was best. Father was as shocked as anyone when, having heard that offer, Stan – aging and fragile – stood up and said with conviction stronger than his voice, 'No.'

His wife Edna, taken aback at what she was now doing and what her husband had already done, stood alongside him, took his hand, and said even more strongly, 'No.' Their granddaughter Simone, as proud as she had ever been of her grandparents and in a moment that would live with her forever, quickly joined them and yelled, 'No'. Andy and his wife Jennifer were next – 'No, No.'

And then Doug and Libby. 'No, No.'

In a scene not witnessed since the students all stood on their desks at the end of the movie *Dead Poets Society* in support of their teacher, played by Robin Williams, the entire congregation – none of whom were given to overt signs of protest – was on its feet. Soon, the chant resonated around the church and could be heard in nearby streets:

'NO. NO. NO. NO. NO. NO.'

It went on for several minutes and only ended when their beloved priest, with a handkerchief to his eye, said in a voice much softer than theirs, "Thank you."

Katherine, deeply moved, nonetheless disagreed with the priest. He bore no responsibility; that rested much higher up.

*

The walk around the point gave her time to process the article she, too, had read before sharing the next chapter in her story.

"Dan Shaw's right about the settlements, too. How much can one person take?" Katherine asked rhetorically, with no answer necessary. It was not unlike a boxer, already knocked senseless, being hit again and again until, finally spent, he says, *'No More.'* It's not bravery to go on in such circumstances; it's stupidity.

They took their preferred seat by the window at the Beach Cafe. It was a perfect day, with a few scattered clouds and a high of around 21 degrees.

Katherine began where she previously left off, with Merryfield telling her he was dying and that, before he did, he wanted to make love to her.

"It didn't take long for him to try to make good on his wish, although making love was not really what he had in mind. A twenty-four-year-old man does not make love to a fifteen-year-old girl," she began, attempting as she did to remain distanced from the emotions she was rekindling.

"I had only just reached puberty and was very inexperienced. I'd never had a boyfriend and was still physically immature. In every sense, I was a very young girl. He wrote me letters, one of which made clear that he had needs. *The needs of a man,* he said, *not of a priest.* This at the same time as he told me he was dying and that he was going to the hospital the next week and would not be coming home. He asked if I could help him pack, and I agreed to his request."

She stared silently at the ocean for about thirty seconds as if remembering the events she was about to describe. The dolphins, oblivious to those watching and what they were thinking, zigged and zagged in a smallish surf. Oh, to be a dolphin, she thought. "He had a favourite song," Katherine said at last, "'If I Only Had Time', and played it as I packed his things."

Jim's Jukebox found it. The singer was New Zealander John Rowles, and the song had been a hit in Australia, the U.K., and much of Europe – the power of music. Rowles possessed a lovely voice, and it was clear that Merryfield's grooming extended to the songs he played. And their lyrics:

Dreams to pursue
If I only had time
They'd be mine

Picture this, then: a priest in his mid-twenties, having already voiced his love for a conflicted teenager ten years his junior, invites her to his home under the pretence that he's dying and she's helping him pack to go to the hospital from where, he has told her, he won't be returning. The girl, confused but wanting to help, begins packing. She's in his bedroom when, again, he says he wants to make love to her. The sweet lyrics played as he attempted to do just that.

If I only had time ...

"After a struggle," she continued, "I pushed him off, trying to comprehend what was happening. A priest was someone a Catholic never questioned. I learned then what hundreds of thousands of boys and girls already knew and what countless others would later learn: how stupid we were to trust all priests. Did he look guilty or sorry? No. He looked angry and told me to get in the car, and he'd drive me home. Except he didn't do that. He drove in the opposite direction, found an isolated spot, and locked the doors from the inside, and this time, there was no pushing him off. He didn't go to the hospital, and he didn't die. Not then, anyway."

That last line landed like a goodnight right hook from Mike Tyson and, as was the case after each week's testimony from Katherine, Jim had little to say. What can you say?

"And now, he *is* dead," the investigator said finally, the only injustice in Merryfield's death being that it took so long to happen. That, contrary to the song's lyrics, he'd had way too much time.

"He most definitely is," Katherine said softly, as an actor sometimes does to add power to the words and to draw the audience in.

Then Jim asked the question he'd asked once before: "Did you kill him?"

At that, she again answered with the enigmatic smile that accompanied her previous response to the same question.

"You'll have to wait until the end of the story."

They walked back around the point to her home, the ocean as always providing solace. We have time, he thought to himself – plenty of it.

30

Thursday, September 12

TRN Sydney

Adam Christopher began his program with a brief editorial on the Presidential debate between Donald Trump and Kamala Harris the previous day. Christopher expressed surprise that the former president had so easily been drawn into the Democrats' trap.

"I simply couldn't believe," he said, "how badly Trump performed. He only had to do a few things: stay calm, smile, treat his opponent with respect, and differentiate his policies from hers. Instead, he became angry and frustrated, exaggerated everything, lacked discipline, and didn't take advantage of Harris's many openings.

He took the bait every time his opponent cast her line. In this morning's *Wall Street Journal*, the respected Republican strategist Karl Rove wrote this:

The debate between Kamala Harris and Donald Trump was a train wreck for him, far worse than anything Team Trump could have imagined.

Many undecided and swing voters will decide less on any single issue than on their visceral reactions to the candidates. Ms Harris did herself much good with that crowd on Tuesday. Mr Trump didn't.

Mr Trump was crushed by a woman he previously dismissed as 'dumb as a rock.' Which raises the question: What does that make him?

Ouch. Rove guided George W. Bush to victory, which was a considerable feat, so he has a pretty good idea of what it takes.

On at least three occasions, Harris flagrantly – but deftly – avoided answering specific questions, and Trump didn't hold her to account. Neither did the moderators, who had no problem fact-checking Trump but let all of her bloopers drift calmly by. Bias can be measured in many ways, and yesterday it was mainly in how they framed the questions and treated the candidates. The level of bias is so entrenched in traditional media around the world now that they genuinely don't even believe they're being biased. One of the reasons media in so many areas is in decline.

Trump knew the moderators would be partisan and agreed to the debate anyway, so he should've been prepared. He wasn't; Harris was. I could almost feel his advisers cringing backstage because, be assured of this, they had not practised for what he did yesterday.

One of the biggest mistakes we can all make is to underestimate opponents, and Trump believed all the nonsense spoken about how unintelligent and unqualified Harris was. A Machiavellian might sense that the Democrats have been choreographing just that – as they did the last-minute removal of Biden for Harris – for many months. Older listeners might remember Muhammed Ali rope-a-doping George Foreman in Zaire. Foreman thought Ali was exhausted and beaten until Ali bounced off the ropes and hit him with one of the sweetest uppercuts in boxing history. Yesterday, we might have seen the political equivalent.

For someone who previously had trouble stringing sentences together and seemed only able to give speeches from an autocue, she emerged as confident, articulate, and likeable. These are qualities that win presidential races. But the debate will soon be in the rear-view mirror, and Harris must answer the questions she dodged yesterday. Her ability to do that will be a deciding factor in the time remaining until election day in November.

I know many listening now want Donald Trump to win – and

he still can – but it was a bad night for the former president. We will learn in days to come whether the debate impacts polls, which currently show things to be very close.

Immediately after the debate, bookmakers reduced Trump's chances of re-election from 51.5% to 50%, and in a tight race, that's a lot. It's still 55 days until election day, but for now, Trump is in strife.

The lines are open for your calls on 1300 TRN. I'll get to them next and then talk with Dan Shaw, who has news on the case of the missing priest."

*

After the ad-break, Adam did as promised and went to the open line.

"You're listening to TRN – call after call of real life – and I'm Adam Christopher. Joining us is Les from Townsville. G'day Les."

"G'day yourself," caller Les replied, with no hint of sincerity. AB, sitting in her office, grinned; this could be interesting.

"I just wanna know how anyone in their right mind could support Donald Trump."

"Is that a question or statement, Les?" Adam said in his disarming way. Les, however, was in no mood to be disarmed.

"Don't be smart with me, mate. It was a statement *and* a question. A fair one. Your correspondent, Steve Anderson, said the other day – and you repeated it a few minutes ago – that the presidential race was tight and that various polls have either Harris or Trump just in front. How is that possible?"

"It's called democracy, Les. We all see the world differently. Not everyone sees it the way you do. Isn't that a good thing?"

"Not when it comes to Trump, mate. Seriously, give me one reason anyone would vote for him."

How would you handle a question like that? This is what Adam said:

"I'll do better than that, Les. Off the top of my head, I'll give you five.

One, they like him more than they like Harris;

Two, they prefer his policies on the Middle East and Ukraine over hers;

Three, they agree with his position on their First and Second Amendments related to free speech and guns.

Four, they prefer his policies on the US border with Mexico; and,

Five, they've had a look at California, where Ms Harris was Attorney-General, and don't want the same woke nonsense happening across the rest of the country. I could go on."

"But you don't believe that, surely?" Les sounded unconvinced.

"You didn't ask what *I* believed, Les. You wondered how anyone could vote for him. I could make the same kind of argument on different points in favour of Harris. It all depends on your priorities. But what we believe in Australia doesn't matter a damn. We're not American. As a supporter of Israel, I hope Trump wins, but that doesn't mean I like him. I liked Scott Morrison but voted against him over the outrageous Robodebt policy. No one presiding over that kind of institutionalised cruelty has any business being in a position of power.

I vote for and against people based on policy, Les, but I respect that others vote for entirely different reasons. People here also forget that Trump was the host of *The Apprentice* for a decade, and millions watched every week and liked him. It's America, and he's larger than life, and there is no way he would ever have led a political party here or in the U.K., where it's first among equals. I understand, Les, that many people loathe Trump with a passion, but equally, that just as many love him. I hate to break it to you, but he might win again."

"Hold on a second, pal," Les said, his voice rising. "The bloke's a threat to democracy. Answer that, you goose."

Alex, noticing that *mate* had become *pal* and *goose,* was keen to hear Adam's response. Hundreds of thousands are listening, pressure on, and the brain somehow clicks into gear. What would you have said? This is how Adam replied:

"How will he be a threat to democracy, Les?" Adam began. "If Trump is elected, it will be the result of a democratic vote by a majority of voters in their Electoral College. Those saying such things have a limited and pessimistic view of the U.S. Constitution and the inherent strength of their democracy. Elon Musk said the same thing if Trump *loses* the election. It's dangerous stuff and just plain wrong. Whoever wins, there will be another election in four years, and life will roll on. I'll tell you what I think is a more pressing threat to democracy, *mate.* Both there and here. When people refuse to contemplate the possibility that others might hold a different opinion and then abuse them for it. Democracy is about people living together despite our differences. Disagreement should be embraced and celebrated.

It's always important to see where the other person is coming from, even when disagreeing. Even *more* so when we disagree. To me, that's the terrible thing happening in America right now.

Relatives and friends are falling out because of their attitude to Trump, and others are moving states. That's ridiculous, and it's even crazier when the same thing happens here. There is something about the man that generates extreme views for and against, but why should that end friendships? I can see why people voted for everyone who has ever won an election.

People ask how Italians could vote for Giorgia Meloni, but Italians like her. They called her a fascist, too, but she's governing from the centre, and the same leftist politicians around Europe who cried wolf now line up to be photographed with her. Mussolini, she's not.

Donald Trump currently has the support of about 48% of American voters, and many of them are sick of being talked down to – a bit like you're doing now. It might be a good idea if, instead of just bagging them, people did what you have failed to do: look at things from their perspective. And if you don't like their point of view, try to change it. Make sense?"

"No," said Les, whose considered response was to hang up. Adam laughed, wished him a good day, and added, "On this program, you always get the final say."

*

When he took over after Ed Bradley's murder, many doubted Adam had what it took to succeed in the cut-throat morning shift. But TRN's owner, Bill Conrad, backed AB's judgement all the way. If any shareholders or senior executives complained, his answer was short: "I'm with Alex 100%". That usually ended the conversation.

Adam combined a good voice and personality with gentle humour, a curious intellect, diverse interests, and easy eloquence. He was an independent thinker, which made his positions harder to predict and more interesting because of their unpredictability. This combination is as rare as the dodo bird in today's media, and if there was cause for optimism for traditional media, this was it: he appeared to be succeeding, and others might follow.

*

Later that hour, he introduced his next guest.

"Many listeners will be following the case of the missing priest, Father Jack Merryfield, through the pages of *The Telegraph* and the byline of their crime reporter, Dan Shaw. These days, Shaw owns and edits The *Lennox Chronicle* in the Northern Rivers, where he broke the story. Good to talk with you again, Dan. Your weekend article suggests you're making progress."

"We are Adam – and thanks for covering this story. It's important. As to progress, I think you're right. We know much more today than we did last week, which is much more than when this all began. What interests me is what we *don't* know, and that will hopefully emerge in time."

"What do you think is most important amongst what you know?" Christopher asked. AB, listening in her office, thought that was a good question. Many interviewers only asked the questions written in front of them, but Adam had been listening closely.

"That will only become clear, Adam, when we have the full story. We know Merryfield is dead; we know he sexually assaulted at least five teenage girls, and we know the Church moved him around and buried the settlements with victims. Those young girls are now women in their 60s and have families that might take extreme action against people who have harmed their loved ones."

Adam Christopher had no inkling of the irony in that statement, given that Danny was describing himself and his actions the previous year, which directly led to Christopher inheriting Ed Bradley's throne.

"What about Merryfield himself? What kind of man was he?" the host continued.

"To many, he was the ageing, friendly neighbourhood priest who enjoyed the footy and a small punt. Those whose lives he destroyed will see things differently."

Adam asked his final question, "What do you think is the most likely scenario?"

"Our investigator, Jim Nicholas, is a great believer in Occam's Razor – that the simple solution is often the right one – but I've been around long enough to know it doesn't always apply. I would ask, Adam, if anyone knows anything about Father Jack Merryfield that they think might assist, could they give you a ring."

"Happy to help Dan. The number is 1300 TRN. Hopefully, someone will know something. Good luck, talk soon."

Someone did know something – and they were listening.

31

Friday, September 13

TRN Sydney

When John F. Kennedy, in the early days of his presidency, asked British Prime Minister Harold Macmillan what he should watch out for, Macmillan replied, 'Events, dear boy, events.'

His point was that the most historic problems are often unanticipated. Whilst you're planning for one scenario, another thing entirely pops up.

As commuters made their way routinely to work in Manhattan on the morning of Sept. 11, 2001, for instance, the skies were blue on a beautiful autumn day. They suggested only sunshine, but in the time it took for two airliners to smash into the Twin Towers, everything changed. Events.

On the morning of December 7, 1941, the sailors, soldiers, and airmen stationed at Pearl Harbour in Hawaii had no sense of their imminent peril, or that the Japanese attack at 7:14 a.m. would kill 2,403 and launch America into the Second World War, which would lead directly to events four years later, when ...

In the early hours of August 6, 1945, the citizens of Hiroshima, having been largely spared the terror of the bombing assault on Tokyo and other cities, quietly began their day. Few, even if they'd seen it, would have paid any attention to a B-29 flying slowly over their city. It was 8:15, and seconds later, they and their city would be destroyed by the first atomic bomb to be dropped. In his book *Even Darkness Sings*, Thomas H. Cook put it like this: 'Perhaps for the first time in human history, to those instantly vaporised, death gave no hint of its own experience.'

On December 17, 1967, when Prime Minister Harold Holt decided to take a swim in the roiling surf at Cheviot Beach on the Mornington Peninsula in Victoria, he had no idea it would be the last he would ever take. His disappearance led briefly to Prime Minister John McEwen, then to John Gorton, then William McMahon, then to Gough Whitlam, and then and then and then ... history changed. All because of an ill-advised afternoon swim.

At a personal level, life is sailing along nicely. You are happy, perhaps planning for the day and years ahead, and then the phone rings. 'Yes, Doctor?'

Events. Things change at unforeseen and unplanned moments. So do investigations.

*

Adam Christopher, unaware of what today's program would bring (and even when he heard it, ignorant of the ramifications), began his day like he did all working days.

The alarm rang at three, and he rose to drink his customary large cup of coffee while browsing the morning papers and noting potential stories of interest. He looked at *The Australian, The Telegraph, The Courier-Mail,* and *The Sydney Morning Herald.* He checked *The Financial Review* and the headline stories in overseas newspapers, including *The New York Times, The Wall Street Journal,* and *The Times* of London. At night and on weekends, he would read articles in greater depth, including English versions of *Le Monde* in France, Germany's *Der Spiegel,* and both *The Jerusalem Post* and *Haaretz* in Israel, with their conflicting views on that country's domestic and international problems.

When he arrived at TRN's Phillip St studios at 6:30, he would check his emails and X to see what various voices were saying about the day's main stories before sorting out topics, possible guests, and writing commentary pieces and questions.

At 7:30, he would meet with his two producers, whom he always encouraged to challenge his thoughts. He wanted to know what was exciting them and to hear alternative views. One, so that he could prepare arguments against them, but also because he was fully aware that there might be a better way to see things. By the time the nine o'clock news finished and his theme song began, he was ready. Game time.

Listeners would often express surprise at his range of knowledge for a young man, but like the sprinter who can effortlessly cover a hundred metres in ten seconds, it was the result of much hard work.

*

Alex was always in by seven to ensure everything was OK. She offered programming thoughts (but never insisted he use them), which was more her way of making a contribution, needed or not, to help ease the pressure. It was also a good opportunity for him to bounce any legal concerns about his editorial content and to get her thoughts on a subject he would cover. He respected her and what she had to say. Everyone did.

He began his program with a general overview of what was happening locally, nationally, and worldwide. He'd done the preparation, but knew that older listeners had much more life experience and a broader frame of reference.

He commented on the parlous state of infrastructure in both NSW and Queensland and how governments had been negligent in allowing such rapid population growth and immigration without making parallel plans to house and accommodate the health and education requirements of the new arrivals. It would be hard to make a case that Adam was anti-immigrant, given that his partner Nguyen's parents had arrived from Vietnam on a small boat with nothing.

He mentioned, as well, that a close source (actually, the press secretary to the Premier) had informed him that the Queensland election would be called within a fortnight, and the election date would be October 26. He was later proved correct on both counts. That kind of thing lends credibility, and politicians of all persuasions liked and assisted commentators they thought were fair and well-informed. He believed the Labor Government would be shown the door after a decade in power.

Annastacia Palaszczuk, when elected in 2015, had been an unlikely premier, but she won the hearts of the Queensland people, something her successor, Steven Miles, had demonstrably failed to do. His very presence caused onlookers to think fondly of Wayne Goss and Peter Beattie. The likely winner of the next election would be the LNP's David Crissafulli, a likeable and energetic man Adam had known for several years. He would have a lot on his plate, including sorting out the mess of the Olympic Games Brisbane would be hosting in 2032. They had no stadium, no funding and seemingly no idea how it would all happen, but the enduring wisdom of the Australian ethos would no doubt prevail: *she'll be right, mate.*

Adam referenced the ongoing turmoil in the Middle East (he was unambiguously pro-Israel even if he did not always agree with their Prime Minister or their tactics), the US election, and the Rugby League finals that weekend. He was a Roosters fan but thought they had little chance against Penrith and predicted Melbourne would easily account for Cronulla. He was confident that the Panthers and Storm would fight out the Grand Final.

*

He then invited feedback, and listeners wasted no time accepting the offer. In the studio, a screen told Adam the names of callers, where they lived, and what they wanted to talk about. That allowed him to mix and match to vary the subject matter or get different views on the same issue. Each person had already been vetted by his phone producer, and a delay system gave him ten seconds to dump a caller who swore or, more often, might have accidentally (or deliberately) defamed someone.

People had every right to ring, but not necessarily to get on. It was something TRN and newspapers did that social media and some FM stations didn't: they insisted on acceptable standards. Adam didn't care whether people agreed with him, only that they had something interesting to say.

Jan from Cairns was keen to argue that Queensland should be building roads and hospitals and not spending limited funds on a two-week party for the Games. It was hard to disagree.

Ken, calling from Parramatta, wanted to say that the Eels teams of the 80s would've been much too good for Penrith. Adam disagreed, and a good-natured debate began. Adam argued that new coaching, training, and dietary techniques saw players bigger, faster, and fitter. The Parramatta teams featuring the likes of Brett Kenny, Ray Price, Mick Cronin, Steve Ella, and Peter Sterling were brilliant in their time but would lose to Penrith by fifty. With the increased pace of the game, they'd be exhausted after ten minutes. Likewise, the great St George sides that won eleven premierships in a row from 1956. Just as Rod Laver, playing now with the same racquet he did then, would have no chance against Nadal, Federer, and Djokovic.

It's true in everything. The women's 100-metre freestyle world record was established in 1908 by German Martha Gerstung. Her time was one minute and 38 seconds (1:38). Dawn Fraser brought it down to 58:0 in 1964, but by 2008 Libby Trickett would've beaten Dawn by six seconds! Progress.

Before taking an ad-break, Adam had time for one more caller. Glancing at the screen, he saw that Charlie from Randwick wanted to talk about the missing priest, Father Jack Merryfield.

"Morning Charlie, how can I help? "

"I just wanted to say I enjoy your show, Adam, and appreciate the coverage you and Dan Shaw are giving to Jack Merryfield, but there is one thing you've both been saying that is wrong."

Adam Christopher, thinking it would be about the seriousness of the allegations and the growing possibility of his murder, hesitated momentarily before saying, "Go ahead, Charlie. I'm always open to correction."

But, it wasn't a big point he was correcting; instead ...

"You and Mr Shaw have been saying that Merryfield was a small punter," Charlie said before pausing, almost as if for dramatic effect.

Of all the things they'd been saying about Merryfield, that snippet had seemed like an afterthought, the type of thing you throw in to give a sense of the man. But the caller was right, even if they'd been giving it no particular meaning, so responded, "Yes, Charlie, we have been saying that."

Then came the answer that would change it all.

"Well, he wasn't a *small* punter Adam. He was a very *big* punter."

Adam quickly tried to process what he was hearing. Was it important, or just a minor detail that Dan Shaw had misreported after being given the information by others? And how would the caller know that? Such was the power of talk-radio: you never knew who was listening and what they might know.

"Can you tell me more, Charlie?" Adam asked, but there was no response. Charlie, like Les the day before, had hung up.

*

Dan, Jim, and Shannon were having breakfast in the Williams St Cafe, Lennox Head, with the radio tuned to the local TRN affiliate. At the mention of Merryfield, Shannon turned the volume up in time to hear Charlie. None of them immediately knew what to make of what they heard but were aware that some of history's biggest stories began with details that felt initially small and disconnected.

On June 17, 1972, a newsreader announced that *'Five men were today charged with breaking and entering the offices of the Democratic Party's election headquarters in the Watergate building in Washington DC…'*

In December 2019, listeners were informed that *'a virus, believed to have originated in wet markets, is causing some concern in Wuhan, China, where people are presenting with flu-like symptoms.'*

The three friends, absorbing Charlie's accented words (and the confidence with which he'd said them), looked at each other with a feeling, born of experience, that their investigation had just taken a significant and unexpected twist.

Events, dear boy, events.

32

Sunday, September 15

The Gap, Brisbane

On the drive to Brisbane, Jim thought more about Charlie's call to Adam Christopher's show. So, as they sat in Father Ralph's presbytery before the 10 a.m. service, he asked him about Merryfield's gambling habits.

Father knew of the stories that suggested his bets weren't always as small as he made out, but not much beyond that. One parishioner, the ageing Stan, had seen him at Doomben races a few years before with a wallet that looked much thicker and far less humble than you might expect of a priest.

Merryfield was smiling at the time and advised Stan, with evident confidence, to back a 25/1 shot in the last race. "It won," Stan laughed when chatting before the service. "I put plenty of my winnings in the plate the next day. Father Jack, I noticed, didn't."

Father Ralph, perhaps inspired by their conversation, also had gambling on his mind in his sermon. Or, more specifically, a wager. Pascal's Wager.

Jim was sitting next to Katherine in the back pew at St Vincent's, listening to Father Ralph talk about the logic of believing in God. She would continue her story over lunch later.

Father Ralph explained that Blaise Pascal was a noted French philosopher, mathematician, and theologian in the 17th Century who thought that individuals engaged in a 'life-defining gamble' about the existence of God. Does He exist, or does He not? Pascal argued that you should believe in God and live your life consistent with His existence. What do you have to lose after all? If God exists, there's plenty of upside, including eternal life in Heaven. You also get to avoid an eternity in Hell. If he doesn't? Well, you're dead anyway and have lost nothing.

Those unaware of Jim's Jukebox might have wondered why he was grinning, but only because they couldn't hear David Clayton Thomas and Blood, Sweat & Tears belting out a few lines from 'And When I Die':

I can swear there ain't no heaven
But I pray there ain't no hell.

Katherine, as she did every Sunday, disagreed entirely with Father Ralph. She thought he should've mentioned that Pascal considered humanity incapable of comprehending God because we are 'a finite being trapped within divine incomprehensibility.'

With that in mind, Katherine thought Pascal's argument (and, by extension, Father Ralph's) that we should live as if God exists on the chance that he does was a singular cop-out. It's a bet each way and an insult of sorts to God. '*I'll believe in you. Just in case*' is not exactly a resounding vote of confidence.

She thought it was better to live a good and decent life regardless of whether God did or didn't exist, and you should never entertain notions of heaven and eternal rewards to do the right thing. Instead, you do it because it *is* the right thing. Golfer Bobby Jones was once congratulated for calling a penalty on himself for an infringement that no one else had seen, but he rejected the praise with: 'That's like praising me for *not* robbing a bank.'

Katherine thought there were plenty of reasons to believe in God (birdsong, flowers, dogs, and the human eye amongst them) and a few not to, but she figured that any God she could envisage would understand her thinking. Unlike Pascal, she wasn't making any bets either way.

She thought Pascal was on more solid ground when he said, 'All of humanity's problems stem from man's inability to sit quietly in a room alone.' Pascal died at thirty-nine, so he discovered the answer somewhat earlier than planned.

*

Jim and Katherine picked up on the subject as they walked the University grounds at St Lucia after the service. This time, they wandered by the lake where the avenue of jacarandas signalled both the arrival of spring and approaching exam time.

Jim, a friend now, asked Katherine if her experience at the hands of Merryfield had impacted her faith. Her answer was interesting. "Yes, it did. I was a teenager who had been raped by a priest and asked myself the questions a fifteen-year-old would ask. What kind of God would allow such a thing, and what kind of religion would tolerate that kind of behaviour? I still went to church and prayed, but I wasn't sure why I was doing either.

As the years passed, and I met and married a most remarkable man who understood and helped me come to terms with everything, I came to believe in the grandeur of things – the perfection. There's a word that describes it: *numinous*. I love that word. I don't think God wants praise – that would make Him something of an egotist – but I offer gratitude and begin and end every day with a word of thanks. We are surrounded by miracles, and neither priests nor philosophers are needed to appreciate them."

*

They made their way up the path from the lake, across the quadrangle and down the hill on the other side to again sit next to the tennis courts at Saint Lucy Cafe. Over sandwiches and coffee, Katherine continued.

"He raped me again several months later. Still trying to process what had happened and still believing his lie that he was dying, I accepted his offer to go to a drive-in movie. He said several others were also going, and for the final time, I believed him. A mistake; it was only me. It's funny how these things stay with you. I was wearing a white skirt I'd made myself and a brown shirt that hung loosely over it. His hands were soon under both."

Jim, aware that every sentence brought back memories etched forever in her consciousness like some irremovable psychic tattoo, told her only to talk about those things she was comfortable discussing. Katherine appreciated it but reminded him he wanted to know *everything* and, if he was to understand the whole story, that's what he needed to hear. So she pushed on.

"A couple of weeks later, I made a half-hearted attempt to kill myself. I went to the bathroom and, with my father's razor, cut one of my wrists. Not deep enough to cause serious injury because I didn't really want to die. More than anything, it was a reflection of my emotional and spiritual pain. I'd been let loose from my moorings and knew that my life was changed forever. I could never be who I was going to be because Merryfield had taken that life from me, but I *could* lead the life I was living. And I've done just that."

Of course, Jim Nicholas had never met Father Jack but now hated him with a passion he saved for the worst offenders.

"My final year at high school was a blur," she went on, "with every day a challenge to keep going. As a result, I became a very average student. My mind was constantly distracted, and I couldn't see the importance of what I was doing. I was depressed and withdrawn. I spent time with a wonderful boy, Isaac, who was two years my senior and would later become my husband. He passed away three years ago, but he is with me every step I take. Always was and always will be.

He told me I must tell my mother, and she took me to our family doctor. His response was initially strange, asking my mother how she could let me be alone with Merryfield. With a resolve and strength I have rarely seen since, she paused as she summoned the right words and then said quietly: *We leave her alone with you, Doctor. We trust you, and we trust priests.*

After that, he had the grace to apologise and called the Church to report my experience. My mother and I went to see the parish priest, who, after hearing the story, said that he noticed I'd been going to Holy Communion throughout this period. It took me a moment to get the implication of what he was saying. He thought that I was committing serious sins with Merryfield and had no business receiving Holy Communion until I confessed."

She shook her head, sipped her coffee, and rhetorically asked, "Can you believe that?"

"He was blaming *you* for being raped by one of *his* priests?"

"He was," she said, looking at him as her mind drifted back to that time. "And, as my mother and I stood to leave, not fully comprehending what we were hearing, he said this – and these were his exact words: *It is time for you to find someone of your own age.*"

Jim put his hand on her arm, and she smiled one of the saddest smiles he'd ever seen and said, "Incredible, eh?"

And then he asked the question that had become the cue for the walk back to their cars before the long return drive to Byron Bay and Lennox Head: "Did you kill him?"

This time, her answer was different. "Would you blame me if I did?"

As was Jim's response, "No. No, I wouldn't."

She hadn't answered his question, but that didn't matter. All bets were off.

33

Tuesday, October 1

Watsons Bay, Sydney

Jim listened to Adam Christopher on TRN as he drove the ten kilometres from Coogee to Watsons Bay to meet Detective Cassie Miller for lunch. He liked the announcer's effortless style and how he was happy to engage with all points of view. His opinions were well formed, even if you disagreed with them. He made you think, and that can never be bad.

In the twenty minutes it took to navigate the coastal roads, Jim passed Clovelly, Bronte, Tamarama, and Bondi before heading on to Watson's Bay via Dover Heights, the home of missing Melissa Caddick (and her rogue foot).

Jim heard Adam chat briefly with Steve Anderson in the U.S. about the presidential election, which was now only five weeks away. He and Steve were surf club mates at Bondi as teenagers and worked well together the previous year when Steve's reporting proved decisive in the Bradley case.

Steve fought hard to stay independent in a time of polarised media. To that end, he thought the race to the White House remained to be won or lost for both candidates. About 70,000 voters would decide the election in seven swing states, and with some 150 million people expected to vote and so many imponderables, it was way too close to call.

Anderson believed Kamala Harris was making a mistake by continually calling Donald Trump a threat to democracy because at least half the country didn't believe it. He thought, too, that she should go on shows with tougher interviewers than the traditional media who, in their attempt to protect her (and their own interests), treated her with kid gloves.

"Should she win," Anderson said, "Vladimir Putin is unlikely to do likewise. Her handlers should realise that candidates often thrive on aggressive interviews and win kudos for them. Australian leaders Bob Hawke, Paul Keating, and John Howard took on all-comers and were respected for it. Besides," he added, "few interviewers can land a glove on politicians who spend many hours studying issues every day before politicising them. A fifteen-minute interview rarely allows for more than five questions, which any decent politician should handle comfortably."

Counterintuitively, Anderson also thought Democrats were erring in making Trump the constant focus: "People have seen him, heard him, and lived with him for many years. For better or worse, they know him, and this election will be less a referendum on him than on *her*. Many want him gone for good, but do they want her to replace him? That's the case she has to make to swing voters, many of whom remain unconvinced. I think things are turning slightly Trump's way."

Christopher thanked Steve and immediately introduced Dan Shaw to provide an update on the missing priest, Jack Merryfield.

"We're learning a few things, Adam, but we're still not sure how it fits together. We are in regular contact with one of his victims from fifty years ago, and we're curious about what Charlie from Randwick had to say to you about Merryfield's gambling habits. Maybe it's important; maybe it's not. We're making enquiries, but if Charlie knows more, and it sounds like he does, it would be good if he could get in touch."

As Jim passed Vaucluse Boys High and the cemetery across the road (a timely reminder to the teenagers looking out classroom windows to fill their years well), Adam returned from an ad-break with:

"This is TRN, Australia's most trusted Talk Radio Network. And, Dan Shaw, your wish has been answered. Charlie from Randwick is on Line 4. Thanks for ringing in, Charlie."

Charlie chuckled before answering, "Sorry, Adam, it's just something you said."

What had he just said? Adam would think about that later (and Jim already was) but wanted to learn more about Charlie. His confidence and the nonchalant way he talked suggested knowledge and authority. Jim thought that he detected a Mediterranean edge to his voice – Italian perhaps – and felt that, despite Charlie's friendly demeanour, he was not a man to be taken lightly. "How did you know Father Jack, Charlie?"

"Oh, we mixed in similar circles for many years, Adam, and shared various interests, gambling amongst them. But our roles were somewhat different. He was a bit older than me, and I never liked him. He had his uses, and a Catholic priest with an interest in girls was not uncommon, but one who liked *very* young girls? That's different."

Charlie had a deep voice and spoke slowly, and a playful tone suggested he was enjoying this, as perhaps he was the fact that Merryfield's disappearance had provoked interest. But why had he rung? That's just one of the questions Adam wanted to ask, but in radio you learn to read voices, and he thought he might test his luck with just one more: "Can you tell me more about his gambling, Charlie?"

"I could, Adam. I could tell you a lot, but the better question is: will I?"

Christopher pushed a little, "Well, will you?"

Which Charlie completely ignored, responding instead with:

"Do you do cryptic crosswords, Adam?"

"Sometimes, Charlie. Why?"

"Here's a clue: *Thin material.*"

"*Thin material,*" the host repeated as if searching for an instant answer. "What's that got to do with anything, Charlie?"

The answer, which could well change the course of the investigation, would have to wait. Charlie had hung up.

34

Tuesday, October 1

Watsons Bay, Sydney

Jim Nicholas believed strongly that environment impacted our personality and thought processes, so he had driven to Sydney to get some perspective and distance on the investigation. He also wanted to spend time with Alex as she dealt with the daily dramas at TRN. For now, he sat with Cassie Miller at the Watson's Bay Hotel, at the same table where, the year before, they had plotted the investigation that changed his life.

The beer garden lent a spectacular panorama of one of the world's great harbours on a perfect spring day. Years earlier, people sitting here saw the former Mr Universe, Hollywood star, and future Governor of California, Arnold Schwarzenegger, arrive in a tight T-shirt, which he proceeded to remove verrry slowly. The crowd cheered.

*

"*Thin material*, Cassie," Jim said as he returned with the beers. "That's what the caller said. *Thin material.* And he did something else. I'll have to get AB to send me a tape of the call, but he laughed when Adam thanked him for *ringing in.*"

Jim already thought he was close to an answer. Like a parcel at the Post Office, it was awaiting collection on the edge of his consciousness. Being a detective means doing cryptic crosswords every day of your life. He had to put the clues together. *Thin Material.* As was his practice, he would let it surface in its own time.

*

It's an odd thing. Kenny Rogers had followed Jim Nicholas in his travels for the past fortnight. Not bad, given he'd been dead since March of 2020. Kenny was eighty-two when the music stopped, although his face was somewhat younger. Barely five. That's the great thing about music, though: *it* never stops.

Since the Sunday of his last meeting with Katherine, when Father Ralph spoke about Pascal's Wager and Stan mentioned his profitable encounter with Merryfield at the races, Kenny's The Gambler was popping up regularly on his internal jukebox. And, as always, he listened. Why was it playing? Was it because he was thinking about gambling, or because his instinct was demanding his attention? He could hear it now.

You've got to know when to hold 'em
know when to fold 'em

It was good to catch up with Cassie, and they swapped information they felt able to share about the missing priest. If this were a horse race, Jim and Dan would be clearly in front, but there was no winning post, and the distance remaining was unclear. They wanted to solve the mystery, but they didn't *need* to. The police had other imperatives.

Know when to walk away
and know when to run

Jim could share with her some of what he knew about the priest's predatory past, and Cassie confirmed that she, too, had heard Charlie's calls to TRN and was trying to learn more. But she wouldn't hear it from Jim.

and the best that you can hope for
is to die in your sleep

Father Jack Merryfield certainly hadn't managed that.

*

She could easily have misinterpreted her former partner's smile as they left the hotel. A lesser detective than Cassie would've thought it reflected his enjoyment of the two hours they'd spent together, but while that was true, he'd also solved the puzzle. Given their different responsibilities, he couldn't share it with her.

He could with Dan Shaw, though, who he rang as soon as he was back in the car. Danny was sitting in the lounge room of his Lennox Head home anticipating the call, and answered quickly,

"I heard Charlie, too," he said.

"You figured it out?"

"I did. My father loved racing, remember?" Danny said with a sense of friendly triumph.

"And I backed Super Impose when it won the Epsom two years in a row when I was a kid," Jim retorted.

Danny went first. "Thin?"

"*Fine,*" Jim answered before asking, "Material?"

"*Cotton.*"

Together, they said, "*Fine Cotton!*" If they'd been in the same room, that's when they would've given each other a high five.

"And," Danny said, "Charlie laughed when Adam thanked him for *ringing in* because?"

"Fine Cotton was the most famous *ring-in* in Australian racing history."

Neither had any idea – yet – what this all meant, but they agreed on one thing: the message wasn't for Adam Christopher. It was for them.

35

Thursday, October 3

Gold Coast

Given their respective backgrounds, it was natural that both Jim Nicholas and Dan Shaw enjoyed extensive contacts in the racing industry. Following Charlie's call to Adam Christopher and their deciphering of his (not too) cryptic clue, they were keen to see where that line of investigation might lead – maybe somewhere, maybe nowhere.

Jim drove back to the Northern Rivers the following morning and used the journey to make plans for the days ahead. He was keen to catch up with Katherine on Sunday, but today he would visit Harry Evans, a legendary bookmaking figure who had often supplied him with information on the opaque and intriguing world of gambling and the characters who inhabited it.

It was 9:30 a.m. when Nicholas arrived outside Evans' home at Bundall on the Gold Coast. The house, not far from the racetrack, was low-set and surrounded by a three-metre wall, which suggested that the owner was selective about who was permitted entrance. Jim wasn't sure what he was after from Evans, but if Charlie from Randwick was right about some connection with Fine Cotton, he might know something.

In his late seventies, Harry was retired but still swam and walked daily. He also paid close attention to sport and racing and made the occasional 'investment', a word he preferred to 'bet'. When he placed his money, it was less a gamble than the result of detailed analysis of the form and odds, which reflected the percentage chances of success – like the best stock pickers.

Harry only invested when convinced he had an edge, a word that had governed much of his professional life.

His reputation as one of the nation's most fearless bookmakers was made at a time when the battles between bookmakers and punters were the stuff of legend. Giants roamed the land: bookies Len Burke, Lloyd Tidmarsh, Bill Waterhouse, and Terry Page, taking on the likes of Perce Galea, the Legal Eagles, and Eddie 'The Fireman' Birchley.

Eddie's nickname came from his fourteen years in the fire department before setting racetracks alight with his huge bets in the 70s and 80s. His habit was to put large amounts of money on short-priced favourites. He bet in cash, which he brought to the track in sacks. Eddie put $100,000 (half a million now) on a horse with Harry in 1978 at 2/5 ($1.40). It won, but as Harry knew would be the case, he eventually got it back – with interest.

"But the biggest bet I ever took," Harry said, after they'd settled down, "was from Kerry Packer. He owned a horse and wanted to have a million dollars on it. Back in 1985, that was a lot of money. Anyway, I'd assessed the horse's chance of winning at 30%, meaning it should have been around $3.30 or, in those days, 13/4. But Kerry was prepared to take 6/4, or $2.50, which equates to a 40% chance. So, the price I was offering gave me an edge. I took the bet, and we were about to see if I was in the right profession."

Evans smiled as he remembered the turning point in his career and life. "To my horror and potential ruin, his horse led all the way … until the last stride. It lost in a photo finish, and I was on my way. It made my reputation as a bookmaker prepared to take big bets, attracting gamblers from everywhere. Kerry didn't miss a beat and told me with a smile he'd see me again the following week. And did – and for many weeks and years after that."

"He was a complex bloke," Evans continued, "and it's no secret that his son has had a tough time. Kerry's dad, Sir Frank, was much worse. Kerry had so much money that he had to keep betting more and more to get the same high."

Jim was enjoying Harry's company.

"But the best Kerry Packer story," he said, with a glint in his eye, "didn't involve me. He was playing blackjack in Las Vegas, sitting next to an oilman from Texas. The bloke was loud and started bragging about his wealth. At one point, he said to Kerry, 'I'm worth $100 million, Aussie!'

Aussie? Without missing a beat or changing expression, Packer calmly reached into his pocket, pulled out a coin, and delivered his famous retort: 'I'll flip you for it.' The Texan was a bit more subdued after that. Talking to the croupier throughout the night, Kerry heard she was struggling. As he left, he thanked her for her professionalism, wished her well, and wrote her a cheque for $150,000. I liked him and owe him a lot."

Harry's knowledge of the racing industry was immense. Jim listened attentively for an hour, interrupting only enough to tease Harry onto more stories: about the punters, horses, characters, and the wins and losses. He knew those pulling the strings; he knew who was being paid off (police, journalists, stewards, and politicians); he knew how much they were all getting; he knew the jockeys who were taking money to get horses beaten, and he knew those who were no longer riding because they'd won when they were meant to lose.

Some were no longer walking.

*

After Harry went to the kitchen and brought back lemon tea and cake, Jim settled back for a lesson on gambling. It began after he asked a question that he was hoping might lead to the reason for his visit:

"Is it possible to rig an entire sports event or race?"

"Well, Jim," Evans began with quiet authority, "you don't need to. Not usually, anyway. The professional punter or bookmaker only needs information that tilts the available odds in his favour. An edge."

"An edge?" Jim was hooked.

"Sure. Let me give you the maths and then a few practical examples. If a football team is $2.50 to win a game, it's a 40% chance. If, however, you have information that their champion goal-kicker will miss 75% of his kicks, as opposed to his average success rate of 90%, then your 40% chance is now about a 20% chance and should be $5. You back the other team. It has a statistical edge, and that edge always wins over time. It's why bookies drive fancy cars, and Vegas has thrived. In roulette, for instance, they pay odds of 35/1 on single numbers for what is actually a 37/1 chance. Doesn't sound much, but 3% of billions over years? That adds up to an edge that has kept the owners and entertainers rich for a long time. Another example?"

"Sure." Jim was enthralled.

"You're a professional punter or bookmaker and like to wager on cricket. In an upcoming game, you have negotiated with two players on the same team – a bowler and a batsman. Neither knows you have spoken to the other. The batsman averages 48 runs but, on the terms agreed, guarantees to score no more than 15. The bowler suddenly has a sore wrist and will not bowl his most famous wicket-taking delivery in the match. The team that had a 70% chance to win is now a 40% chance. You back their opponents – an edge.

Sometimes, players like the former South African captain Hansie Cronje get greedy or, like the Pakistanis who went to gaol after a

Test at Lords in 2010, stupid. But gambling is a multi-billion-dollar international business, and most know the rules. Do you want to know the best sting of them all ?"

Jim looked at him expectantly.

"We don't know," he laughed. "They didn't get caught. Happens all the time."

*

Sipping his tea, Harry told Jim about some of the more famous failed stings.

He told him about the baseball World Series of 1919 when 'Shoeless' Joe Jackson and eight of his Chicago White Sox colleagues fixed the result. The shattered fans had only one request of the man they idolised: *Say it ain't so, Joe.*

He told him about the Italian Football Scandal of 2006 when clubs, including the mighty Juventus and AC Milan, were found to have been involved in match-fixing – sometimes, the entire results; sometimes, just the number of goals.

He explained how that was the most common form of 'spot-fixing' in sports, including basketball, football, ice hockey and anything else where an edge can be gained and a profit made. You don't necessarily need a team to lose, only for them to win within a selected margin.

He told Jim that Australians weren't immune and cited a case from a 2010 rugby league game in Townsville between The Cowboys and Canterbury. The Bulldogs' Ryan Tandy gave away a penalty in front of the posts to favour his opponents after large bets were placed on them to score the game's first points – with a penalty goal! Most unusual. Typically, that kind of exotic bet attracts about 10% of the total betting pool, but it was well over 90% on that day. You didn't have to clear the sinuses to smell a rat.

He said that the dozens of cases we'd heard about were only the tip of an enormous iceberg that remains mostly submerged.

*

Jim was intrigued and was trying to fit what he was learning into the case they were investigating. So, he tried again.

"But sometimes they do get caught, right? I was only a kid when it happened, but what about the Fine Cotton ring-in?" Jim asked, pleased with how he'd eased effortlessly into it.

Evans laughed as he recalled the day.

"Eagle Farm racetrack, Brisbane, August 18, 1984. What a bunch of clowns they were. They painted the damn horse." He laughed again before going on. Harry liked to laugh, but looking at the house, the art that adorned the walls, the bookcases and the Olympic-sized pool in the backyard, he had a lot to laugh about. The Gold Coast skyline was a spectacular backdrop.

"The plan," he began, "was simple enough. A horse called Dashing Solitaire, which looked identical to the much inferior Fine Cotton, was purchased to take its place. The problem was that Dashing Solitaire injured itself, but with the plan already well-advanced, they brought in another horse, Bold Personality, as the new substitute.

That's where things got tricky. Fine Cotton was brown, and Bold Personality was a bay – a much lighter colour. Fine Cotton had white markings on its legs, and Bold Personality had none. The solution? Buy some paint. Can you believe this? The funniest part is it's all true. So far." Those last two words hung in the air briefly as he continued.

"Those in the know – and I was one of them – backed Fine Cotton to win. A huge edge." His laugh gave way to something more serious.

"After the horse won narrowly – and it had been backed from

33/1 to 3/1 (a 3% chance to a 33% chance) – people in the crowd started yelling *ring-in, ring-in*. How could they know that? I'll tell you how they knew." And now Harry leaned towards Nicholas and said conspiratorially, "They knew because a senior Sydney underworld character who had been left out of the caper was mighty angry and had an employee ring the stewards to tell them to check the horse before correct weight was signalled. After correct weight – in racing, that means all clear and you can pay out – organisers of the sting would've made millions. Instead, the horse was disqualified, and they lost the lot."

He sat back and smiled as he remembered events four decades in the past before going on. "They gave the dopey trainer Haydn Haitana a lifetime ban, and Bill and Robbie Waterhouse, the father-and-son bookmaking family, were warned off racecourses for fourteen years for having prior knowledge of the ring-in. Fine Cotton never knew what all the fuss was about and died in 2009, aged thirty-two."

Jim listened with rapt attention to this insider account of a piece of Australian folklore before asking the question others had done a thousand times down the years, "Why would intelligent, sophisticated businessmen get involved in something the Three Stooges couldn't make up?"

He took a moment to ponder his response. "In my experience, Jim, powerful people aren't like the rest of us. They see themselves as puppeteers, organisers of events. They start wars, hang stolen Rembrandts on their walls and kill presidents. Why? Because they can. Never underestimate the stupidity of supposedly intelligent people. In this case, it wasn't about money; it was about power. The thrill. Why did Kerry Packer bet? He didn't need the money, but he did need the excitement. And arrogance can be fatal. Not many of them are as smart as they think they are." Pointing to his bookcase, he said, "Ask Napoleon why on earth he thought he could take Russia in winter. He had as much chance as the real Fine Cotton."

*

Not wanting to outstay his welcome and not sure he'd achieved much, Jim stood to leave. "I appreciate you seeing me, Harry." He placed his card on the table and went to shake his hand.

"A pleasure, Jim. They were good times, and I like to share them. Some of them, anyway." And then Harry said: "In fact, there's someone who knows much more. How? Because he *organised* much of it." Harry Evans wrote a name and a number on a piece of paper, folded it in two and handed it to Nicholas, who thanked him and put it in his pocket. "He lives not far from here. Tell him Harry sent you."

As Jim stood and prepared to leave, Evans had one more thing to say. "Funny," he said, pushing himself out of his chair to walk his guest to the door, "I could never see how they planned to keep the Fine Cotton stuff secret when they had people running all around the country with bags full of money placing bets. Including a few priests. Can you believe it?"

"Priests?" Jim asked, doing his best to control his surprise.

"True. Plenty of them loved a bet and a drink. The one they caught was Father Edward O'Dwyer, but there was another bloke they never heard about."

At that, he paused, trying to recall the name. "Merryweather," he speculated, "or Mayfield. Something like that. It's a long time ago," he said apologetically.

"No worries, mate. Take care."

Harry was close; it was Merryfield. That's an edge.

36

Thursday, October 3

Gold Coast

Back in his car, Jim unfolded the paper Harry Evans had given him with the phone number and name. Sam Cassavetes. Sam Cassavetes! For a moment, he wondered what kind of rabbit hole he was going down.

Sam Cassavetes was the kind of man every major city has or, just as true, every major city is the kind of thing people like Cassavetes have. He dominated the Sydney underworld for half a century, and his name was treated with respect and caution. In his days as a detective, Jim heard all the stories, unsure of how many he should believe. In retrospect, the answer was clear: most.

He emerged when Abe Saffron ruled Kings Cross and George Freeman controlled SP bookmaking – and much else. Names like Roger Rogerson, a detective who went bad (or was bad all along and became a detective), and Christopher 'machine gun' Flannery made the headlines, while Sam made the money and kept ambitions and revenue streams under control. He generated large profits and spread them liberally enough with competitors, police, and politicians to be mostly left alone, as he was content to be in retirement.

Jim dialled the number, and it rang four times before being answered with a simple "Hello."

"Mr Cassavetes, my name's Jim Nicholas. Harry sent me."

On the other end of the line, Jim could hear pleasure in the older voice.

"He doesn't do that often; he must've liked you." He then invited Jim to his home.

It came as no shock that Evans and Cassavetes were friends, or that they had retired within a seven-minute drive of each other. That's how long it took Jim to drive down Racecourse Drive, cross Ashmore Rd into Campbell St, turn left into Freyburg St, and, after two-hundred metres, arrive at Marseille Court in neighbouring Sorrento.

Situated right on the canal, it was a two-story mansion. A kidney-shaped pool, the water turquoise against the house's white, was surrounded by palms imported from Perth and adjoined a tennis court on which he played daily. He would occasionally hire top professionals to play exhibitions for selected friends. Security cameras were prominently displayed around the stylishly rendered fence, topped with electrified wire that would've sat comfortably on the Berlin Wall. You get the idea.

Jim's later research would tell him the house was designed by the much sought-after Michelle Marsden, whose signature on a contract on the Gold Coast brought the same credibility and value as Pablo's simple *Picasso*.

*

He was met at the front gate by an assistant, who didn't bother introducing himself. The man was tall, perhaps 200 cm (around 6' 6" in his employer's language), and had a deceptively gracious and benign demeanour. Jim, a lover of old movies, thought his manner was not unlike that of actor Max von Sydow in the superb *Three Days of the Condor*. He signalled Jim to follow him.

Like the smiling assassin in that movie, this 'Max' had a pleasant disposition, which Jim imagined wouldn't stop him from doing *un*pleasant things if his boss required it. Jim followed him to a cabana by the pool where Sam Cassavetes sat. What do you say when you meet a legend? "Thanks for seeing me, Mr Cassavetes."

"My pleasure, Jim. Please, take a seat. A drink?"

"Water's fine. Thank you."

He looked at Jim with eyes that had seen a lot. He was only small, about 170 cm, but something about him projected strength. These things are hard to define, but it could be an absence of fear or a disregard for the opinion of others – knowledge that he had navigated some of life's more treacherous waters and was now in safe harbour.

Many people think they're tough, but only a few know it. Sam knew it and, therefore, paid it little attention. It was just a part of who he was, and for better or worse, he knew who he was.

Something about such people has intrigued historians down the years: Was it a combination of qualities in that person that created the power, or did the power invested in the holder create the aura? When asked why so many attractive women should surround a man as odd-looking as himself, Henry Kissinger replied: 'Power is the ultimate aphrodisiac.' Jim made a mental note to tell AB.

Even now, there was nothing in his orbit about which Sam Cassavetes was unaware, because being *un*aware could be financially and physically disastrous.

Sam had presided over elements of the Sydney underworld for decades, but his tentacles (and those of his contacts) reached way beyond the confines of even one of the world's great gambling destinations. The casinos and racetracks of the Harbour City were a trusted means of laundering the profits of local and international criminal activity, and Sam knew the details. Hell, he'd been the architect of many of them.

Some of the proceeds had been poured into plumb real estate along the East Coast, for which you would need a strong microscope to find the owners, who would usually be camouflaged inside fictitious shell companies in the Bahamas or Geneva. The real names might surprise you. Good luck sorting all this out when AI takes over.

Sam Cassavetes knew where the bodies were buried, both literally and metaphorically, and whilst that can be helpful, it can also be dangerous. But Sam never gave anyone cause to doubt his loyalty or that secrets and promises would be kept. That's why, notwithstanding the wall and security cameras, he was living a happy and peaceful life at eighty-four.

Many of his former colleagues who'd possessed far less self-discipline hadn't made it to half that. Others spent years in prison, whilst some, like Rogerson and hitman Neddy Smith, died there. Sam had lived free and planned to die that way – in his own time.

*

Did you see *The Godfather Part II*? Sam reminded Jim of Hyman Roth, the wizened character played by the famous acting coach Lee Strasberg. In the movie, Roth is behind the assassination attempt on Michael Corleone, who is superbly portrayed by Al Pacino. In real life, Al had studied Strasberg's Method acting philosophy in New York.

Marlon Brando, Don Vito Corleone in the original, was the most famous graduate of Strasberg's school, which taught the idea that you bring your own life and emotional experience to a role. You must become the character. Brando believed that we're all actors who design a face to present to the world, and he was probably right. Wear the mask long enough, though, and it can be hard to remove. They say he drove Trevor Howard to distraction during the making of *Mutiny on the Bounty*, with the Englishman at one point yelling at him: *Marlon, just say the f...ing words.*

In *Godfather II*, Roth was based on the mafia's financial maestro,

Meyer Lansky, who was a driving force behind the creation of Las Vegas as a place to make and wash money.

Meyer would've liked Sam.

*

Jim was thinking how strange it was that, whilst investigating the death and presumed murder of a paedophile priest, he was now sitting in the cabana of a luxury mansion with the long-running boss of organised crime.

With luck, he would learn more about the Fine Cotton affair and Father Jack Merryfield. He, therefore, chose his words carefully, and Cassavetes, guessing that he was doing just that, grinned. Not unlike a spider as the fly approached.

"Mr Cassavetes, I'm working with journalist Dan Shaw, and we're looking into the death of Father Jack Merryfield. That involves investigating his past and his alleged paedophile activity. Our enquiries uncovered his gambling background, and I was talking with Harry Evans about Fine Cotton and other things. He thought you might be able to share more. I'm hoping that you can, but understand totally if, for whatever reason, you can't."

The old man acknowledged the question – and how it was asked – with a nod, before taking a full minute to respond. That's a long time when you're waiting. Count it.

"I knew Merryfield for many years, Jim," he began. "From around 1982. It was the year Gurners Lane won the Melbourne Cup. It narrowly beat the champion Kingston Town, which my colleagues and I had backed to win a huge sum. Malcolm Johnston rode it. Badly. It should've won." He grinned nostalgically, but there was a message in what came next. "I never forget these things, Jim. Some people remember places, faces, or names. I remember when people did the wrong thing by me. Same as when they do the right thing.

I never forget. Never." The *never* came with compressed ferocity, which was then replaced quickly by another smile.

"But back to Merryfield," he continued, realising that, like the jockey Johnston, he had wandered slightly off the track himself (or maybe he hadn't?). "I liked him well enough back then. I was brought up a Catholic, and I've known a lot of priests, although their collar never fooled me. I learned early on that some were good, others not. It's the way of the world. But he loved a bet, and he loved the intrigue of hanging around people like me and my colleagues. He thought it was romantic or something. Maybe he liked what he saw as the potential danger. So, yeah, we used him to put on bets in races where we had an interest. Who would suspect a priest? We were also turning bad money into good, but he didn't know that."

Translation: the illegal proceeds of organised crime were placed on horses in races where he and his, ahem, colleagues had already organised 'an edge'. The winnings were then declarable as profits from gambling. When they declared them, that is.

"Fine Cotton's race," he said with an air that said this was it for the day, "was one of those cases."

Jim didn't ask another question. He could see Cassavetes was tired and had said enough. The tall assistant stood, but said nothing. He didn't need to.

"I appreciate it," Jim said. He would sort out later what it all meant. "Can I visit again?"

"I'd like that, Jim. I'll tell you more about our activities and Father Jack Merryfield. Just one thing," Cassavetes said seriously, taking Jim by the elbow (the grip still firm) and looking at him directly. "I never knew about the other stuff – the girls – until much later. Do you believe me?"

Jim's response came quickly. "I do, Mr Cassavetes." And he did.

"Thank you, Jim. Like I said, I never forget. One final thing ... "

Again, Jim looked at him.

"Next time you come? Call me Sam."

37

Sunday, October 6

The Gap, Brisbane

I t was another perfect Spring morning. At 6:30, as Jim headed out of Lennox Head for the journey to Brisbane, Jason Dasey told him on the local TRN affiliate, 2LM, that the temperature was 16 degrees and headed for 26. It would stay fine with scattered clouds.

Jim thought Jason was a good broadcaster. He knew his music and talked confidently about many subjects, including politics and sport. Jim would tell Alex about him later, and wondered briefly if this was the break the talented announcer needed and where it might lead.

It also led him to think about how many gifted people lived their entire lives without that talent being recognised or its potential fulfilled. Some of the greatest poems have been read only by their writers. It's also true that nobody who achieves greatness does so in isolation. They've all been recipients of parental encouragement, good advice, assistance, friendship, dedicated teachers, or luck – an edge. The smartest of them know that.

Another thing struck the investigator as he drove up the freeway to St Vincent's Parish, The Gap: he was looking forward to it. To seeing Katherine and hearing more of her story, to seeing Father Ralph and listening to his homily, to seeing Stan and Edna, Andy and Jen, Doug and Libby, and all the others.

In an increasingly disconnected age where loneliness was reaching critical levels, it offered a connection – family. It wasn't necessarily the religious component but the company, the atmosphere, and the idea of being part of a group you liked. That's comforting.

The poet Donne, he recalled, wrote that *no man is an island unto himself*, but more and more people were living in not-so-splendid isolation. As he contemplated that, Jim's Jukebox began playing 'Get Together' by The Youngbloods. It was a hit during a period of deep division over Vietnam when societies and families were being torn apart. The song urged people to *smile on their brother and try to love one another right now.*

It struck Jim that, sixty years later, Father Ralph was doing something similar, and it seemed to be working.

*

Jim arrived at nine, which gave him a half hour alone with Father Ralph before the priest would go outside to welcome his congregants, a number that appeared to be growing with every visit. As a courtesy, Nicholas told him (without naming names) what he had learned about Merryfield, including that his gambling wasn't as small as previously thought and that he mixed with some 'interesting' characters. Or, in racing parlance, 'colourful identities.'

He then explained some of what he'd been thinking on the way up, to which Father Ralph replied with a smile, "Ah, God works in mysterious ways." Jim instinctively wondered how Sam Cassavetes might fit into that idea.

As he sat down for the traditional pre-service tea and biscuits, the investigator noticed Kris Kristofferson playing softly in the background. It was 'Sunday Mornin' Comin' Down', one of the saddest of all songs, written when Kris was going through a marriage breakup.

There was nothing sad, however, about what Father Ralph provided every Sunday morning. Jim knew (of course, Jim knew!)

that Johnny Cash recorded it and that it was the breakthrough song for Kristofferson, who would go on to become one of the finest songwriters of his generation. He'd died the previous week.

Father Ralph saw his younger friend listening to the song and said, "I loved his music and was saddened when he passed away. And I loved *his* version of his music. I plan to talk about that this morning."

"I'll look forward to that, Father," Jim said, sincerely interested in hearing what he would say. But something the priest said caused him to ask, "You know I say this with respect, Father, but why would a priest be sad when someone dies? Doesn't that mean they're now with God? What's sad about that?"

"Ah, another good question, Jim. You're right. Sadness at the passing of a loved one is a personal thing, selfish in a way, but understandable. In our religious teaching, the person we're mourning has gone to a better place, but we're still in *this* place, and if we love someone, by definition, this place is now diminished because of their absence. Our environment has changed, and our life has changed. So, in mourning them, we acknowledge our loss and what they meant to us. I've mourned writers I've never met because there will be no more of their books, just as I mourned John Lennon and all the others we lost along the way. I will miss Kris, but I'll listen to one of his songs whenever I do."

Jim acknowledged the answer, which he liked, and together they rose to talk with the parishioners who were now arriving.

*

At ten, Father Ralph welcomed everyone, and the service began. Katherine was early, arriving a full two minutes before he commenced. Jim looked at her and smiled. She returned it, knowing they would meet and talk later.

He was surprised when Father Ralph began by indicating his presence, which sparked many to turn their heads and wave. Most knew him by now, and he waved right back.

Father related to those who weren't aware that Kris Kristofferson had died recently and that the two of them were listening to his music a little earlier. He told the congregation a bit about Kris: he was a Rhodes scholar at Oxford, a Captain in the army, a helicopter pilot, and an actor. He talked of how Kris had been a part of the soundtrack of his own life, just as music was for all of us. Father Ralph then travelled two roads Jim had never considered, another reason for his growing admiration of the priest. This was the first:

"There was a spiritual component to Kris's music, and one of the things that led me to God as a teenager was music. The beauty of it, the combined simplicity and complexity, and its capacity to express and convey emotions. In fact, some theologians think music is one of the most powerful arguments for God's existence. Listen to his song 'Help Me Make It Through The Night' this week if you can.

There was a lot of controversy when it was written because people thought it was too provocative, but I never heard it as that kind of song. I heard Kris asking for help, just as we all do at some point in our lives.

Let the devil take tomorrow, he sang
Lord, tonight I need a friend

And the Lord is always there, helping us through the nights and days when things are tough. You only have to ask for it. Lots of artists sang that song, but I liked Kris's version. Let me tell you why."

This was the second point Father Ralph wanted to make, and Jim was curious to see where it led. He looked across at Katherine, who was also listening intently, as she always did. She liked Father Ralph, even if she rarely agreed with a word he said.

"When Kris was trying to break into the music business, he took a bunch of songs he'd written to a record producer called Fred Foster. Kris thought they were good songs for other people because he didn't rate himself as a singer. His voice was gravelly or croaky, and he didn't like it. Fred asked Kris to sing the songs, and after he did, he offered him a contract to record an album. Kris was puzzled and told Fred, *But I sound like a frog,*" at which some of the congregation's younger members laughed – some of the older ones, too.

"Fred's response," Father Ralph continued, "has stayed with me since I read it many years ago. *Yes, Kris, but a frog that can communicate.* The point, I guess, is that when Fred heard the lyrics, they were connecting. He didn't care if it was a frog singing; he liked what he heard and figured others would, too. That applies to all of us. We're all frogs of one kind or another. Don't let it stop you from singing, and don't let it stop you from trying to communicate. We all do both in our unique way. Kris had also defined himself in a way that wasn't true. He thought success required him to be something he wasn't when what made him successful was what he had been all along. Have a wonderful week – go in peace."

And you had a feeling they would.

38

Sunday, October 6 (afternoon)

Wategos Beach

Jim and Katherine were walking on Wategos Beach early that afternoon with Kris Kristofferson still on their minds. It didn't surprise Nicholas that the musician and teacher knew and admired his work, or that she would be able to quote the lyrics of one of his greatest songs, 'To Beat The Devil'.

If you waste your time talking to
The people who won't listen
to the things that you are saying
who do you think's gonna hear?

Like all great songs, paintings, or books, the words contained universal truths, and it was clear why she related to them.

"I talked to many people, Jim," she said, "and most didn't listen. So how could they hear?"

They walked along the water's edge, where a slight northeasterly breeze pushed a gentle half-metre wave around their feet. They settled on the rocks at the eastern end of the small bay, the lighthouse above and behind them, its presence unseen but always felt. With the water providing comfort, Katherine picked up unprompted from where she left off.

He was listening, and she knew it.

*

"After the experience when the parish priest virtually blamed me for what Merryfield had done, I did my best to get on with life, but with limited success. My schoolwork was far below what it had been, and, as I reflect on it with all we now know, I was clearly in depression for several years and suffering some form of PTSD. My mother thought it was the teenage blues.

I didn't want her to have to deal with any of this, and I didn't want to deal with it either. But, and I learned this later, you need to deal with it at some point, or it will deal with you. Isaac and I went out for the remainder of our high school years and married soon after. He was a high school teacher and was loved and respected by all. Until his death, his former students would keep in touch and occasionally visit. One became a champion golfer, another captained the Brisbane Broncos, and a famous ABC current affairs host would ring regularly to see how he was. His surname was always preceded by *Mr.*"

That prompted Jim to think momentarily of one of the great movie scenes from *In the Heat of the Night*, in which Rod Steiger played a racist southern detective, and Sidney Poitier an African American detective from the North. In a condescending and patronising way, Steiger asks Poitier: 'What do they call you where you come from, boy?' Poitier responds with the power that only the experience of entrenched racism can evoke: 'They call me *Mister* Tibbs.'

The reflection took only seconds before Katherine went on.

"Isaac did something remarkable, and it took years before I understood the full nature of his achievement. He succeeded in stopping me from running away from my past and, instead, had me walking confidently, even if still warily, towards the future. And he never once said that's what he was doing. One day, the fog I had been living in since my teenage years lifted, and for a while, I didn't even notice. Many victims never get that opportunity. It was the day this victim became a survivor."

She paused momentarily to reflect on that pivotal moment in her life, which gave Jim's Jukebox time to play a few bars of Johnny Nash's 'I Can See Clearly Now'. In the song, the rain had gone, and he could see all obstacles in his way. We can all be shrouded in one thing or another until, like the child who gets glasses and can suddenly see the blackboard or the cricket ball, the world becomes a different place – more defined and colourful, easier to navigate.

He wondered what else we might be missing if only we had eyes to see.

*

"Merryfield, meantime," Katherine continued, "was quietly moved a long way away. Only later did we learn that was a commonly used tactic by the Church, causing even more pain. Out of sight, out of mind. Out of theirs, anyway. By my mid-thirties I'd found a place for all this and life was good. It was not what it would have been because something essential had changed forever, but it was good nonetheless. Demons lurked, but mainly in the shadows. It was then that I decided, with Isaac's encouragement, to go to the police. I was strong enough by then."

The water still lapped, like a loving puppy more interested in giving than taking, as she explained what happened after she made the complaint.

"The police were incredibly kind and sympathetic. They also knew how to listen. Closely. Details were important and turned out to be a problem. They asked if I could remember his underwear. I could, white Y fronts. But there were things I couldn't remember, and they told me small details were important if it ever went to court.

One of the officers, Janice, also explained why so few did. The Church would hire aggressive lawyers who would force you to relive the trauma. They would prey on any confusion or mistakes in the timeline. And, after so long, even that was fuzzy. I could recall the smell of him, the feel of him, the sound of him, and these took precedence then – and in memory – over other particulars. Forgetting some of it also works as a protective mechanism, allowing a future where those details don't dominate every second of every day. That's one of the reasons most abuse victims don't acknowledge the abuse – or get treatment for it – until their 40s. If ever.

The Church lent no support, and Janice was told by the Archdiocese's Chancellor, who was responsible for the archives, that there was no file on Merryfield. But later, Royal Commission documents showed that Catholic Church insurance had paid out another of his victims just a few years earlier.

After seven hours of extensive questioning by three caring police professionals, they said it was up to me but that they'd seen too many cases where the court experience, even if they thought they had enough to *get* to court, was devastating and counterproductive. Isaac and I didn't want him to get away with it, but we didn't want him to have a win in court either. That brought with it the threat of him taking legal action against us, which would have been devastating.

We determined there had been enough devastation and decided against it. Several months later, though, Isaac and I went to see the Archbishop. At the very least, we could put it all on the record. Are you happy for that to wait until next time?"

Jim was happy to do whatever she wished. As they strolled back up the beach towards her house and his car, he asked his usual question:

"Did you kill him?"

"Soon," she smiled somewhat sadly. "You'll find out soon."

He was happy to wait for that, too.

39

Monday, October 7

TRN Studios

Adam Christopher began his show that morning with a brief outline of topics and guests coming up over the next few hours. A little radio theory: forward-promotion is important in maximising Time Spent Listening (TSL), which, combined with the cumulative audience (the number of listeners), determined ratings. They then influenced revenue, salaries and futures.

When Adam took over from his late predecessor, Alex spent several hours explaining how ratings work (knowing that most announcers have no idea) and showing him a few ways to do it. She reinforced the message regularly.

TSL was calculated in fifteen-minute units, and you can dramatically increase the overall figures by keeping just a few people listening longer. Many broadcasters thought their audience listened to the entire program and were often astounded to learn the average listener managed about forty-two minutes during the breakfast program and even less on the drive home. Knowing when they listen was important in prioritising the content.

It was no accident that talk announcers launched their strongest editorials at 7:10 a.m. or that Kyle and Jackie O were at their most outrageous at the same time. That's when they maximised their available audience. The trick – or, in the hands of the best, the skill – was to spread that listenership over the next hour or so, which might also encourage more to listen at the end of the day. That's another thing many announcers are ignorant of: other programs doing well also benefits them. There's a mathematical flow-on effect.

Partly to tease Alex but also to give his audience a sense that there was always something happening, Adam would occasionally point to guests a week or, sometimes, a month away. He was very good at it.

So, at the end of the nine o'clock news, as his introductory theme (courtesy of Mark Knopfler) played, he began his show like this:

"Good morning and welcome. A big few hours ahead. They're still celebrating in Penrith after the Panthers made it four in a row last night; I'll talk with their coach, Ivan Cleary. If he's up. The Prime Minister will join me after ten, and I'll ask him why the government is still going so soft on Hamas and Hezbollah sympathisers. Investigative journalist Ross Coulthart has the latest findings from the U.S. Congress on UFOs, and, as always, your calls are welcome. We already have a full board, including Charlie from Randwick, who dropped that cryptic clue related to the missing priest last week. I'll get to you soon, Charlie."

Sitting in her office, Alexandra Burns smiled like a proud parent. The basic stuff was good, but the reference at the end to caller Charlie was a zinger, and people would stick around to hear him. She rang Jim to let him know.

"Ahead of all that, a few words as we mark the first anniversary of the Hamas attack on Israeli civilians, many of whom were attending a rock concert and others living a peaceful life in small communities close to the border with Gaza. You may agree or disagree; all views are welcome on 1 300 TRN. And remember, on this show, you always get the last say.

The events in southern Israel one year ago that we commemorate today represent one of the most infamous massacres in modern human history and caused the largest single loss of Jewish life since the Holocaust. More than 1,400 men, women, and children were murdered in the most barbaric manner, and 251 were taken hostage. Ninety-seven remain in captivity, held in tunnels and used as pawns by their terrorist captors. As a result of the actions of Hamas that day, the Gaza Strip lies in ruins, a tragedy for all who live there.

This is a common theme when dictators rise: ordinary people pay the price. Many more innocents died in the firebombing of Tokyo in World War 2, than perished because of the atomic bombs, and nearly three million German citizens perished as the Allies brought down Nazi Germany. There was peace on October 6 last year, and it was not Israel that broke it.

From an Australian perspective, it has been challenging to see the response. The day after – *the day after* – the attack, protestors cheered outside the Opera House, as they did in London, New York and all around the world. Women and their babies stabbed, raped and murdered ... and they cheered.

Thousands gathered at the Israeli embassy in London. One reporter said the mood was 'celebratory, almost jubilant'. Anyone who loves London and England, as I do, would have been horrified.

What fools we were to think antisemitism is dead. And what fools these people are. Most of them have no idea that the river is the Jordan and the sea is the Mediterranean, but they are chanting from the river to the sea. And they have no idea, either, that their chant implies that Israel would cease to exist, along with the nearly ten million people who live within its borders.

This is not about a Palestinian state; it's about removing the Israeli state. Until the actions of Hamas one year ago, most Israelis wanted a Palestinian homeland, just as most Palestinians wanted Israel destroyed. The great Israeli Prime Minister Golda Meir famously said that 'if Palestinians put down their weapons, there would be no war, but if Israel put down its weapons, there would be no Israel'. She was right.

Australia's Jewish community has suffered its most traumatic year with more than 1,800 antisemitic incidents reported across the country, an increase of 324% on the previous year. If it wasn't about antisemitism, why would Jews here be getting targeted? What have they to do with what's happening 14,000 kilometres away?

Do the protesters not know that the majority of Jews have wanted a just resolution to the Palestine question since Israeli independence in 1948 and that one of their Prime Ministers, Yitzhak Rabin, was murdered in 1995 for his advocacy. Palestinian leader Yasser Arafat, knowing the same fate would befall him if he accepted, never did. Even after he initially endorsed the agreement negotiated by Bill Clinton that featured a Palestinian State on 96% of the West Bank. If the Arab world had not invaded Israel from all angles in 1967, Syria would still control the Golan Heights, Jordan would control the West Bank, and Egypt would control the Sinai and Gaza.

The Jewish community has played an integral role in our country, and their contributions are a shining example of hard work, intellectual excellence, dedication to family and generosity towards charity and the arts. And this is their reward? Our way of saying thank you? Politicians and police, scared of their own shadows and with an eye to possible unrest in the Muslim community and seats they need to retain at the next election, stood by and neither said nor did anything. What a gutless bunch they are.

After World War 2, we accepted Jews who had escaped or survived the Holocaust. They felt safe here; this was their home. Shelter from the storm. They were deeply grateful and embraced their new homeland. But now, the ugliness of the Middle East has arrived at our front door and barged its way in.

In December last year, a Harvard poll found that 51% of Americans aged 18 to 24 favoured a one-state solution in which the

Jewish state would be brought to an end and the land handed to Hamas. Most of them couldn't point to Israel on the map and had no idea that Israel withdrew from the Gaza Strip in 2005, where the leadership, instead of taking care of the people they pretend to care so much about, has spent billions on tunnels and weapons. We even see groups like Gays for Gaza marching proudly, blind to the fact that in Gaza they would be thrown from the tallest buildings for the simple accident of their sexuality. Islam is the only religion that still codifies death for homosexuality.

As always, churches that have preached antisemitism for more than 2,000 years have said too little, too late. And with way too little conviction. The silence from most of the imams, meanwhile, speaks loudly.

Some say that these protests were unAustralian, but because they were performed in Australia *by* Australians, it follows that they were *very* Australian. Not the Australia most of us remember and have lived in, but the Australia it has become. We must ask ourselves: How did it come to this?

One commentator in the U.S. recently asked, 'Did you ever think you'd see this kind of thing in America?'

But America is a divided, noisy country prone to mass shootings and violence. It always has been. There are now more people serving life sentences in U.S. prisons than were serving any sentences in 1970. They have seen plenty of this kind of thing, and they've assassinated four of their presidents, so nothing surprises.

We like to believe we are different, so the more relevant question is this: Did you ever expect to see this in *Australia*?

As always, I welcome your calls on 1 300 TRN."

Alex thought it was Adam's finest moment as a broadcaster and man. She knew that what he said would anger some listeners, others would vilify him online, and the ABC would no doubt attack him, but he said it anyway. That takes courage.

*

After the ad-break, Adam took several calls on his editorial, none of whom disagreed with a word he said, and held Charlie from Randwick until the end. Today, he was on Line 6.

"Good to hear from you again, Charlie. You have more on Father Jack?"

"Oh, I have much more on Merryfield, Adam. You'll excuse me for not calling him Father."

"Why have you rung, Charlie? What is it you want to share about him?"

"I like your style, Adam. You sound like a reader. Books are good; you learn a lot. I'm a reader, too. All the classics, including Crime and Punishment."

Put yourself in Adam Christopher's position. He's talking to a well-spoken man, speaking quietly but with authority, about a missing priest Adam knows to be dead (because Jim Nicholas and Dan Shaw told him he was).

What did this caller, who may or may not be Charlie from Randwick (he could just as easily be Henry from Grafton), know about Merryfield? How did he know it, and why was he ringing a talk show?

Adam pushed him to say more, with: "Crime and Punishment? Dostoevsky. Timely."

"More than you know, Adam. That book dealt with moral complexities about good and evil."

"But what does that have to do with Jack Merryfield?"

"Well, Adam, a priest who did the kinds of things he did, *crimes,* invites a response. *Punishment.* Once that is agreed upon, it remains only to decide what that punishment is." Again, there was the hint of a smile in Charlie's voice, tinged with a slight European accent of some kind, as if he was enjoying this cat-and-mouse game. Adam, feeling increasingly like the mouse, asked the caller why he was ringing.

"I like how you and Dan Shaw are covering this case. I like his style as well. Would you like another cryptic clue?"

The call was nearing its end.

"As I told you, Charlie, I'm not very good at them."

Laughing, the caller said, "Oh, that's alright Adam. Others might enjoy them. Here you go: *Poetic Beacon.*"

Adam really wasn't good at them. *Poetic Beacon?* What on earth?

"Hey, Charlie, give me another clue."

But there would be no more clues today. Charlie from Randwick on Line 6 was gone.

*

Adam might've been stumped, but it took Jim and Danny, listening over coffee in Lennox Head, fifteen seconds to look at each other and smile.

From Shaw: *Byron.*

From Nicholas: *Lighthouse.*

Adam had no reason to worry. Like the first clue, the second wasn't for him; it was for them. But why? And who the hell was Charlie?

40

Wednesday, October 16

Lennox Head

It was a week of catching up.

From the time Danny became involved in the Merryfield case, both he and Shannon had been busy. She came to the Northern Rivers after completing a university degree in History in Brisbane and falling short in her aspiration to become a professional surfer.

There had also been personal traumas in her university years, and she'd been keen to start afresh in a new environment. Shannon was much loved by both locals and Shaw, who acknowledged her skills – and his regard for her – with a share in the business several years earlier.

She was fully aware of all that had transpired with Danny and Big Ed the previous year and the reasons for it. She would never mention a word, and they would not talk about it again unless he felt the need, which she knew he wouldn't.

In the small second-floor offices of the *Lennox Chronicle*, the smells from The Bakery below wafted through the spring air: croissants, meat pies, vanilla slices, and newly baked bread. The olfactory glands were doing their thing.

Our sense of smell is intense, but the family dog's is a hundred times more. A bloodhound's is three times that, and the average bear's another seven times more powerful still, which makes it 2,100 times more potent than ours! They can smell a sea lion at three kilometres and the carcass of a deer at ten.

Evolution at work. That kind of ability keeps you safe from predators and guarantees dinner. Elephants, too, are strong on memory and long on survival, it being no coincidence that they can smell even farther than bears. Smelling danger is no bad thing; ask Father Jack.

*

Following recent events, Dan Shaw wrote an article for the *Chronicle* while Shannon worked on another book review. Danny thought his 350 words were enough for the local paper, and the challenge was to fit everything you needed to say into so few words.

Danny would often remind himself of Abraham Lincoln's memorable Gettysburg Address. Written in 1863, it told the tale of America, the cause of the Civil War, the lessons of the decisive battle he had come to commemorate, and the promise and hope of democracy: government of, by, and for the people.

He did all that in only 272 words. The main speaker that day was the famed orator Edward Everett, who spoke for two hours, but no one remembers a word he said.

Sometimes, less is more.

*

In his piece, Danny brought readers of *The Chronicle* up to date with the investigation into the body last seen on the rocks below the Cape Byron Lighthouse. His previous article on September 8 detailed Merryfield being moved from parish to parish by the church. That was then picked up by Adam Christopher, who was championing the story on TRN, and it was his involvement that led to caller Charlie ringing in with his cryptic clues, which Shaw would now use as the basis to move the story forward. This was often how the media worked.

In a famous Queensland case, a book was written about the conviction of Graham Stafford for the murder in 1991 of twelve-year-old Leanne Holland. Criminologist Paul Wilson and former detective Graeme Crowley detailed the many flaws in the police investigation, which raised serious doubts about Stafford's guilt.

The *Courier-Mail* covered the story before attracting a broadcaster's interest in Brisbane. That, in turn, led to the jury's foreman ringing into his program to express his disgust at the false and limited information the jury had been fed. The juror went on to say that, had they been aware of *all* the facts, there is no way Graham would've been found guilty. He served fourteen years as a model prisoner before being paroled in 2006.

Thanks to the chain of events set in train by the book, the newspaper, the broadcaster, and the juror, Stafford's conviction was quashed in 2009. He and the juror became firm friends.

Why Charlie had involved himself in the Merryfield case remained – for now – a mystery, but he was providing details to both Jim Nicholas and himself, Shaw thought, that he was keen to expose and which most certainly added to the sum of knowledge (none of it positive) about the late priest. The headline was meant as an invitation to Charlie, or anyone else, to come forward with more information. This is some of what he wrote.

Who was Father Jack Merryfield?
by Dan Shaw

Father Jack is still missing, and the chances of his body being recovered become more remote by the day. He has now been in the ocean for three months, and it's long odds he will ever be seen again. In fact, odds have become a new feature in our investigation.

On September 8, we reported exclusively on the allegations concerning Merryfield's abuse of young girls and the way the Church covered up those crimes, but now the investigation has branched in a new direction.

A caller to respected broadcaster Adam Christopher's morning program on TRN has hinted at his possible connection to illegal gambling activities as well. This was one busy priest, and he seemed to have only a nodding acquaintance with the Ten Commandments.

The caller to Christopher's program identified himself as 'Charlie from Randwick,' but there is no guarantee that either the name or suburb is real. This newspaper would be delighted if he felt inclined to tell us more and, importantly, share why he's telling us anything.

Listeners to TRN were given cryptic clues by 'Charlie,' clues we believe we've cracked. We also think it will lead to the imminent resolution of the case.

The next day, when 'Charlie' read the last line in *The Chronicle*'s story, he smiled and said quietly to himself, 'Wanna bet?'

*

Shannon spent the morning writing a review of *The Echo Chamber*, the latest book by the fine Irish novelist John Boyne. She thought it a joyful journey through the absurdities of the modern age – from much of the nonsense of the woke left to the dangers (actual and potential) of technology. He managed to do it within the context of one family and their various friends and colleagues.

'The book,' she wrote, 'is as funny as it is wise and full of insight. It's also a cautionary tale about how events we believe are small and irrelevant can quickly pick up speed, often with unimagined consequences that consume you before you even know you're approaching quicksand.'

Many of Shannon's loyal readers were disappointed when she

strongly criticised Boyne's book *The Boy in the Striped Pyjamas*. It was an international bestseller, and millions watched the film version, but Shannon thought it troubling. Boyne's idea was to have two young boys, the mirror image of each other, sitting on either side of the wire fence at Auschwitz, the German concentration camp in occupied Poland during World War 2. One free, one doomed.

The debate centred around whether you should mythologise Auschwitz and turn what happened there into fiction when the facts were so terribly real. No children in Auschwitz experienced that; most died. Shannon believed some things were off-limits. That was also the view of the Auschwitz Memorial Museum, whose job of keeping awareness of Auschwitz alive was made more complicated by the various things Boyne got wrong.

They said that the book *should be avoided by anyone who studies or teaches about the history of the Holocaust.*

Shannon then wrote, 'When dealing with this subject, you just can't afford to be wrong. Boyne's goal was not to be disrespectful, but when you set a fictional story with a feel-good element in one of the worst places ever created, you enter hallowed ground where facts are important. Eighty years from the liberation of the camp, there are still too many Holocaust deniers around to play literary games with the horribly real events that happened there, including the murder of more than a million people, 200,000 of whom were children and young people.'

Not everyone agreed with her take, but none would question the integrity and passion with which it was written. Danny was her greatest fan. What he didn't know was that she would soon provide the breakthrough on their current case.

41

Wednesday, October 16

Coogee

At their home in Vicar St Coogee, Jim and Alex spent the evening doing some catching up of their own. They ordered a pizza with the works and enjoyed a bottle of Margaret River Chardonnay while she brought him up to date on what was going on at TRN, and he did the same about the investigation.

The radio survey figures came out the week before, and Adam, just a year into the shift formerly dominated by Big Ed Bradley, was rating the same as Ed's final results, with a 14% share of the market. She was thrilled for him and delighted to again prove the naysayers wrong.

Alex had anticipated the early loss of 3% but was always confident Adam would build his audience and win back some of those who initially left. His style differed markedly from Bradley's, and it would take time. She kept telling him, '*You get the listeners you deserve.*'

During the early volatile months, she encouraged him to remain confident that things would turn around. Confidence, like a lack of it, creates its own momentum. Alex commissioned the renowned demographer Bernard Salt to provide a detailed analysis of the market they were appealing to: people over fifty, with a focus on those over sixty.

There was a time when that demographic was scorned in radio as being 'old', but with Jagger, McCartney, Springsteen, and the rest still performing in their late seventies and eighties, *old* had taken on a new meaning. It was always at least ten years north of where you were now. These were baby boomers, most of whom owned homes whose value had gone through the roof. They had time, an interest in doing things, and money to spend. That is not a market to be either ignored or scorned.

Moreover, Alex impressed upon him the importance of psychographics – the attitude people bring to their lives and how they view the world. For a range of reasons, seventy-year-olds now think very differently to those of previous eras, so that age becomes somewhat irrelevant – a state of mind.

Alex thought it best to let the FM stations fight for the 10–39s, and good luck with that, too. With new technologies and more available options, it will be an increasingly futile exercise. Few were making money now, and it would only get tougher. Alexandra Burns' job was maintaining fortress TRN, which she did brilliantly.

When FM was introduced in the 80s, many predicted it would mean the end of AM radio, so it was a sweet irony that TRN was making more money and rating just as well as any of them. As Kyle and Jackie O, along with many of their FM colleagues, edged closer and closer to the gutter, Alexandra aimed somewhat higher. And, to the surprise of many, it was finding a ready market.

In Adam's early days on the 9–12 shift, she conducted focus groups weekly and soon figured out what his audience saw as his strengths and weaknesses. Success, therefore, was relatively 'simple': maximise the former and minimise the latter. Adam listened and did both.

From TRN's perspective, it was a win/win: He was on half of Big Ed's inflated salary, and they were yet to be sued. Big Ed used to take pride in landing at least one writ a week.

*

Jim was heading back to Lennox Head the next day with plans to see Sam Cassavetes on Friday and catch up with Father Ralph and

Katherine on Sunday. He had told AB all about both, and she was looking forward to meeting them.

Alex wasn't overtly religious but never understood atheism and the level of egotism it takes to say definitively that there is no God. If even the smartest minds are only beginning to comprehend quantum physics, let alone what lies beyond it, how can anyone say with confidence how and why it all came into existence?

There are many who think that the more science uncovers, the less likely it is that people will believe in God, but what if all these extraordinary discoveries of previously unknown intricacies lead to even more appreciation, questions, and wonder? Perfect mathematical equations – the kind by which we are surrounded and of which we are part – don't just appear.

Max Planck, the founder of quantum theory (that looks at energy and matter at atomic and subatomic levels), believed that 'science cannot solve the ultimate mystery of nature because we ourselves are part of nature and therefore part of the mystery we are trying to solve.'

New technology and the perspectives they offer have a big impact. Jim Irwin was one of the first astronauts to stand on the Moon: he went there an agnostic, but when looking down at 'the little blue planet,' he had a profound experience and came home a devout Christian.

Alex believed all religious convictions were subjective and influenced by personal beliefs, cultural background, and individual experiences, so that any certainty was built on shifting sand. We're meant to respect all religions, but she wasn't convinced of that either. Why should she tolerate any religion that preached hatred to those of different faiths or no faith?

We were all part of something amazing, she thought, and treating others well and giving thanks was enough. She realised that Father

Ralph probably wouldn't agree, but then again, given his love of Kristofferson and his belief in the majesty of music, he just might.

*

When they went to bed at 10:45 (she rose every morning at 5:30 to hear what the breakfast show was doing), Alex said: "I'm pleased you're enjoying your visits with Father Ralph, but I have two questions," she said mischievously. "One, you won't take a vow of poverty?"

"No," he grinned.

"And, two, you won't take a vow of chastity?"

"Let me think about that, Alexandra," he teased. That's when she hit him with the pillow.

"Have you thought about it?" she asked, raising it again.

"I have, I have," he said with mock seriousness, covering his face to ward off her attack.

"And what's the answer? Are you taking a vow of chastity?" she asked, her eyebrows raised, along with the threatening pillow.

"No."

That's when she laughed, turned off the light, put the pillow down, held him tight, and said, "Good."

42

Friday, October 18

Gold Coast

Two days later, Jim Nicholas was again sitting with Sam Cassavetes, who looked relaxed in a dark blue polo shirt, cream pants, and sandals. His grey hair was combed straight back. This was a man who felt no need for pretension.

Cassavetes was no Gotti or Giancana, infamous American mafia figures who thrived on fame. They'd featured far too prominently in the newspapers for the liking of their associates, who didn't appreciate the attention their infamy attracted. Likewise, officialdom can accommodate criminal activity (and profit from it), but it can't allow itself to be mocked. People might begin to notice.

Sam preferred to fly under the radar and live a quiet existence. The story goes that the old-time mafia bosses like Carlos Marcello, the New Orleans kingpin believed to have been involved in planning the assassination of JFK, watched James Cagney movies to see how they were meant to talk and behave. It was a novel version of life imitating art. These days, the role models are likely Tony Soprano and his band of psychopaths from the magnificent TV series.

Sam Cassavetes took his cues from nobody – and never had.

*

Jim was met at the front gate by 'Max', the tall assistant with the gracious manner and disarming smile. He said little but left you with the impression that words were of minimal importance and that, when used, they should count. He wore a loose-fitting jacket, which gave effective camouflage to the gun he was undoubtedly wearing on his right hip. He'd guided Jim with his dominant hand; it pays to notice these things.

His host awaited him in the cabana and put out his hand, signalling Nicholas to join him.

"It's good to see you again, Jim."

"You, too ... " he paused and smiled, "Sam."

"Ha, you remembered. Good. Now, how can I help you?"

Jim felt Sam was happy to see him, but he wasn't entirely sure why. What reason would a man who guarded his privacy so zealously have for speaking with a former detective investigating the possible murder of a priest? Time would no doubt tell. For now, he liked the old man's company and was fascinated by his presence.

Cassavetes was the product of an outlier life. He had made his own rules, lived by them, and insisted others do the same. And, as he'd previously told Jim, he never forgot.

"The Merryfield connection, Sam. Is there anything you can tell me that helps put the puzzle together? I'm aware from various sources about the girls, but the gambling angle came out of nowhere, and I don't know how it fits in."

"Might be," Cassavetes said with a hint of pleasure, "that someone wanted the truth told about the bloke. The Catholic Church was able to cover up his sins, but maybe other people weren't happy to do the same."

Jim heard the words *other people* but wasn't going to ask about them. He knew he wouldn't get an answer because, in his way, Cassavetes had already given it. Someone wanted Father Jack exposed. The better question was: "Why?"

As now appeared to be his custom, Sam processed the complexities of what seemed to be a simple question.

"You asked about Fine Cotton last time. Merryfield was one of several priests running bets for us that day. But not only that day, Jim. He helped out on many occasions and was always rewarded handsomely. We invested in all kinds of things – football, tennis, golf, cricket, boxing – and always had an edge." At which he stopped for a moment and smiled. "Harry probably explained what *an edge* is in our world?"

"He did, Sam, but he also said he never actually organised it."

"True, and I admire his modesty. I always found it half the fun and would sometimes share it with Harry in advance. Because Harry, too, served our purposes. He was able to say that my associates and I had won half a million dollars on a race when we hadn't even had a bet. In my experience, placing the bet *after* the race was a handy – and profitable – edge."

Sam grinned at that as Jim made sense of what he'd just been told. Sam hadn't backed the horse at all, but Harry would vouch for the fact (courtesy of a bet later detailed in a space left in his ledger) that he had, thus paying out the $500,000 Sam's people had given him the day before. Dirty money instantly washed. '*Where did that money come from, sir?*' asked the taxman. '*I won it.*'

"Merryfield," Sam continued, "knew all about that as he did many of our greatest stings. Want to hear about a couple?"

Jim nodded. He wanted to hear as much as Sam would tell. The storyteller remembered them all vividly.

"There was an outstanding footballer who also loved to bet. His problem was that his skill on the field far exceeded his talent with a form guide. Over a period of months, he accrued a debt of over $150,000 with us. A colleague had a quiet word with him, suggesting a way out. It would be simple. The player's team won 80% of the games he played, but only 20% when he didn't. We would back the opposing team earlier in the week at a much longer price than when our player withdrew on the morning of the game. That's a serious edge, Jim," he said, enjoying the memory before continuing.

"To optimise our profits, everyone had to think he was playing until the last minute when he pulled out with a 'hamstring injury' suffered when warming up. They were a $1.50 chance when he was playing, but the price would be closer to $4 after he withdrew. The 75% chance had become a 25% chance."

So simple, Nicholas thought, that he wondered how regularly that kind of thing happened.

"It's too easy," Sam said. "Same in horse racing. I preferred the ones where it took imagination. One of my favourites happened during a tour by an overseas cricket team years back," he began. "They were playing a game against a provincial side and had a player who was an excellent bowler but a poor batsman. To the astonishment of most, we backed that man to score a century, something he'd never previously done. Happily, he did just that: 125 not out. The odds were 100/1."

Jim could tell there was a punchline coming.

"The thing people never knew, Jim, is that the fast bowler who was a bad batsman had an identical twin brother who was an average bowler but a brilliant batsman. We flew the twin brother over, and he made the hundred and then went home again – with a handy bonus. That's one of many ring-ins they never found out about."

Jim acknowledged the story with a smile and saw 'Max' do the same, as he had when Sam used the word 'colleague' when talking about the footballer. He made a mental note of it. These two had been through a great deal together, and the assistant's look suggested total and absolute loyalty to his friend – a look that said he would do anything for him, and perhaps had.

"Oh, one thing I left out," Sam said as 'Max' rose, thus signalling an end to today's chat. "That footballer I was telling you about? He started to feel guilty about it a couple of years later when he retired, so I sent Father Jack to see him. The player soothed his conscience by giving $20,000 to the Church, which only saw about $5,000 of it. A greedy man was Jack Merryfield. I hope I see you again soon, Jim."

'Max' escorted Nicholas wordlessly to the front gate, where he farewelled him with a slight nod and a pleasant half-smile.

Jim would process the conversation on the way back to Lennox Head, not least Sam's suggestion that the priest *was* a greedy man. Past tense. How did he know that, or was it just an accidental slip? It seemed to Jim that there wasn't much accidental about anything Sam Cassavetes said or did.

He'd noted that as well.

43

Sunday, October 20

The Gap, Brisbane

Father Ralph welcomed Jim warmly. He was also looking forward to their chat and learning the latest about the still missing Father Jack Merryfield. He'd made peace with the fact that he would likely never see him again and remained somewhat mystified that he knew so little about the man.

"I've seen that a lot, Father," Jim said, seeking to put the priest at ease. "People often have a private life, a public life and a secret life, and one sometimes dominates the others, particularly when their secret life needs to stay hidden. As was the case with your former assistant. He had much to hide and seems to have done it well."

"Too well," the priest said, "and the Church helped. Disgraceful. It shames me as it should shame everyone who shares our faith and could have stopped him and all the others like him. It still shocks me how those in charge – those at the top who knew what was going on – chose to do nothing. The great journalist George Orwell wrote that any institution is only the lengthened shadow of one man, so the organisation must reflect the people who comprise it. And their values. That applies to politics, sports organisations and businesses. He was right, Jim, and it worries me about what it says of those who have risen to the top in *our* organisation and the values they think they represent. How could they, Jim? How could they?"

It was a question that had been asked down the ages. How did such foolish people reach the top of his organisation, just as they did politics? It says something about the ego and ambition it takes to attain those levels. There's a paradox at work here: we want the finest among us to emerge as leaders, but those best suited would want nothing to do with it. Humility and wisdom don't last long in the political slaughterhouse.

No occupation is immune, and Jim had seen the same thing at close quarters: individuals reach the top, and then, bit by bit, ethics are replaced by expediency and decency by pragmatism. And so it goes. Modesty and introspection aren't typical in those who make the headlines.

Jim knew some of what Merryfield had been hiding, but not all of it. With the help of his new friend in the cabana, that might soon change. That's what he was hoping, anyway.

*

Father Ralph was rarely sad in front of his parishioners. He saw it as part of his mission never to burden them with anything that might be bothering him. They came here, after all, to escape problems, enjoy their time with each other, learn more about their faith, and go away better prepared for the challenges of the week ahead.

Interestingly, that attitude seemed to be contagious. Stan, looking more frail by the visit, nonetheless offered Jim his hand and asked him how *he* was. Stan didn't have much earthly time left, but his concern was for someone he hardly knew. And he did it with genuine warmth.

"I'm fine, Stan. Thanks. And you?" In asking, Jim hoped the older man (by some forty years) could hear that he, too, genuinely wanted to know. That he cared, because he did.

"Oh, I'm OK, Jim. Better than the doctors think I should be anyway." At that, he smiled. And then coughed. "They told me three years ago that I had about two months. It was a profoundly stupid thing to do, and I told them so. People might be inclined to believe them, and that would be a mistake. They look at averages and possibilities but bet against the human spirit, and that's never wise. I wanted to see my granddaughter graduate from high school, which she does in two weeks," he said. Simone, standing nearby, smiled. "And I wanted to celebrate my wife's 80th birthday." Edna held his arm. "That falls on December 24th, so you can back me to be here on Christmas morning. Will you be here, Jim?"

"It's a date."

"I'll look forward to it."

As they prepared to go inside for the ten o'clock start, Stan said, nearly as an afterthought, "One thing about Father Jack, mate. He was no more a priest just because he wore the uniform than I would be a Brisbane Bronco simply because I wore their jumper. I reckon a few players wearing the jumper these days don't know what it means either." At that, he laughed. And then coughed.

After the service, Katherine and Jim drove separately to the University of Queensland at St Lucia, where they parked their cars by the river before walking to the lake and then up the hill to Wordsmiths Cafe, which was adjacent to the bookstore. It was one of the more peaceful and beautiful spots in Brisbane.

*

"Amongst the worst aspects of the entire experience," Katherine began, "was when I sought compensation years later. By then, I was in my 40s and seeking acknowledgment from the Church about what had happened to me. I wrote to the Archbishop, but after several conversations during which he looked uncomfortable, we received a letter from the Church's lawyers requesting us, and I will never forget the words, *to refrain from contacting our client and that all future contact between the respective clients should be between their solicitors.*

What we were doing wasn't really about money but more a recognition of the damage done and their responsibility for it. That was rejected. Instead, they offered a token amount, for which I had to agree to the settlement terms of never talking about it and never taking civil action against the Church."

"Did you sign?" Jim asked, giving Katherine a moment.

"I had no choice." She took a legal document from her bag and handed it to Jim, who took several minutes to read it. It was from the Church's solicitors to Katherine's lawyer. Part of it said:

We are disappointed we cannot reach an agreement with your client, particularly because the agreement would be to her advantage. From a personal point of view, we think it would be a shame because we cannot see any basis upon which the action can succeed and the consequences of that would be a cost order against your client.

"You thought they would attempt to bankrupt you?"

"We did. First, one of their priests abused me, then they covered it up, then they moved him, then they refused basic compensation, then they threatened to destroy us financially – such fine Christians. I rang the Archbishop one final time in an attempt to reach an accommodation and told him of our potential financial peril. His response?"

Jim waited, knowing this would be it for the day.

"He told me, and I'll never forget these words either: *That's your problem.*"

*

"Now, let me ask *you* a question," Katherine said. It took him by surprise, but given her transparency, the nature of her disclosures, and what now felt like a friendship, he could hardly say no – even if he wanted to, which he didn't.

"I followed that case last year of the murdered radio announcer."

She had his attention. "You were mentioned in some articles as the lead detective, and it seems you visited Lennox Head to talk with Dan Shaw. I read the *Lennox Chronicle* every week and admire his work, and what he's doing with this story. Please give him my best. I was just wondering what your relationship with him is."

Well, that came out of nowhere. Jim, like Sam Cassavetes the previous day, now had to balance various ethical quandaries, so he took his time forming his answer. "We're close friends," he began after thirty seconds of silence, during which Katherine speculated on the cause for the delay. "Yes, I met him during that investigation and liked him immediately. And that grew into respect. When the case was resolved, we stayed in touch, and the friendship grew."

"But that's the interesting thing," she responded with mock puzzlement. "It never *did* seem to resolve itself. You came to Lennox Head with your assistant, Detective Miller, to ask questions about Mr Shaw. A friend of mine who works at the hotel even saw you having lunch with him, and then you went back to Sydney, where you resigned from the police force. After which nothing more was heard of the murdered shock-jock, or Dan Shaw." And now she looked directly at him with the hint of a smile. Jim interpreted her expression as understanding that he couldn't tell her everything, but might tell her something.

"As we both know, Katherine, life can sometimes be complicated, and I have various competing loyalties. That's one of the reasons I resigned as a detective." That answer told her a lot, as did the following sentence.

"I went to Lennox to pursue leads, and satisfied with what I learned, I returned to Sydney secure in the knowledge that justice had been done."

She had followed the case closely and was aware of the letters written by the killer, under pseudonyms, to the newspaper and the argument for revenge he was presenting.

"The writer was pretty convincing," she continued. "Bad things happen to good people all the time, and they then have to make a subjective decision about how to respond. The law can be too black and white and often forgets that grey is also a colour. My feeling is that you found some grey."

"I found plenty of grey, Katherine," was all he could, or would, say.

"You're a good man, Jim Nicholas."

Jim put his hand on her arm. Nothing definite had been said, but neither would leave the other needing to know more.

"Thank you," he said. As they walked back to the car, more out of habit than any real hope of an answer, Jim asked: "Did you kill Merryfield?"

She looked at him, put her arm through his, and smiled. No words.

*

Two hours and thirteen minutes later, she drove into her garage at Wategos Beach. After a quick change, she ran into the surf and let the first small swell wash over her; the residue of the day and life washed away.

The years receded with the ebbing tide, leaving only a young girl, innocent and perfect. It's strange that she should feel this way now because, back then, Merryfield had stolen that as well.

44

Tuesday, October 22

TRN studios

Adam Christopher began his program with the usual rundown of issues exciting interest, amongst them the looming U.S. presidential election, now only two weeks away, and the reception given across the weekend to the visiting monarch King Charles and his wife Camilla.

As Prince of Wales, Charles previously visited with his then-wife, the enormously popular Princess Diana, in 1983. Oh, how people loved Lady Di. That was thirteen years before their divorce and fourteen before the tragic accident in Paris that claimed her life.

The years again take their inexorable, inevitable and ever-surprising toll.

During Charles' previous visit, people assumed an Australian republic was not far away. However, the 1999 referendum showed (by 55% to 45%) that the majority liked things as they were and saw no need for change – at least, not until they knew what they were changing *to*.

The Republicans were divided about what kind of republic they wanted, and the then-Prime Minister, John Howard, played on those divisions to encourage a No vote. Malcolm Turnbull, who headed the Australian Republican Movement (ARM), blamed Howard for the defeat but, as was underlined during his sad stint as PM, Malcolm was always reluctant to look in the mirror. The Republicans misplayed their cards, as they have ever since, to the extent that more people oppose a republic now than was the case twenty-five years ago.

Adam, who was a Republican in sentiment but was more than happy with the status quo, thought the movement's leaders must share much of the blame. He believed change would inevitably come, but that there was no need to disrespect the Royal Family or fellow Australians with a different viewpoint.

He liked and often interviewed Peter FitzSimons and thought Craig Foster was an exceptional soccer analyst. He also believed that both had been dreadful leaders of the ARM: noisy, divisive, ignorant, and unconvincing.

"In fact," Adam said in his editorial, "Craig was invited by the premier to a function with the British Royals on the weekend and tweeted:

Thanks … But, no thanks. I look forward to being in the presence of our first Aussie Head of State … When we put our big pants on, as a country.

Most Australians, and I'm one of them, think that is both childish and rude and that there is no reason why you can't be both a good host *and* a Republican. Most would look at Craig's response and have no problem deciding who should have their big-boy pants on.

But that's the kind of attitude we see too often in this country, where those who believe they know best are dismissive of other views. We saw it as well with this year's Voice referendum when, from the Prime Minister down, to disagree with the idea was to be branded as ignorant, racist, or un-Australian. Like the referendum vote, it lost convincingly even after a majority were initially supportive. Telling Australians they're stupid and worse is never a winning argument. The irony regarding the republic issue is that Charles has always loved Australia and made it clear at the time of the referendum that what Australians did was entirely their business. He welcomed the result either way."

Adam wrote this part of his commentary because he wanted to make specific points, but then ad-libbed the rest. Alex encouraged him to do this when he was especially passionate about a subject. You don't *read* your thoughts to a friend, after all.

"The Republican movement makes the same mistake now as the Yes argument did during the referendum on The Voice, which made the same mistake the Republican movement did back in 1999 when they argued that Australia would be a better country if we voted Yes, and a lesser one if we voted No. That was nonsense related to both The Voice and the prospect of us becoming a republic. Most Australians have only marginal knowledge of our history and constitutional arrangements, with a recent poll suggesting that 47% think Captain Cook and the Endeavour were part of the First Fleet.

They argue, too, that we will be more independent if and when we become a republic. But how? Does anyone seriously doubt our independence? Unlike the American Revolution, our break with Britain was incremental and amicable, but it was just as decisive. As independent people, we have settled on a system that has served us well. In time, we will change that arrangement a little. But *little* is the operative word and one that neither FitzSimons nor Foster is prepared to accept.

The country wouldn't change much, and suggesting otherwise was a tactical mistake and a total misunderstanding of the people they needed to convince. Australians are open to change but prefer it not to be dramatic. Republicans would do better to undersell what is being proposed rather than exaggerate any likely impact. But that's their irreconcilable problem: how do you argue for change when you can't explain its compelling reason?

Nobody in government will even talk about it for the foreseeable future, which makes you wonder how serious they are. And, if the republicans think they have problems now, what happens when the far more popular William and Katherine take over?

Many thought that a republic would come quickly after the death of the much-loved Queen, but the smooth transfer of the Crown to her heir highlighted that it was never really only about Elizabeth. The more England declines politically and culturally, the less likely it is to want to break the ties to an institution that acted as a binding thread during its glory years. That same attitude might prevail here as well.

I believe that, somewhere down the road, we will become a republic, and I much prefer the minimalist option, but people who hold a different view are no less Australian and care no less for Australia. We have different viewpoints, which is what democracy is all about. I welcome your calls on 1300 TRN."

*

Adam's words provoked a lot of reaction, with callers offering various opinions, most being considered and well-argued. It confirmed his thinking that if you're ever worried about Australia, talk to some Australians.

As Bob Hawke wisely advised, never underestimate their decency or common sense. Adam liked his audience, and they could sense it. But there is always one. Les from Townsville was back, today on Line 8 and in no mood to be placated.

"You're no Republican, mate. You're a monarchist sucking up to those foreign inbreds. It's time to grow up and get rid of those royal bludgers. Why should we let the King of England be our Head of State."

"Well, he's not Les. Since Bob Hawke signed the Australia Act in 1986 ..."

"Who cares what Hawke did! He was a womaniser and a drunk." Les was at his thoughtful best.

Hawke was one of Adam's favourite Prime Ministers and, by any measure, among our best. His failings were many, but they were easily surpassed by his political skill and ability to relate to his fellow Australians. A coin, he thought, depicting the complementary qualities of the Australian character, might well have John Howard and Bob Hawke on either side.

"The point, Les, is that Australia is already independent, and our Governor-General plays no active role in our day-to-day governance."

Les was not deterred. "The point, you clown, is that Australia deserves better than a bunch of aristocratic hacks."

Adam, smiling now and prepared to tease his caller into even greater depths of exasperation, explained that the royal family has, at best, a limited role. It's about the Crown and its enduring, nonpartisan link between past and future. People come and go, yet the Crown remains forever as it is. In an ever-changing world, a lot of people like that idea.

It's also true that many Australians neither know nor care – and couldn't explain – what a Republic or Constitutional Monarchy is. There's no shame in that. It's an endearing quality and saves us from much of the nonsense we see in other places, where people have been fighting wars long since decided. Some intellectuals look down their noses at that, and the response to them is: *Who will win on the weekend?* It drives them mad.

Adam was enjoying his chat with Les and figured the audience would be, too. It took the edge off the seriousness of previous calls.

"It doesn't matter who the King or Queen happens to be, Les. That's the whole point. It could be you, mate. King Les from Townsville has a nice ring to it, don't you think?"

King or not, Les was nobody's *mate*, and wasn't in the mood for humour. Once again, he'd hung up.

Adam laughed.

45

Wednesday, October 30

TRN Studios

It was a good news cycle, which was exciting for Adam Christopher and all commentators. There was no going to sleep the previous night restless about what the new day might bring. The unexpected was never far away.

His program that morning began by promoting that Steve Anderson would join him soon from Philadelphia, Pennsylvania. With the U.S. election only a week away, Pennsylvania was a key state, and both candidates were spending much time and money there.

Adam could also see that the phone lines were already lighting up with potential callers – one of them being Charlie from Randwick on Line 3, who no doubt had another cryptic clue about the missing priest. It was Charlie who initially mentioned that Merryfield was actually a big gambler, which led Jim Nicholas to the bookmaker Harry Evans, who'd aimed him at Sam Cassavetes. Adam would get him on soon and was looking forward to it.

First, though, he touched on the controversy surrounding American commentator Candace Owens, who had been refused an entry visa into the country because of her incendiary comments about Israel and her apparent antisemitism. In The Australian newspaper, the fine writer Brendan O'Neill criticised the ban, arguing that Owens should have the right to free speech. Adam couldn't have disagreed with him more. And said so:

"Brendan says, and I quote, *a dangerous precedent is being set. The*

Australian state is assuming for itself the staggering power to determine which ideas its citizens may hear and which ideas their dainty ears may be protected from.

In a way, that's true, but it happens on a daily basis. Governments and courts already have a say on what can – and can't – be said, and being *dainty* has nothing to do with it. Nor is it a *staggering* power. It's simply the government doing as requested by the people it represents. Candace Owens questions whether Nazi doctor Josef Mengele conducted experiments on Jewish children during the war. She calls it 'bizarre propaganda', evidence that she hasn't read the testimony of those who survived to tell the story, or maybe she has heard and read those accounts and says it anyway. Even worse.

Owens has said many equally repugnant things, so the question is whether we want that kind of person visiting our country and spreading her garbage to people who might be inclined to listen. We are already seeing a level of antisemitism that most thought impossible in this country.

Do we want to throw fuel on that ugly fire? This is no slippery slope, and I believe Brendan is wrong to suggest that it somehow threatens free speech. You and I practice free speech every day within the limitations that come with it. We know that it's not entirely free and that there are limits for me, as there are for you. I act as the judge on the callers I put to air, and you and the courts keep an eye on me. If a caller says something defamatory or uses language that vilifies or unfairly insults, I use our delay system to cut them off. With people like Candace Owens, there is no delay system.

If I said what she said, I wouldn't be sitting here now; I would be in contravention of the laws that govern our industry and the laws that govern our country. And the newspaper in which Brendan argues for free speech would never publish the garbage he says Owens should be allowed to articulate.

Listen to public discourse in America, which is dominated by the likes of Owens, and ask yourself whether we want that here. There is one other question worth asking: if the Federal Minister believes it's right to ban the antisemitic Owens, why is he granting visas to residents of Gaza who are indoctrinated from the moment they go to school to hate Jews? And why, in our own country, do we allow imams to call Jews rats, pigs, and termites?

On October 7 last year, we saw where those lies and hatred lead. I welcome your calls on 1300 TRN."

*

Adam took five callers with slightly different perspectives, four agreeing with him and one taking O'Neill's position. All were worth listening to. He felt good about that, remembering Alex's words: You *get the listeners you deserve.* He then deftly changed subjects.

"Talking of America, their election is now less than two weeks away. Steve Anderson has been covering it for us and is in Pennsylvania, a state that will be vital on election night. G'day Steve."

"Greetings, Adam, and you're right. This is a swing state with a popular Democratic Governor, Josh Shapiro. Many Democrats are convinced that if President Biden had withdrawn earlier, as they believe he should have, there would have been more time to find a successor. In that scenario, either Shapiro or one of the other popular Democratic governors would easily have beaten Kamala Harris for the nomination and been far more formidable candidates. If the Democrats are serious about the threat Trump poses, they should have done everything possible to find the best candidate to thwart his return. For reasons born of self-interest, they didn't do that, and I sense the mood swinging Trump's way.

After allowing her people to call him a Nazi and a Fascist for weeks, which by implication says his supporters are of similar mind,

Kamala Harris says she wants to unite the country. Swing voters might not be convinced. Trump must be the only Nazi with a street named after him in Jerusalem, from where the Israeli PM will be cheering him on. It's a cynical and self-defeating tactic and displays massive ignorance of both Nazism and history. By comparing their actions in any way with what's happening here, it diminishes the diabolical nature of what the Nazis did.

The election is tight, although the bookies now have the former president a slight favourite. Last night, I talked with one-time Independent candidate for the presidency, TJ O'Hara, and he believes the polls are again underestimating the Trump vote and that he will win more comfortably than most are saying. He thinks the policies and performance of the Biden government favour Trump, as does the parlous campaign being run by the Democrats. And TJ's rarely wrong.

Meantime, after comments from Biden that Trump's supporters are 'garbage', the former – and perhaps future – president turned up at a campaign rally yesterday in a garbage truck. It's not a bad metaphor for the entire election. I doubt we'll ever see this kind of campaign in Australia, Adam, and that's probably a good thing."

"I appreciate it," the host laughed. "We'll talk again after the election. I'll get to your calls next."

*

Listening in her office, Alexandra thought Adam was covering the U.S. election well, providing a balance that the ABC and the commercial TV networks were finding difficult to achieve. If you watched them, you would think Harris was a certainty, and they would be stunned should Trump prevail. Their loathing of him prevented even a cursory approach to objectivity or anything but a superficial understanding of the complex country they were covering.

Also on her mind that morning was the radio industry's discussion about a local program on music station 4MMM in Brisbane being axed to make way for a networked show out of Sydney. 'Local versus networking' had been a vexing issue in radio for years, but Alex – unlike many of her peers – saw it as one of the only ways the medium could hope to survive.

Like Big Ed Bradley before him, Adam Christopher was heard on stations around N.S.W. and Queensland, which enabled them to create revenue streams that otherwise would not have been possible, while giving listeners in those places access to the best broadcasters and the guests they could attract.

For generations country radio was the breeding ground for announcers who became household names, but that was no longer the case and hadn't been for some time. John Laws, who recently announced his impending retirement, made his way from Bendigo to Parkes to Orange to Sydney and became, for fifty years, the most successful and listened-to networked show in Australian radio history.

These days, survival is the challenge for most provincial stations (and capital city ones, for that matter), and low-cost networked shows and the national revenues they attract are helping to slow the inevitable. New technologies and the ad-free choices that came with them were the single biggest challenge since the inception of television in 1956. Radio was meant to die then, but reports of its demise were still premature. Alex thought that broadcasters like Adam Christopher were its last best hope.

Brisbane's *Courier-Mail* nonetheless found an 'expert' academic (of whom Alexandra Burns had never heard) who was critical of MMM for axing their local show. He said, 'Commercial radio worries too much about the bottom line.' That kind of comment generally comes from people entrenched in positions where economic survival is rarely a factor – usually universities or the ABC. Commercial radio, like any business, *must* worry about the bottom line in order to give owners a return on investment and secure their employees' futures. At the moment, most legacy media was losing money and jobs.

The academic, who in all likelihood has never worked a day behind a microphone, also said, 'Listeners want local shows'. Alex thought it would be interesting to see the evidence of that claim. Listeners want entertaining and stimulating radio and, increasingly, don't care where it came from. The *world* is local now; people can access information and entertainment in ways not imagined ten years ago. Good luck, she thought, predicting where things would be a decade down the road. Perhaps they should ask the expert academic.

Or, she smiled to herself, perhaps not.

*

Alex was shaken from her musings when she heard Adam say, "Charlie from Randwick is back. Good to hear from you again."

"Thank you. I'm enjoying the program, Adam. Well done," Charlie said with a resonant voice that hinted at a Mediterranean background, perhaps Italian, and placed its owner somewhere in his 60s. In radio, you learn to detect such things.

"For what it's worth," Charlie said, "I agree with you about Candace Owens and the issue of free speech. We should be free to say what we like, just as others should have freedom from us impugning them or their character. That requires respect and restraint, Adam. No organisation or country long survives without them. Jack Merryfield survived longer than most, and that's a pity."

"Are you prepared to tell us more about your relationship with him, Charlie?"

"No," he said quickly, but not in an unfriendly manner. "But I am prepared to give you another cryptic clue. I hope they're helping."

"I still haven't figured out the other two, Charlie." But they weren't meant for him, and he knew it. His role, as discussed with Jim Nicholas and Dan Shaw early on, was to draw someone out who could help, and in that, he had succeeded.

"Perhaps your listeners can assist, Adam. They sound like a clever bunch. *Think of a famous line in a White House classic.*"

"Is that the clue, Charlie?"

Silence; Charlie was gone.

"I guess that was the clue," the puzzled host said. "*Think of a famous line in a White House classic.* If you can help, call me at 1300 TRN. I need it."

No one could.

46

Wednesday, October 30

Lennox Head

It was another perfect day in Lennox Head, sunny with a high of 22 degrees. Jim and Shannon were with Danny in his Williams St home, the sun pouring into the lounge room. The ocean, no more than 150 metres away, provided background vocals.

Adam Christopher spoke through the local TRN affiliate, discussing freedom of speech and the U.S. election. His producer had alerted them, at Adam's request, that Charlie from Randwick would be speaking soon.

They'd been talking about the brilliant *Bronwyn* podcast, in which investigative journalist Hedley Thomas again pointed his journalistic torch into dark corners. Bronwyn Winfield disappeared in May 1993 from her Sandstone Crescent home between Boulder Beach and Lennox Head – no more than five minutes by car south of where they sat.

It is clear now, as it should've been then, that any 'disappearance' was not voluntary. It was an explanation too often accepted in those years. The perverse logic was that suspects were rewarded for their ability to hide the bodies of their victims. The Chris Dawson case was evidence that a strong, circumstantial case could have been made all those years ago.

In *Bronwyn*, Hedley was asking serious questions about the story her husband told at the time, and Jim Nicholas was confident that there would soon be movement on a mystery that should've been resolved by the police then rather than by a journalist more than thirty years later. This was happening more often as dedicated teams of journalists prioritised a single case, which, for the police, was just one of many.

The tranquil tea-leaf-stained Lake Ainsworth, where some speculated evidence of Bronwyn might be found, was no more than a five-minute walk to the north of Danny's home, which opened on each side onto the garden he cared for with the same diligence as he did the *Lennox Chronicle*. A bookcase took pride of place, and paintings adorned the walls. They included a quality Monet print and a piece by renowned Tyalgum artist Meron Somers that didn't look out of place alongside her more famous colleague. Shaw had explained her history, and connection with some of Australia's greatest artists, to Jim on the day they'd met last year. His surfboard and bike lay exhausted after recent workouts against the wall that granted the privacy he savoured, rather than the security desired by Sam Cassavetes.

The journalists, Shannon and Danny, discussed Steve Anderson's U.S. election coverage. They were impressed and endorsed his concern about how journalism was going in that country, but Jim was more intent on hearing from caller Charlie and was ready with his pen when he came on. He knew Charlie was aiming these clues at them, but remained unsure as to why.

The three of them speculated that he knew something about how Merryfield went missing because he had knowledge of aspects of the priest's life that nobody else did. But why share it? They were confident that the answer would soon surface, unlike Merryfield, who was now making his way lifelessly across the Southern Ocean.

For the living, however, there were cryptic clues to solve.

*

The three of them shared Adam Christopher's confusion. The

answers to the first two clues – *Fine Cotton* and *Byron Lighthouse* – had been easy enough, but this one was tougher. Jim repeated it.

"Think of a line in a White House classic."

They looked at each other, more than slightly baffled.

"OK," Shannon said, looking at Jim and Danny. "You two are the movie buffs. What are some famous movies involving the White House? Then, we can think of some lines from them. Just yell them out, and I'll write them down."

Jim began, "Nixon." Danny chimed in with, *"Lincoln."*

Then they rattled off a few more as Shannon, enjoying this moment immensely, made notes. *"Vice, Being There, Independence Day, The Contender, The Sentinel, White House Down."*

"Did Forrest Gump end up in the White House?" Jim asked.

"Good call, mate. He was in the All-Star football team, and they met President Kennedy there in 1963."

Talk of Forest had Shannon thinking of chocolates. "I'm not sure that's cryptic, though," she said before adding, "What about *The American President*? I loved that movie. Michael Douglas, Annette Bening, Michael J. Fox, and Richard Dreyfuss. As a teenager, I wanted to grow up to be the Sydney Ellen Wade character played by Bening. She was the president's girlfriend and was way beyond cool. *Inteligente y hermosa*, as my Spanish surfing friends would say. Smart and beautiful. That was before I wanted to be Layne Beachley, which was before I wanted to be Steph Gilmore, which was a few years before I travelled and surfed with both of them in Spain. Great beaches, great ladies, great times."

These days she was happy being herself – never a bad thing.

Jim and Danny were enjoying her reflections before Shaw interrupted.

"But is it a classic film, and are there any lines that might be cryptic?"

"I don't know about cryptic," Shannon replied, "But the Dreyfuss character ..."

"Bob Rumson," Jim reminded her.

"Yeah, Bob Rumson had been attacking Sydney, who was struggling with being in the spotlight. That happens when you're dating the President," she laughed. "Rumson was trying to undermine him by damaging her, so President Shepherd holds a press conference and says ... "

Shannon stood and used her best presidential voice, pointing to the two-person audience.

"Sydney Ellen Wade has done nothing to you, Bob; she has done nothing but put herself through school, represent public school teachers, and lobby for the safety of our natural resources. You want a character debate, Bob? You better stick with me because Sydney Ellen Wade is way out of your league."

Jim and Danny clapped; Shannon smiled, bowed, and sat down.

*

They determined that *The American President* wasn't a classic but had some great lines, none of which were cryptic. Jim, as ever a great believer in instinct and the power of the subconscious, suggested they sit quietly for a few minutes and think of the clue and the key words. It's a classic movie and involves the White House.

He did what he often did in investigations: he wrote the clue on paper and gave Dan and Shannon a pen to do the same.

"O.K. Let's look at that for a few minutes and let our minds sort it out." He reminded them of the advice of his old mentor, Bruce Mac, who told him early in his career that the synapses in our brains work in milliseconds, and a millisecond is to a second as a second is to about seventeen minutes. Time is a tricky business.

They took several minutes, each bringing a different approach to the task. What happened next was not the Eureka moment that Isaac Newton experienced when he saw the apple fall from the tree and 'discovered' gravity, but was impressive nonetheless. It was Shannon who spoke.

"We heard the clue," she began, "when Charlie gave it to Adam, and we heard Adam repeat it. That's the thing: we *heard* it. But, what if the clue is meant to be *read*, not heard? As we're doing now. We all assumed it involved *the* White House, but that's not what Charlie said. He said *a White House classic.* We presumed it was the White House in Washington, and the movie was about that, but maybe it's not."

Jim and Dan both looked at her, acknowledging the possibility.

Inteligente y hermosa. Smart and beautiful.

"But," Shannon continued, excitement building, "what if it's not *the* White House at all, but is *a* white house, with the 'w' and 'h' in lower case, not capitals? So, now we're looking for a famous line from a classic movie with something to do with *a white house.*"

Shannon knew the answer but was going to draw it out. They knew she knew and were happy to let her own the moment.

Her experience surfing on the circuit was about to pay off.

"Boys," she said. "I stayed in lots of white houses in Spain, but they didn't call them a *white house.*"

With a look of admiration and recognition, Jim had caught up and said, "They called it a casa blanca. *Casablanca.* Humphrey Bogart and Ingrid Bergman. One of *the* classics." The rest made instant sense to the film lover, who had his own Eureka moment as Dan watched his friends at work and play.

Jim had watched the movie a dozen times. It was a film about many things, including loyalty and love. Rick (Bogey) and Ilsa

(Bergman) met in Paris at the start of the war but found themselves in Casablanca, Morocco, and very much in love.

They have a song, 'As Time Goes By'. At one point, Ilsa sits with the piano player, played by Dooley Wilson, in Rick's Café. She wants him to play their song, but he says he can't remember the words. And then she says,

"Play it, Sam. For old times' sake, play 'As Time Goes By.'"

"Sam," says Danny.

"Sam," echoed Shannon, her face bathed in delight at the moment they were sharing.

"Sam!" Jim exclaims, thinking immediately of his friend on the Gold Coast sitting calmly in the cabana while his tall assistant 'Max' stood protectively nearby. And that, of course, is exactly what 'Charlie from Randwick' wanted them to think. The question remained: why?

"You're a genius, Shannon," Danny said, stating what he thought to be the obvious.

"Nah," she said playfully, before adding, "Well, maybe just a little."

"Si," Danny agreed with a smile. "Inteligente y hermosa."

47

Friday, November 1

Gold Coast

For the two days after Shannon unravelled Charlie's latest cryptic clue, Jim's Jukebox played 'As Time Goes By' on high rotation. Radio stations do this with the most popular songs, and it was playing now as he drove the 110 kilometres from Lennox Head to Marseille Court at Sorrento on the Gold Coast.

You must remember this
A kiss is just a kiss
A sigh is just a sigh

It was written by American Herman Hupfelt, of whom few have heard. He wrote it in 1931 for a Broadway show that lasted only 139 performances, yet the song and movie have endured and touched the lives of millions worldwide for more than eighty years. Rudy Vallee recorded it that year, but it wasn't until the movie came out in 1942 that he re-recorded it, and it became a massive hit. Sometimes greatness takes a while to be recognised, and sometimes it never gets recognised at all.

The fundamental things apply
As time goes by.

*

Jim Nicholas was again greeted at the secured front gate by the tall man, 'Max'. He stood about 200 cm, with what seemed to be a permanent half-smile, more on the right side of his face than the left, and the same bulge on his hip nicely hidden by a loose-fitting jacket. He was, as ever, gracious as he escorted Jim in but, as usual, said nothing.

Sam Cassavetes – formerly Mr Cassavetes, but now Sam – was sitting in the cabana by the tennis court, only a drop-volley from the turquoise infinity pool that blended seamlessly into the canal beyond. He pointed Jim to the chair opposite, poured his visitor a glass of water, and, after telling him how good it was to see him again, said: "I think, Jim, that in another life, I was a crow." That was some opening line, and Sam smiled at Jim's reaction.

"I've just been reading the *New York Times*, which I do most days," the former head of the Sydney underworld continued. "There's a story that says crows can hold a grudge for up to seventeen years. If you annoy or hurt a crow, or one of its immediate family members, it will remember you and attack when least expected. Can you believe that?" Sam was delighted he had so much in common with the animal world.

"It says so right here. *Researchers wore masks of Dick Cheney, the former Vice President, and the crows remembered it.* I think if I were a crow, I'd attack Dick Cheney just for fun."

Sam was amused at the image of Cheney being dive-bombed and thought Iraqis would laugh even harder. He then read again from the article.

'*Researchers say that crows are either unable or unwilling to forgive threatening behaviour. Instead, they use their renowned intelligence, including an alarmingly good memory for faces, to pursue their abusers.*'

Sam stopped, contemplated what he'd just said, and then laughed again. "Maybe I'm not such a crow after all. I usually only need to attack once. But crows and I have one thing in common, Jim," he said with a straight face. "We never forget."

'Max' held the half-smile as his head nodded slightly up and down.

*

Sam put the increasingly partisan newspaper, no longer the paper of record, down and turned his attention to his guest. He liked Jim's understated confidence and the fact that he was not intimidated by either him or his reputation. Then he said something else the investigator would never have imagined.

"*Big*. That's who you look like. We were talking about it after you left last time." Fascinating, Jim thought: 'Max' could speak, just not to him. Was there a reason? "Yes, Big. That bloke in *Sex and the City* who died on his exercise bike. Carrie's husband. I loved that show. Mind you, Samantha was more my type. Back in the day." He knew he'd surprised Jim (again) and grinned at his expression.

Jim had heard the comparison before and thought it fit nicely, even if his self-image was more in the style of Bryan Brown and James Garner (circa *The Rockford Files*). Like his favourite songs, he enjoyed TV shows and movies of an earlier generation. The characters were more laconic and laid-back, and that's how he preferred to conduct his life, too. He smiled at his host's reflections before doing a little surprising himself.

"I would've thought some of those old-time movies would've been more up your alley, Sam. Something like, say, *Casablanca*."

The octogenarian, though, wasn't one to be surprised. He chuckled before saying, with evident admiration, "Bogey, what an actor," as he put on the actor's voice and recited from his famous speech at the end of the film.

"*Ilse, I'm no good at being noble, but it doesn't take much to see that the problems of three little people don't amount to a hill of beans in this crazy world."*

Yesterday, it was Shannon with a monologue from *The American President,* and now Sam Cassavetes doing Humphrey Bogart. Seriously?

Jim wasn't entirely sure whether Sam was doing a great version of Bogey or that, years earlier, Bogey had channelled Sam. He also knew that one played a tough man, and the other *was* a tough man. Bogart died at fifty-seven; Sam is still going strong at eighty-four.

"Why are you doing this, Sam?" Jim asked.

"Doing what exactly, Jim?" Sam replied, with all the innocence a man could muster who was many years removed from any semblance of innocence.

"Organising cryptic clues on a radio show that all lead to your door. It's taken our investigation into Merryfield's disappearance in an entirely different direction."

"I'm not admitting to anything, Jim, but let me offer a hypothetical." The investigator was intrigued and gestured for him to go right ahead. Sam took his time, again organising the words to avoid unintended misunderstandings. Nothing cryptic.

"Let's imagine that in someone's dealings with Merryfield, they came at one point to learn that he was skimming from the profits of the bets he was placing. And let's assume, as well, that soon after his actions were discovered, the Church moved him for other reasons. The hypothetical people with whom he was involved in the gambling industry were happy to let him disappear. But what if those people learned much later about the young girls and why the Church was moving him? They would feel some responsibility for what he had done and, in the world such people inhabit, would need to make amends. And what if they found out one more thing, Jim?

Something he did when working for them that they only recently learned with certainty."

"What would that be, Sam? Hypothetically, that is." He said it gently and with genuine curiosity.

"Next time," he said, as 'Max' rose to guide him out, his half-smile and gun firmly in place.

"There's one other reason for the clues, Jim. I read you were investigating Merryfield's disappearance and wanted to meet you. I'm glad I did. I like you. I think you try to do the right thing."

"So, what's the right thing, Sam?"

"Telling the truth about Merryfield. Remember what I said about crows, Jim? They hold a grudge for a very long time."

48

Sunday, November 3

St Vincent's, The Gap

Jim Nicholas rose with the alarm at 4:50, precisely one hour before the sun. He recited the same mantra he had every morning since reading the quote by author Christopher McDougall more than a decade earlier:

Every morning in Africa, a gazelle wakes up, knowing it must outrun the fastest lion, or it will be killed. Every morning in Africa, a lion wakes up. It knows it must run faster than the slowest gazelle, or it will starve. In Africa, it doesn't matter whether you're the lion or a gazelle – when the sun comes up, you'd better start running.

For him, it was less about running than it was thinking. The point was to get moving. So he walked on Seven Mile Beach before driving north to see Father Ralph and Katherine. He wanted to play out a hunch. There was a strange connection between Sam Cassavetes and Katherine that he couldn't quite sort out. He knew of their respective experiences with Merryfield, but what linked them?

He'd spoken to Alex the night before, and they made plans for the following weekend when he would be in Sydney. Watching *Casablanca* was on the list. He'd also talked briefly with Detective Cassie Miller, his former partner, who was heading the official police investigation into Father Jack Merryfield's disappearance.

The day after Shaw published the priest's name, Cassie travelled to Brisbane to see Father Ralph and learn more. Without a connection to Katherine, however, and possessing no knowledge of Sam Cassavetes, she and her colleagues were sailing in light winds – not quite becalmed, but unlikely to get line honours. Jim felt the wind at his back, and the metaphorical spinnaker was out, even if he wasn't entirely sure he was headed in the right direction.

*

Father Ralph awaited his arrival with tea and biscuits – today, Tim Tams. He looked troubled, and the investigator soon learned why. They were relaxed in each other's company and talked of various things in the news, including another Church scandal.

This one involved the Archbishop of Canterbury, Justin Welby.

Father Ralph explained to his visitor that the head of the Church of England was reportedly much closer to a man called John Smyth than was previously known. Smyth was a barrister who used his relationship with the church to gain access to, and then abuse, one hundred boys in England and Africa in the 70s and 80s. One hundred! And they knew.

His behaviour was revealed to the hierarchy forty years ago, and they covered it up. Welby knew him then and stayed in touch but says he didn't know the 'full extent' of Smyth's crimes until 2013, when he admits he should've done more.

"The words *full extent* and *more* are interesting, Jim," Father Ralph said. "How much did Welby and the others need to know before they did something? What was the *extent* they thought was OK? Ten boys? Twenty? And when he says he should've done more, why didn't he? I ask myself the same question. Like Hollingworth and many in my Church, they just don't get it."

"But you didn't know about Merryfield, Father."

"But I should've made it my business to investigate what the rumours about him entailed. I should have been more curious, Jim."

Father Ralph was confident that Archbishop Welby would soon have to resign, joining the growing list of church leaders to leave in disgrace. The similarities to the Hollingworth case and many of those in his own Church were stark. Welby knew something was happening with Smyth but chose to do nothing. Then, when they finally acted, they did far too little. The man from Nazareth wept.

*

Before going outside with Father Ralph to meet the congregants – and to make sure that Stan was still in the land of the living – Jim played his hunch.

"Over the past year or so," he asked the priest, "have you noticed any new faces in the congregation, someone who stood out?" He asked the question casually, not wanting to prompt a particular answer.

Father Ralph considered his response seriously as if he had asked himself the same question and stumbled upon an answer, or at least a fact that troubled him. "I'm happy to say, Jim, that we're getting new people every week, but if I understand you correctly, that's not what you're asking. You want someone who might be different, or looks out of place?"

"That's exactly what I'm after, Father."

The priest had been thinking about it because he answered quickly.

"There was an unusually tall man who was coming here for several months before the disappearance of Father Jack. Like the lady who sits in the back pew, he would arrive just before I started and leave as soon as I finished. But they never sat together and left separately. I sometimes wondered if they knew each other. And the man had an almost permanent half-smile as if he was in on some cosmic secret he was reluctant to share. Interestingly, he never spoke a word and kept his silence in a dignified way, as if he were here for a reason that didn't include talking."

Don't feel bad, Jim thought. *He doesn't talk to me either.*

"The funny thing is, he stopped coming about a month before Jack disappeared. Does that help?"

"It might, Father," Jim said, before quietly adding to himself, *More than you could know.*

*

"You look shocked to see me," Stan said with a grin, before coughing. Jim hoped it wasn't that apparent, but he was pleased that his old friend was hanging in there.

"I told you," the old man said, "I have two reasons to be here until Christmas, and I plan to do just that. Are you still coming on Christmas Day?"

"Looking forward to it, mate." And he was. "My wife, Alexandra, will join me, Stan. I've told her all about you, Edna, and Simone. You'll like her."

Stan struck him as a man who'd made a lifetime habit of sticking to his commitments and was not about to start breaking them with the finishing line in sight. The best athletes are coached to 'run through the line.'

Thinking you're already at the end can change the entire psychological dynamic, and the brain might send the wrong direction to the body. A horse stops quickly when a jockey drops their hands, and many golfers start thinking of the victory speech only to discover that it's no longer needed. It might also be why more than 70% of motor vehicle accidents happen close to home. You're already thinking of what you'll do when you get there.

On farms, it's different – they call them five-minute accidents.

You're tired and trying to complete a task that could easily wait until the next day. That's when the cow charges or the stallion rips your arm off.

Those doctors who told Stan that he had, at best, a couple of months should have listened more to their patient. Telling him his race was run signalled him to stop running. Dumb. Jim wondered if the medical profession's reliance on statistics might also be counterproductive, given that those numbers are compiled from many different personality types. Until recently, Japanese doctors rarely told patients of terminal diagnoses, prioritising the patient's well-being, family cohesion, and the maintenance of hope.

Jim thought that was an interesting idea. He also believed it better to focus on the overachieving minority and what they'd done to beat expectations. Stan knew precisely what he was going to do: he was going to be there on Christmas Day, and that created the reality.

As Sam Cassavetes would agree, that's an edge.

*

In his sermon that morning, Father Ralph returned to the subject of prayer and its various forms: acknowledging dependence on God, asking God for something physical or spiritual, making requests on behalf of others, thanking God for all He does, and expressing love for God.

He discussed the meaning of each prayer and asked the congregation to engage in Petition Prayer, which asks for something specific. He then explained his reasons, and that's when what was troubling him became clear.

"I received bad news this week and wanted to share it with you so we could all pray together," he began. "As you know, real estate values have gone through the roof in this area recently, and the

Archdiocese wants to sell this land. I was very upset and argued against it, but all they saw were dollar signs. These are difficult times even for the Church."

The priest laughed when Jenny, sitting beside her husband Andy, yelled, "Why doesn't the Vatican just sell a painting and send the cheque?"

"A fair question, Jen, but don't hold your breath. The auction is scheduled for December 14, which means this parish will likely close sometime early in the new year. I'm sorry to bring this news to you so close to Christmas, but with your help, who knows? The Lord works in mysterious ways. So, let us pray together for a Christmas miracle."

Father Ralph would be pleased to know that his homily had the iconic 'I Say A Little Prayer' as its soundtrack on Jim's Jukebox. One of the dozens of songs written by Hal David and Burt Bacharach, it was intended from a woman's perspective for her man serving in Vietnam.

The moment I wake up
Before I put on my makeup
I say a little prayer for you

They wrote it for Dionne Warwick, who sang the original in 1967. Aretha Franklin's exquisite album version was released the following year.

My darling, believe me
For me there is no one but you

Jim could tell Father Ralph was finished because Katherine was already gone.

*

They sat together three hours later at the Beach Cafe in Byron Bay, and Jim sensed that her story was nearing its conclusion. Like reading a book with the page marked, she seamlessly picked up the narrative.

After the call during which the Archbishop was dismissive of her concerns – and, by implication, her experience – Katherine got on with her life. She paid close attention to the Royal Commission into the Institutional Responses to Child Sexual Abuse and was keen to see what came out of it. She and Isaac had juggled whether she, too, should come forward, but plenty of others already had, and she doubted if she could deal with being disbelieved again.

To her initial surprise and immense gratitude, the Commissioners were in no mood for a cover-up or whitewash. Nor was Katherine shocked that so many cases echoed her own, including what came to be known as Case Study 4. The findings were tabled in Federal Parliament on February 11, 2015.

In Finding 5 of Case Study 4, the Commission found, in part, that *the church,* its *lawyers, and insurer engaged in protracted legal negotiation for over two years before making a monetary offer.* It also found that *the Church heavily relied on advice from insurers and lawyers when negotiating compensation.*

In Finding 7 of Case Study 4, they found that *it was not compassionate, fair, or just* to require the complainant to sign a deed with clause 7 in it. That clause related to the silencing of victims, a callous thing to do to people who had already been silenced for too long. Silencing a victim is itself a form of abuse because it denies survivors the ability to do all in their power to heal. They should be able to yell their story from the rooftops, and it was that possibility the Church was disgracefully (and far too diligently) seeking to prevent.

In a case with similarities to her own, they found that in 1998, Father Francis Edward Derriman was convicted of two counts of indecent assault. Yet, his superiors did nothing... until September 2011. Unbelievable.

Katherine told Jim all this from memory as if she had read the findings many times, which – of course – she had.

"But there were no findings against Merryfield?" Jim asked.

"No. He slipped the net, and it underlined how many other stories there must have been that went untold because of the ruthless behaviour of the Church and its enablers. But justice comes in many forms and at different times, doesn't it."

It was more a rhetorical statement than a question, although the reference to Father Jack's demise was apparent, and she was clearly close to revealing her knowledge of it. Jim was keen to nudge her in that direction but also wanted to further explore the recent appearance of Sam Cassavetes and his colleague, the tall man of perhaps 200 cm with the gracious presence and permanent half-smile, who – for a couple of months – had been a regular attendee at St Vincent's. 'Max'. Father Ralph had noticed him, but had she?

"He was hard *not* to notice," she laughed softly. "He came every Sunday throughout May and June, but never again." Nicholas did some quick calculations: the German tourists saw the body on July 14, the same day photographer Mark Taylor unwittingly photographed it, which was two weeks after his last visit. Coincidence?

Michael Connelly's acclaimed detective, Harry Bosch, didn't believe in coincidence, but Jim thought all of history was determined by random meetings and actions. Is it a coincidence that this or that happened at the place and time it did, or was it just something that had to happen – or not – somewhere?

At a micro level, was every meeting of our ancestors that led to this living, breathing moment pre-determined, or just coincidence?

If your great-great-great grandmother hadn't locked eyes with that naughty-looking Irish boy across the hall in County Limerick, you wouldn't be here today. And to think she had a cold and nearly didn't go to the dance!

"Did he ever speak to you?" Jim asked, returning to the subject at hand.

"No, but he did something else. He followed me home on several occasions. As you know," she grinned, having done the same to Jim, "I'm pretty good at spotting someone tracking me. I don't think he was even trying to hide his presence and didn't seem to care one way or the other. It was as if he was somehow doing his job."

"Were you scared?"

"That's the funny thing, Jim," she replied. "No, I wasn't. It felt comforting, as if he was protecting me in some fashion. My personal guardian angel. He made me feel safe."

"Did you ever see him again after he stopped attending church at the end of June?"

"Only once." There was no smile, just the hint of a memory never to be forgotten. Jim was betting that the meeting was no coincidence. As they returned to Wategos Beach, Katherine promised to tell him about it next time. She was going to Tasmania to see her sister before Christmas, so agreed to meet him at the Cape Byron Lighthouse at one p.m. on Sunday, December 15. By the rail, exactly 139 metres above the rocks below.

Her words would stay with him until they met again: *only once.*

49

Thursday, November 7

TRN Sydney

The nine o'clock news finished, and with his theme song playing, Adam Christopher began another three-hour journey. Part of the excitement of radio was the spontaneity and unpredictability, which was the reason for the adrenaline hit that accompanied him every time he turned on the microphone. What unplanned subjects might come up, what were callers going to say, and what news might break that required instant, professional coverage?

He and his partner, Nguyen, enjoyed kayaking, an activity Adam believed bears similarities to radio. You enter the water upstream with a destination in mind but with no clear idea of what might happen along the way. There are some benchmarks and things you must do, but the joy was exploring unknown tributaries before returning to continue the trip downstream.

Burt Reynolds and his fellow paddlers in the terrifyingly wonderful movie *Deliverance* probably have a different view about that, particularly Ned Beatty's character, Bobby Trippe. Poor Bobby. The scene featuring the duelling banjos remains an enduring masterpiece.

Adam had taken a call at home the previous night from Dan Shaw, who was keen to come on the show briefly with an update on the missing priest, a request to which he instantly agreed.

He began, however, with the story most shows of his kind around the world would be leading with: Donald J. Trump's extraordinary victory the previous day. The 45th president was also going to be the 47th. Two non-consecutive terms, a feat performed only by Grover Cleveland in 1884 and 1892.

Adam knew that his audience – like audiences everywhere – was divided about Trump, so he needed to navigate the territory with that in mind. That didn't mean pandering or changing his views, but it did mean treating alternative opinions with respect and making listeners aware that, within limits, they are perfectly entitled to hold them. Try doing that on the ABC.

On TRN's programs, the presenters held vastly different views on Trump, and listeners knew that. In all of Australia, how many ABC hosts do you think would have voted for him? The answer would be zero or close to it, which, with allegations of regular bias against the national broadcaster, makes it worth asking this question: How is that possible? They speak a good game on diversity, but not with political views.

"Whatever people think of Trump," Christopher began, adding with a laugh, "and they think many things, this was a victory historians will be writing about hundreds of years from now. What they will be writing as they try to make sense of this period remains to be seen and largely depends on what unfolds in the next four years. The jury is out on that for now, but a decisive verdict was delivered yesterday. Steve Anderson has been covering the campaign for the last few months and joins us for the final time from Washington, D.C. Not many saw that coming, Steve, but you did predict when last we spoke that the momentum was swinging his way." It was less a question than a comment that would begin a conversation.

"Morning Adam. You're right. As you said, it is a comprehensive and historic result, and it has taken the Democrats only a few hours to begin the recriminations and start levelling blame. There's enough to go around. I was talking to one senior Democrat last night who was scathing about the candidate, Kamala Harris, and the campaign. He was equally critical of Joe Biden, who should've stuck to his pledge to be a one-term, transitional president and given his party a chance to choose a more formidable alternative.

From Australia's perspective, the United States can be a confounding place, and you will hear the normal demonisation of the new president. But it's a remarkable country with twenty-thousand cities, towns, and villages filled with bright, friendly, resilient people. The ties that bind are strong, and we don't always get that perspective from far away. They have problems, and the last few months highlighted the dangerous divisions in the country, but it would be a mistake to count them out."

Adam then asked Steve what he thought decided the outcome.

"As I've mentioned, Adam, I always saw it as a referendum on Ms Harris and the policies she and Joe Biden have pursued. People already knew more than enough about Mr Trump and had made up their minds. She was a bad candidate and ran a poor campaign, and none of her proxies helped. Most, including the Obamas, hurt. Barack and Michelle, neither of them fans of Harris, suggesting black men should vote for her because she was a 'sister' is, by definition, racist and patronising.

Mr Obama has travelled some distance from his successful campaign in 2008 when he wanted the country to be 'race-neutral' and for people, as Martin Luther King dreamed, to be judged by the content of their character and not the colour of their skin.

It's no coincidence that Trump's vote went up amongst African Americans by more than 10%. I reckon most Americans, like most Australians, are completely over the entire identity politics nonsense. Diversity, Equity, and Inclusion have permeated all areas of life here, and people might have just said, 'Enough.'

And trotting out all the high-profile celebrities was

counterproductive, as senior Democratic operatives – including the highly regarded James Carville and David Axelrod – have been saying for weeks. People can do without lectures from billionaires when most here are doing it tough. They are far removed from the problems confronting their fellow citizens. So, as much as people might admire Springsteen and Oprah, they are more than capable of making up their own minds on politics, and resent the idea that they aren't. Again, it's no surprise that many in the old working-class areas who bought Bruce's albums voted for Trump."

"That's interesting about identity politics." Adam prompted. "Some commentators on the left are saying that Harris lost because of sexism and misogyny."

"As Mandy Rice-Davies said long ago during the Profumo Affair in England, *they would say that, wouldn't they*? It's rubbish, mate. They said the same when Trump beat Hillary Clinton, but she was also a terrible candidate. America has twelve female governors and twenty-five female senators, and Nikki Haley mounted a much better challenge to Trump than any of his previous male opponents. Had anything happened to him, which it almost did, she might've beaten Harris even more comfortably. Most Americans have no problem electing female candidates but prefer them to be good ones. Kamala Harris is many things, but Margaret Thatcher she's not."

Adam then said, "And she gave her concession speech just a few minutes ago?"

"She did. Harris says she will continue to fight for what she believes in, which is odd given that most voters were left confused about what those beliefs might be. It's also strange because she and the issues she talked about were comprehensively rejected by the American people yesterday. What part of 'no' does she not understand? Better, perhaps, to stop telling people what *you* want and listen to what *they* want. In a country where fully 95% of people think it's absurd that transgender males can play sport against biological females, she couldn't even bring herself to say that."

Adam asked one final question: "What about the media over there, Steve? Did their coverage have an impact?"

"As a journalist, I've been appalled at the partisan nature of the press and how too many have become shills for the respective parties. Opinion writers and commentators can do that, but once-prestigious newspapers and television networks no longer have even a pretence of fairness. Many people are losing faith in the institutions here, and cynicism is rife. So, the more they piled on against Trump, the more independent voters went his way. In the end, it proved decisive. The press played a significant role in helping elect the man they profess to loathe.

Politically, Adam, the loss gives the Democrats a chance to recalibrate, ditch the woke policies, and reconnect with middle America. They would likely do it best with someone far from California. They will need a strong candidate, not a politically correct one. This has been an enormously consequential election, and not only for America. From Tel Aviv to Kyiv, and even for Australia, political and policy ramifications – for better or worse – will be wide-ranging. In an uncertain world, one thing is guaranteed: the next four years will be fascinating to watch. It might be wise to buckle up."

Adam thanked him for his coverage, wished him a safe trip home, and mentioned that Dan Shaw would be on next.

*

Shaw, the one-time mentor to Steve Anderson, was intrigued by the turn of events that saw them on the same radio program in roles neither could have imagined. After being introduced, he told Adam they were learning more about Jack Merryfield daily and hoped to have something more definitive before Christmas. And then Dan added this:

"Adam, I just want to thank Charlie from Randwick for his cryptic clues. They've been most helpful. We've sorted them out, Charlie, and we know what they mean. We share your view that *Casablanca* is a classic movie and 'As Time Goes By' a timeless song." In his best Bogey voice, he then repeated the lines he told Adam the night before he would so that he could have the song ready. *'Play it, Adam.'* Which the host did.

Listening in her Program Director's office, Alex said two words: *Great radio.*

*

An old man and his loyal colleague were listening in the cabana of a mansion in Marseille Court on the Gold Coast. Sam looked at 'Max' and added with a wink, "His Bogey's not as good as mine."

50

Monday, December 2

Gold Coast

"Welcome to my Casa," Sam Cassavetes said as Jim entered the cabana and shook his outstretched hand. Once again, 'Max' had met him at the fortified front gate. He put his hand softly on Jim's back (much as Prime Minister Paul Keating did, to the horror of monarchists, with Queen Elizabeth) to guide him to the destination adjoining the tennis court and the infinity swimming pool that created the illusion of reaching to the canal and beyond.

Near the pool was a new addition: a large, decorated Christmas tree with an angel sitting at the top watching events below. Given the history of the home's owner, it struck Jim as somewhat discordant and out of place. Sam noticed his expression and said it was honouring his late wife, Rosa.

"I loved her very much, Jim. She loved me, and she loved Christmas and all it meant. She was an extremely devout woman," he said, then laughed. "I have no idea what she said about me in confession. I lost my faith early on, and instead of following the rules of an unseen God, I created my own. And, rightly or wrongly, I've lived by them. Mostly fairly, I think, although I've always liked an edge." At that, he grinned, paused, and drank some water.

"Funny," he said. "Lately, I've been looking to make things right in various areas. At eighty-four, you know you don't have the luxury of putting things on the back burner. We shouldn't at thirty-four either, but you don't necessarily know it then."

Jim sensed that this would be a crucial conversation, and so it turned out to be.

*

Cassavetes asked Jim what he'd been up to, and he responded that, apart from working out cryptic clues, he was spending time with Katherine, who was also sharing her past experiences with Father Jack Merryfield.

"I've been up to the church in Brisbane where she goes and where Merryfield assisted. Before he disappeared, that is."

The host noted the last comment but focussed on the first. "Are they good people? The priest and Katherine?"

"They are Sam. They're wonderful people. The church is like a family, and Father Ralph's a fine man. Katherine is an intelligent woman and has made a good life despite what Merryfield did to her early on. As she pointed out, it's a different life than she would've lived – in ways she will never fully know – but is thankful for all she's enjoyed. She loves music and has taught it for many years. And you'd like Father Ralph. You should come up with me at some point." It was an unscripted comment, and the look on Sam's face suggested that he would think about it.

"Sadly," Nicholas continued, "the Archdiocese wants to sell the church and land at auction in December, so they might have to find a new home. It's not easy with rising prices these days. I hope they can do it."

"I hope they can, too, Jim. People need a place to go, and, by the sound of it, the world could do with more Father Ralphs and a lot fewer Father Jacks." He paused again and looked at his assistant, 'Max'. Jim hardly discerned a nod between the two, but communication had occurred subtly, like a conductor signalling his string section to get ready.

*

It struck Jim again how the twin threads of this investigation had seen him form friendships with a humble parish priest and a much-feared underworld chieftain. He wondered what it said about him that they both felt comfortable in his company – and he in theirs. He knew Father Ralph and Sam Cassavetes possessed a deep moral code, even if they were ethical opposites in many ways.

Nor could he imagine Sam condoning cruelty to innocent or decent people. In this, at least, he had something in common with the priest: they shared a love for the downtrodden and a desire to protect the vulnerable. Not that this qualified him for sainthood, but it did add depth to an easy stereotype. It's also true that most saints wouldn't survive close scrutiny.

"As I told you, Jim," Sam began after some quiet moments, "I knew nothing about Merryfield and the girls until much later. When I found out, I felt responsible for balancing the scales. To set things right by his victims and to do something about it. I wanted to make amends but never knew how to do it. And then, I became aware through associates in Brisbane earlier this year that he was working in the parish you mentioned. By then, he was in his mid-70s and wasn't exactly wearing a disguise. His days of doing damage were over, but for his victims the damage was already done.

I still have contacts, Jim, and I used one of them to identify all those who had made allegations against Merryfield and tracked them down. If I could help them, I would. We found several in faraway places, and without them knowing who'd done it, I paid off mortgages, helped children, and settled debts.

There was another woman in her mid-60s, who we learned lived at Wategos Beach, so we followed her for a while and discovered that every Sunday she went to the church where Merryfield worked. It naturally puzzled me as to what she was going to do. Did she have revenge on her mind? I didn't know, but we kept an eye on her. We weren't going to let her do anything silly. It turned out to be Katherine. Let's have a sandwich, Jim, and then, if you're interested, I'll tell you a tale."

"I'm very interested, Sam."

"I know," he replied. "First, let's eat."

*

Sam ate his sandwich slowly. He was deliberate about every bite, an attention to detail that had served him well in other matters. After 'Max' cleared the plates, Sam began to speak and asked that Jim repeat it to no one. He spoke slowly as well, as if pacing himself for the task ahead.

"At the start of this year, a strange thing happened. I discovered what happened to a horse I owned that, many years ago, was the favourite in a Melbourne Cup. Her name was Rosa Corragiosa, which means courageous Rosa in Italian. I bred her in New Zealand and named her after my dying wife. Rosa and I loved that horse; there was just something special about her. And, despite all she was going through – or, perhaps, because of it – the two Rosas were incredibly close. Who knows about our relationship with animals, but that horse came up to my Rosa every time we went to the stables and put its head on her shoulder. It would sometimes make me cry." As he remembered this, his eyes watered, and then, like Rosa Coraggiosa and his wife after whom the mare was named, he pushed on.

"Well, some colleagues and I bet a substantial amount on our horse and hired security guards to keep a good watch on her. We didn't want the same thing to happen to her as it did to Big Philou in 1969. I was a young man then, but I remember it clearly. The great Bart Cummings trained the horse, and it won the Caulfield

Cup and would've done the same in the Melbourne Cup. But they poisoned it the day before the race. The horse survived, but the bookies kept all the money when it was scratched. Rain Lover won and became the first horse since Archer to win the race in consecutive years.

The night before the Cup in 1992, our horse started vomiting. Soon after, she lay down in her stall and couldn't get up. She never did. The vet told us he didn't know what the problem was. He guessed it was colic or a bad batch of supplements. They weren't as advanced about things back then. Rosa Corragiosa died the following day, and it broke my Rosa's heart. She passed away not long after."

"I'm terribly sorry, Sam. Did they ever confirm what happened to the horse?"

"They didn't." And now there was the same simmering anger that, for thirty-two years, had never gone away. "But that's what I found out earlier this year, Jim. The vet was dying and went to confession, where he admitted that he'd poisoned the horse. He wanted it off his chest. The fool confessed to another one of the priests who used to run bets for us, who told me soon after. So much for the sanctity of the confessional.

It turns out the vet poisoned the horse after being paid more than $200,000 by another syndicate, which stood to lose millions if our horse won. I'd asked Jack Merryfield to go down and bless the horse. Instead, he carried the cash to the vet with the instructions from the rival syndicate. The 1992 Melbourne Cup was won by a horse called Subzero, a lovely animal but not in Rosa Corragiosa's class. She would've won easily."

Sam paused again and looked briefly at his tall colleague, who wasn't smiling; he knew what was coming next.

"When my Rosa died," the old man said, suddenly looking every one of his eighty-four years, "Merryfield conducted the funeral."

There was a pause as he again reflected on the nature of the priest's betrayal, before adding with simple incomprehension, "Can you believe that?"

Even after all this time, Sam couldn't. He had seen and done a lot but could not envisage a world where anyone would do such a thing.

"Katherine wasn't the only one who hated that man."

The investigator reached across and put his hand on the forearm of his host, who then put his on top of Jim's.

The smile had returned to Max's face.

51

Thursday, December 5

Coogee

J im was talking with God.

It was one of those dreams where you know it's a dream, but you dream it anyway. It feels real even though you know it's not. It couldn't be real, could it?

There are all kinds of dreams, and science remains in the dark about what causes them. Various theories are offered: they are the unconscious filtering of the day's affairs, the continuation of our thought processes at night, or a way of clearing the brain of unwanted material. That could be true, but if you don't know what they are, how can you know what they're not?

Many songwriters and authors awaken to write down their dreams. Keith Richards was getting no satisfaction until he dreamed of the opening chords of the Stones' classic. After dreaming 'Yesterday', Paul McCartney checked with John Lennon to make sure he hadn't stolen it from someone. Likewise, scientists for whom the dream makes clear what they had long speculated. The Theory of Relativity was just one of them.

Then there are predictive or precognitive dreams, where you somehow get ahead of time and glimpse the future. The scientists say it's impossible, but those who have done it would tend to disagree. After Charles Lindbergh's baby was kidnapped in 1932, scientists ran a study in which they asked more than a thousand people who claimed predictive powers to dream where the baby's body was. Only one succeeded, so it was deemed a failure. A failure? Better, perhaps, to study how these people are able to do it. Not that they would necessarily know.

Mark Twain dreamed of the death of his brother the day before it happened and even pictured the coffin he would later see him in. On April 11, 1865, Abraham Lincoln told a friend about a dream in which he heard that someone was dead in the White House. He asked a guard who it was, and the guard replied, "An assassin killed the president."

Ten days after the dream, John Wilkes Booth shot Lincoln while he was attending the theatre.

*

At one point in his dream, Jim said to God, "By the way, Lord, you really do sound like Morgan Freeman."

"Sometimes," He laughed. "But you forget, my son, that I can sound like whoever I choose. I have always enjoyed Richard Burton, and in some of my more playful eons, I'm more Bogey than Bogey. He had a point about that 'hill of beans', by the way. He and Bacall are around here somewhere, together forever. *Casablanca*'s one of my favourites, too.

They're all here, Jim. Olivier and Brando are organising movie nights, and Jack will join us soon to help. Whoops, spoiler alert," he laughed. "*You can't handle the truth*. He was right about that. Laurence still doesn't get all that Method acting stuff, but I do. You have to inhabit the character. I used to have fun doing Charlton Heston until he started to believe he was Me. Not good. I haven't seen Chuck in ages. And I remember turning up at a Democrat prayer breakfast sounding like Trump. Scared the hell out of them," He chuckled, before adding, "So to speak."

"Anyway, good to chat Jim. I'll see you down the road. A long way down the road, you'll be happy to hear. Please give my best to

Father Ralph and let him know he's doing a great job ... and that *all shall be well*. Remember those words; he'll understand. And let Sam know that Rosa and Maria are both fine. Oh, and tell Stan I'm looking forward to seeing him, but not just yet. He has promises to keep." In that state between sleep and consciousness, Jim made a mental note of his instructions.

And then, God was gone.

*

It was Jim's Jukebox, the one that only he could hear, that woke him. Kenny Nolan's 'I Like Dreamin'' was playing. In the song, he dreams of being with the woman he loves from afar, only to wake up and she's gone. In this case, however, Alex was smiling down at him.

"You were dreaming," she said. "You OK?"

"Better than I thought. Seems like I'm going to be around for some time."

"Good," she grinned. "Let's use it wisely."

And they did.

52

Saturday, December 8

St Vincent's, The Gap

Auction day had arrived, and they were all there. With Christmas approaching, a festive mood filled the air, and hope was high that perhaps the property might not reach its reserve, which could force the Church to reconsider its plans to sell.

Stan was coughing more regularly now, but with a stoicism born in another era, he looked forward to Christmas Day. There were promises to keep. His many friends gathered around, and they laughed about other times. Father Ralph looked on and tried to maintain an outward calm he didn't feel. It would please him to know that his congregants – his family – thought he was how he looked. He wasn't thinking too much about what-ifs, but the possibility of moving out of here (and going where?) was weighing heavily on his mind.

Jim had flown back to Lennox Head from Sydney the previous day and then driven to Brisbane to lend support – and to deliver a message. On the way, he stopped briefly in Marseille Court at Sorrento on the Gold Coast to share his dream with Sam Cassavetes, who paid close attention. The older man knew that Jim was not a frivolous man.

Sam appreciated him dropping by but, whilst respecting the sentiment, initially placed little credence in the dream. That changed dramatically, however, when Jim mentioned that Maria, too, was just fine. The words, of course, meant nothing to Jim, but they did to Cassavetes.

"Maria was my mother, Jim," is all he said.

*

"All shall be well, Father Ralph," Jim told his friend after arriving at St Vincent's. He said it matter-of-factly, without emphasis, and was keen to see any impact the words might have. The priest was initially taken aback and asked Jim where he'd heard that, to which the investigator responded, "In a dream, Father. A bizarre dream. I was asked to pass it on and that you would understand. Do you, or am I crazy?"

Jim knew that every religion embraced visions and dreams, so if he *was* crazy, he wasn't alone. After all, the Archangel Gabriel supposedly foretold the birth of Jesus to the Virgin Mary, and the Archangel Daniel revealed the Koran to the Prophet Mohammed. It's a pity the archangels couldn't have better synchronised their messages. On a spring day in 1823, 19-year-old Joseph Smith received an ancient record from an angel known as Moroni, which led to Mormonism and the Church of Latter-Day Saints.

Jim's message looked tame in comparison.

*

"No, you're not crazy, Jim," Father Ralph replied. "Those words are amongst the most sacred in Christendom. Mother Julian of Norwich first uttered them in the latter part of the 15th Century. In those days, Norwich was the second city in England behind London.

She lived through the Black Plague and wrote the longest surviving book by a woman, *Revelations of Divine Love,* which detailed 16 visions she said came straight from God. Many people laugh at that, but they might do the same about your dream as well," he said with a smile. "Just because we don't understand these things doesn't mean we should mock them. Her words have been interpreted in many ways, but I've always thought they were saying to trust God, and the rest will take care of itself. In that sense, it's about the optimism of faith."

On this day, Jim thought, they could use all the optimism they could muster.

*

St Vincent's was built in 1965 on a double block of mostly farmland. The total cost in pounds was the equivalent of $7,500. A renovation was undertaken in 2007 for $95,000. Situated on Waterworks Rd, near where it intersected Settlement Rd, it was prime real estate for developers keen to take advantage of the housing shortage. The average price for a decent house in the area was now around a million dollars, and because it was set on a larger block, agents for the Catholic Church were confidently anticipating a price somewhere between two and three million.

In years to come, it will be remembered as the fastest successful auction in Brisbane real estate history. The auctioneer opened the bidding at the reserve of $1.5 million. Precisely fourteen seconds later, respected local agent James Monaghan, acting on behalf of a silent bidder, raised his hand and said in a voice just loud enough to be heard, and with all the drama of someone asking you to pass the sugar: "Ten million."

And that was that. The place was sold.

Father Ralph and congregation members were as stunned as they were disappointed. He told them that just because things don't always work out how we would like doesn't mean they don't work out for the best.

He urged them to continue praying, reminding them that God worked in mysterious ways. He tried his best to believe it himself, taking comfort from the words in Jim's dream.

All shall be well.

53

Sunday, December 15

Cape Byron Lighthouse

Wen Jim arrived at the designated spot a few minutes before one p.m., Katherine was already there. She was standing at the foot of the lighthouse, exactly 139 metres above Father Jack Merryfield's last known resting place. Five months earlier, his body had been briefly glimpsed here by two German tourists and was fortuitously (and quite accidentally) snapped by the esteemed Brisbane photographer Mark Taylor.

"And so, Jim," she said, greeting him with a hug, "we reach the end. This is where it happened." He thought of the distance they'd travelled together and the story she'd shared. How would it finish? He had no idea, but was about to find out.

*

Katherine attended St Vincent's at The Gap for most of the time Merryfield worked there, but they first spoke the week before he disappeared – Sunday, July 7. On that day, he waited for her outside the church as she attempted her usual fast getaway at the end of Father Ralph's service.

"I was initially surprised but wasn't going to show it," she told Jim. "I was even more shocked when he said he knew it who it was the first day he'd seen me at the church fifteen years earlier. He said he could still see the young girl in me. That was horrifying, and I told him I had no desire to speak with him. He replied that he understood, but he didn't understand at all. It was still about him and his needs. But instead of leaving it there, he said he was dying. Again. I suggested he try a different line and that I wasn't a child anymore. This time, he insisted, he really was dying and wanted to talk with me before he did.

He needed my forgiveness and was happy to meet me *anywhere, anytime.* Why I said what I said next remains a bit of a mystery, but if I've learned nothing else listening to Father Ralph, it's to pay attention to the voice inside. So, before I could stop them, I uttered these words: *Next Sunday night, July 14, at the Cape Byron Lighthouse. 11 p.m. Don't be late.*

I couldn't believe how calm I sounded. I'd imagined this moment for fifty years, only guessing what words would emerge and what I might do. Agreeing to see him alone – *anywhere, anytime* – was never a possibility I'd seriously considered. I turned and left, wondering why I'd said 'yes.'"

A woman in her mid-sixties meeting an allegedly dying man in his mid-seventies with only the ominous sound of breaking waves on the rocks below for company. The two of them at a place where, in the morning light, hundreds would gather, blissfully unaware of what was soon to unfold.

Years earlier, Katherine's husband Isaac had bought a gun to be left in their house. He said then that it was for their security, but she knew it was primarily about *her* security – both physical and, more than that, psychological.

Could she use it against Merryfield? She didn't know. She was a peaceful person, but the violence inflicted on her had sparked an anger that all who had been through something similar could understand. How vast, she wondered, was the chasm between wishing violence on another and committing the act yourself? She took the gun with her.

*

Merryfield wasn't late. With much on her mind, it took Katherine twenty minutes to walk slowly up the hill from Wategos Beach. When she arrived, the priest was leaning on the rail below the lighthouse, looking at the ocean. Was he contemplating his mortality, and if so, what did he make of the life fast approaching its conclusion?

"I've wished you dead many times," Katherine told him, "so I'm not about to pretend sympathy."

"I understand, Katherine." But, of course, he didn't, and she briefly pondered how someone so lacking in empathy could pretend to understand so much.

"Don't call me that; you have no right. It's what my husband called me."

Left with few alternatives, he cut to the chase. "I have only one request and then I'll go. I want to die with my sins forgiven, so I need your forgiveness." The priest looked at her with optimistic anticipation of immediate agreement. Another mistake.

"What does that mean exactly?" she asked with a furrowed brow and a genuine desire to know. "Explain it to me, *Father*," her contempt evident in how she highlighted the word. "Forgiveness. People talk about it a lot, but what does it mean?"

"You know what it means. I *forgive* you, just as the Lord forgives *our* sins."

"How do you know that?" she responded, as more questions surfaced. "And isn't it a bit presumptuous? How can He forgive *you* for what you did to *me*? And why would He? And why do you priests talk so often of Hell if all sins are forgiven? Doesn't Hell, in which I don't believe but you do, reflect a fundamental refusal by God *to* forgive? Do you worry that you're going to Hell, Jack? Is that what this is about?"

She'd never called him by his Christian name, and it seemed to add even more power to her refusal to acknowledge any sense of holiness in him. Yes, *Jack* it would be.

Merryfield was disturbed by this line of argument. "Corinthians tells us forgiveness is about pure love and keeping 'no record of wrongs'. We have to let things go and leave it up to God."

"That only works if I believe in your God, and thanks to you, I don't. Mine is bigger and kinder, and I can't imagine He or It has any time for paedophiles, particularly those who pretend to speak on His behalf. This is not an act of contrition; it's about you trying to save your soul. It doesn't wash with me, so what chance do you have with God?"

The priest looked about to interrupt, but she wasn't finished, and the hour was becoming late. "Am I meant to have no record of what you did to me? To wipe your disgusting slate clean and leave your conscience pristine? The answer is *no*, Jack. I won't forgive you."

"But, what about what Mother Teresa said?"

"Mother Teresa?" She almost laughed. Now, he was like the punter who, losing going into the last race, bets on the outsider. As she would later learn, the priest knew a bit about punting. "She was a very stern lady, Jack, and I don't think I would've liked her much. But tell me what she said anyway."

"*If we really want to love, we must first learn how to forgive.* Isn't that magnificent?"

The word 'surreal' is much overused these days. What was it like? Surreal. How did you feel? Surreal. How was dinner? Surreal. But if the word retained any meaning, it could be used to describe being part of this conversation, at this place, at this time ... with this man.

"I'd say," Katherine replied, "it's more like nonsense. I've loved many people in my life and never thought of forgiving them – for anything – and I wouldn't expect them to forgive me in a million years. Nor would I ask. Love implies a depth of knowledge of the other person that negates the need for forgiveness, Jack. And why would the parents of Daniel Morcombe or Sian Kingi ever contemplate the idea of forgiving their murderers? No, forgiveness is too easy. Understanding and empathy are better, and when necessary, punishment."

In circumstances like these, with her gun now hanging by her side awaiting instructions, those last words carried added weight.

*

Many books are out there repeating Merryfield's argument that 'you must forgive to move on', but you never move on from what Katherine and millions of others have experienced. It becomes a part of your life, and you deal with it, as we deal with everything, as best you can. Damaged and changed, but still standing. And, of course, there are others who can't move on at all.

The word 'must' is the problem. There are people who find peace in forgiving those who have wronged them, and it's true that even some family members of murder victims have done just that. It wasn't a request from the murderer, however, but the grace of the injured. For their sake, not the perpetrator's – a big difference.

For now, and this was more bad news for Merryfield, she totally rejected their advice.

It struck Katherine then that Merryfield was requesting forgiveness, but hadn't offered an apology. Why should it be up to her to take the positive action? Consistent with lifelong practice, he had placed total responsibility on his victim. After all he had done, he was asking forgiveness without the need for him to do anything. Not a bad deal ... if you can get away with it.

Katherine thought the apology was the critical thing, with the recipient then free to do with it as they wish. Accepting an apology is not granting forgiveness but, rather, is recognising an admission of poor behaviour. It's entirely possible – and happened often – to accept an apology, yet never talk to the person again. And that's the point: it's a choice and one that Merryfield was conspicuously failing to provide.

Yes, forgiveness is a concept designed by those who either gain power in the forgiving or who so badly need to be forgiven that they are prepared to pay a considerable price to achieve it. In a stroke of genius, the Catholic Church came up with indulgences as a way to pay your way out of purgatory. It was a lucrative market.

As self-help advocates discovered long ago. They sell millions of books and live in increasingly luxurious houses at even greater distances from those whose lives they care so much about. Tony Robbins, a one-man industry, once said he couldn't sit quietly on a beach and read a book. We should worry about people like that, but instead, we give them megaphones.

In Australia, we do it differently. '*Sorry, mate*,' usually says it all. There is no need for more. It's done. Lessons are learned, and life goes on. But there are times – times like these – when that just isn't enough. Sensing the inevitable futility of his request, and with Katherine's gun still close, the priest attempted a figurative last throw of the dice.

"Forgive me, Jesus," he cried, bypassing Katherine and sensing (correctly) that his pleas to her were falling on deaf ears. He was no doubt hoping for a more willing heavenly listener, and that, all along, needed only to invoke a higher authority.

Well, maybe not.

*

If photographer Mark Taylor had been there that night, he would have again used the Rule of Thirds to immortalise what happened in the next few minutes. The Cape Byron Lighthouse remained the dominant character, covering the left third of the frame. Below and to its right, two people were caught in fraught conversation: a man and a woman, both over sixty, and the man older than her.

The darker third was the ocean, so much of its menace implied and hidden, with only the reflections from the moon and the crashing waves suggesting its presence. The starlit sky would fill the frame on the upper right-hand side.

Mark learned early on from his brother Viv that the three rules of photography, in no particular order, were: get closer, get closer and get closer.

With that timeless advice in mind, he would choose a shorter fixed lens because his favoured long-focus lens would make the lighthouse look unnatural. 50 mm is standard and replicates what the human eye sees, but he would go for 85 mm or 135 mm, creating a mild compression. He would then walk towards the lighthouse to get the image he wanted in the frame. The lazy way is to stand still and use a zoom to frame the image. That's for amateurs.

Later, when processing his work, he would notice a man in the shadow to the left of the lighthouse, on the opposite side to the two main protagonists, but no more than ten metres from them – a tall man, perhaps 200 cm. The photo would not pick up the half-smile on his face or the Mediterranean skin tone.

But Mark Taylor wasn't there, and there was no photo.

*

The thing about photos is that they capture an isolated moment, and you never know what happened immediately before or, significantly in this instance, immediately after.

On the day President Kennedy was assassinated in Dallas in November of 1963, for example, amateur photographer Abraham Zapruder recorded it all on a silent 8mm colour motion picture with a Bell & Howell home-movie camera. In seeking a memento of the president passing by, he had no idea that his film would ignite a debate that would never end.

By demonstrating that the president's head jolted backwards when hit, the film demolished the theory that Lee Harvey Oswald was the lone assassin. All evidence, including the large exit wound in the back of the president's head, says that the bullet came from the front, and the Texas Book Depository, from where Oswald supposedly took the shot, was behind and to the right. Not possible. It raised questions that the American security establishment has never wished to answer, so they did what they've always done: they covered up, and they lied.

Zapruder began filming as the motorcade pulled onto Elm Street and recorded 486 frames over 26.6 seconds. Kennedy was enjoying himself and waving to the crowd. He clutched his throat when the first bullet hit, and then frame 313 shows the appalling fatal shot. At 12:30 the world was one thing, but by 12:31 it was another entirely.

History on the grand scale is changed in frames and seconds, as are our lives.

Ask Merryfield.

*

It's also true that Taylor's photo, had he been there, would not have picked up the tall man as he walked smoothly and silently towards the other two, nor would it have recorded the look of surprise on her face and something more like shock on the priest's.

The tall man said only a few words when he reached them. Indeed, a conveniently placed listening device would have heard him say kindly to the woman, "You won't be needing that," as he reached out and took her gun. At the same time, he removed his own; a suppressor was attached.

He would also have been overheard saying it was time for her to go, before adding assuringly, "I'll take it from here." The tall man then watched her walk down the hill towards her house near the beach. She didn't look back. The waves beat to their eternal rhythm, neither knowing nor caring what was happening at the lighthouse above.

Had they been interested, they would have heard Father Jack Merryfield – paedophile priest, destroyer of lives, killer of horses and disloyal associate of gangsters – say to the tall man, "Tell Sam I'm sorry."

To this, the tall man put his fingers to his lips. Merryfield had said enough and would say no more. Two seconds later, as the tall man raised the gun, the priest turned his head sharply to the right.

There would be no divine intervention.

54

Christmas Day, 2024

St Vincent's, The Gap

A fine day with a maximum of 28 degrees was forecast, a pleasant change in what had already been a volatile summer of storms and high temperatures. It was the first Christmas Jim and Alex would spend together as a married couple. If you'd told them, when they'd exchanged vows, that this is where and how they would share it, the newlyweds would scarcely have believed it. They drove north from Lennox Head, with Danny and Shannon sitting in the back seat. There was something faintly surreal about it.

Jim put the idea to join them the previous night, and a bit to his surprise, they accepted. Curiosity about the place that had figured so prominently in the investigation was part of the reason, but Christmas, with its accompanying memories, had been difficult for Shaw since his daughter Rachel's death. As it was for many others for whom the past loomed large on this day. They were on their way to St Vincent's; Jim, too, had promises to keep.

*

As they approached the outskirts of Brisbane, Celine Dion was singing 'O Holy Night'. It was one of the most played Christmas songs on Jim's Jukebox, but today it was coming from the radio and they could all hear it.

Oh holy night
the stars are brightly shining

It was based on a French poem written in 1843 by Placide Cappeau. As he often did of those who'd created masterpieces in the distant past, Jim wondered what Placide would make of his song being sung worldwide – and in this car – nearly two-hundred years later. It was set to music by Adolphe Adam, and with a few minor changes to the initial melody, the English version came courtesy of John Sullivan Dwight.

Canadian Anne Murray sang it with a simplicity and honesty that accentuated the lyrics, whilst Celine, like an Olympic gymnast getting points for difficulty, hit notes that the composers would never have imagined. Sometimes, she tried too hard to make a great meal from a meat pie, but her version of this song was sublime.

A thrill of hope the weary world rejoices
For yonder breaks a new and glorious morn

But there would be no glorious morn for Father Jack, of whom nothing had been heard, save for the telling of Katherine's story to Jim, since mid-July. As she'd recounted Merryfield's final moments, there was no listening device and no camera, so what was said of his fate would remain forever between the two of them and, with her permission, Dan Shaw and Shannon Leary.

Others only needed to know, as Dan and Adam Christopher informed their respective audiences, that a remarkable woman had given testimony about a man now dead. And that she hadn't killed him. They told their readers and listeners that they would leave it to the police to provide any further details. Detective Cassie Miller laughed when she heard that, aware that Jim Nicholas knew much more than he would (or could) ever share. For the second year in a row, her former partner was content to let the story drift quietly away.

A little like the missing priest.

*

As he said he would, and about which Jim harboured few doubts, Stan had made it. That only a few days remained for him was unimportant compared to the ones navigated to reach this one. Edna celebrated her 80th birthday the day before, and Simone's exam results indicated a bright future. Stan told her he would watch over her, and she never for a moment questioned it. Why would she? He kept his promises.

Jim introduced Alex, Dan, and Shannon to other congregants. They were made to feel welcome, and nobody cared about what they did or why they were there.

At 9:57, a stretch limousine of the type favoured by dignitaries and Russian oligarchs pulled up outside St Vincent's. Jim had last seen the car in its garage at Marseille Court on the Gold Coast and, hiding his surprise, walked toward it to welcome Sam Cassavetes.

Sam had left his casual clothes in the cabana, instead opting for a grey suit two shades darker than his hair, black loafers, and a white shirt. He wore sunglasses, which he removed and put in his left inside pocket; he knew a lot about respect. The driver had exited the car and opened the door for his much smaller and older passenger, who thanked him before saying, deliberately loud enough for Jim to hear it, "Park it around the back, Carlo."

Carlo?

Until then, Jim hadn't heard his name mentioned, and the tall man acknowledged it with his usual slight nod and half-smile. Carlo? He paid it no particular attention, but as Jim approached Sam, the penny dropped. Carlo. Italian for Charles. Charlie! And, at the first sign of his understanding, Sam's smile grew as he took Jim's outstretched hand in both of his. "After you gave me that message, I thought it was time to go to church again."

*

In recent weeks, with the closure of the parish looking inevitable, the numbers had grown dramatically as the local community thanked Father Ralph for all he had done. Before commencing his homily, he made the Sign of the Cross and extended his hands in greeting. He then looked out at all the faces, young and old, that were gathered, perhaps for the final time.

He welcomed everyone and made mention of those here for the first time. Father Ralph wanted them to know that in this place, they had no past and that this day was all they had – and it was enough. He looked down at Stan, who nodded his approval. He then spoke for no more than seven minutes, enough to give both the devout and the questioning plenty to think about.

"It's wonderful that we can share Christmas Day," he began. "It is a day of celebration. As Christians, we celebrate the birth of the child we believe to be the Son of God. This is a strange concept for many, and it can sometimes be a struggle for the rest of us. But it is, perhaps, not as complex as we occasionally make it sound." He said that with a self-deprecating smile before continuing, being sure to find the eyes of some of the children.

"The birth of every child is special, but on this day, we celebrate the birth of the most precious of all children. God was making the point about the miracle of life, even for those born into the most humble circumstances. We believe that He sent Jesus in human form to live amongst his creation and ultimately to die for it. In doing so, he told us there is nothing to fear in death. That *all shall be well*." And now Father Ralph, at the mention of the words from his dream, saw Jim smile and returned it.

"We live in a cynical age, in which we see many of our leaders and public institutions, including our Church, acting badly so often that it is easy to think that is how things always are. That, too, is part of the message of this day: it doesn't have to be that way.

Today, we see love all around and people being kind to each other. We celebrate family and friendship, reach out to the lonely, and give thanks to something bigger than ourselves. The great scientist Albert Einstein was once asked whether he believed in God, and responded with these words:

> *The problem is too vast for our limited minds. We are in the position of a little child entering a huge library filled with books in many languages. The child knows someone must have written all those books. It does not know how. It does not understand the languages in which they are written. The child dimly suspects a mysterious order in the arrangement of the books, but doesn't know what it is. We see the universe marvellously arranged and obeying certain laws, but only dimly understand these laws.*

They are beautiful words, but as Christians, we believe we do know something about the mystery – not all of it, but enough. We believe there is a God and that Jesus, in whose existence Albert also believed, was his son. Unlike scientists, we think faith – which can never be proven – counts as much as facts. That faith, like the birth we celebrate today, is itself a miracle and we can feel this way every day. Each new sunrise brings with it the chance of doing better, of being better. Today, we celebrate that together – as friends, family, and strangers. For Christians and non-Christians alike, that is quite something. I wish you all a very happy Christmas."

*

With Father Ralph's words still resonating, the congregation sang 'O Come All Ye Faithful', the words of which took on new meaning.

Then came the collection, and people gave what they could.

Father Ralph always made it clear never to give what you couldn't afford, and that he and 'head office' would get along just fine. As the plate made its way from hand to hand and then back to him, Father Ralph wondered where they would all be next Christmas. He looked at the money, blessed it, and gave thanks.

It was then that he noticed the Manila envelope that the small man of advancing years with swept-back grey hair had placed in the offertory plate. It was 228 mm x 304 mm (9" x 12") and the priest opened it, as curious as any child to see what lay beneath the wrapping. Therein were some official-looking papers and a brief note:

Dear Father,
I hope you don't mind if I visit from time to time.
Happy Christmas.
From Sam, Rosa and Maria

He looked at the papers. They were the deeds to the land and church, signed over to Father Ralph.

God, he thought, really does work in mysterious ways.

*

From his vantage point in the pulpit, Father Ralph could see all eyes were on him, and the sudden change in his demeanour. A burden lifted and a gift bestowed. They would learn the details later. He mouthed a silent *thank you* toward the old man and his tall assistant, who wasn't Max at all. He was Carlo, Charles, Charlie – and his smile had spread to both sides of his face.

There were five people in the pew at the front to Father's right. Alexandra, on the aisle, was sitting next to Jim and holding his hand; further along, Danny and Shannon looked at each other and grinned.

Seated between the two couples was a woman in her mid-60s of medium height and above-average looks. Her hair, which she wore loose and didn't quite reach her shoulders, was grey and her eyes a colour of blue you might see on the Barrier Reef.

She listened to Father Ralph talking about miracles and Einstein and, for the first time, agreed with every word he said. Many years ago, another priest had stolen her faith and identity, but she'd never lost her sense of awe and wonder. To herself, as the congregation now sang 'Silent Night', she spoke the words from the poem 'Invictus' by William Ernest Henley that had travelled this journey with her:

I am the master of my fate,
I am the captain of my soul

A careful observer would notice the hint of a tear in her eye and a tentative smile forming.

Her name was Katherine.

The End

Acknowledgements

This book is a mix of fact and fiction. Katherine, whilst uniquely herself, has much in common with Joan Isaacs, whose experience is chronicled in these pages. She and her husband, Ian, are good friends and have fought a long and courageous battle against the Catholic Church. They have also supported other victims of abuse in their attempts for recognition and justice.

With Joan's permission, I have at times used her words and story, including her family background and meetings with church officials.

It was Joan, not Katherine, who became Case Study 4 at the Royal Commission into the Institutionalised Responses to Abuse, the findings of which are accurately recorded in Chapter 48 and are available online. But it was Katherine, not Joan, who had the decisive meeting – and conversation – with Merryfield at the Cape Byron Lighthouse. By happy coincidence, the words at the end from 'Invictus' have been part of Joan's journey as well.

Father Jack Merryfield is a fictional character but did engage in some of the behaviours of another priest, as detailed by Joan at the Royal Commission. They should not be considered, however, to be the same person.

Father Ralph is also a creation, although he shares the qualities of my old school friend, the much-respected Anglican Reverend Dr Ralph Bowles, who is also a kind and gentle man. Wise, too.

The explanation of Canon Law in Chapter 28 is taken from Kieran Tapsell's 'Canon Law Through the Ages'. Professor Nicole Silver, who appears in the same chapter, does not exist, but the cases she highlights do. Forensic entomologist, Dr Gail Anderson, whose work is chronicled in Chapter 6, most certainly does.

The commentary by Adam Christopher, Dan Shaw, and Steve

Anderson is based on the news of the day as taken from various media outlets, including *The Australian, The Sydney Morning Herald, The Courier-Mail, The Wall Street Journal, The New York Times,* and *The Spectator.* Adam is a creation, but as fate would have it, I agree with many of the views he expressed, particularly on the appalling and tragic spread of antisemitism.

I am indebted to Mark Taylor for his explanation of the Rule of Thirds and his detailed knowledge of photography. Without Mark's photo, Father Ralph (and the rest of us) might still be wondering what happened to his assistant.

Likewise to my good friends on Bribie Island, Bruce and Helen McLachlan. Not only for their support, but for making me (and Jim Nicholas) aware of the Dunning/Kruger Effect in Chapter 27 and the wonderful story about Kris Kristofferson.

Michelle Marsden most certainly exists and designed the home occupied by Sam Cassavetes, who doesn't. You will find the house in Marseille Court, but not Sam. He and Harry Evans are creations, although some who have mixed in those circles might think they recognise them. The deeds they recall are mostly real.

T.J. O'Hara is a long-time American friend and commentator on my radio programs. He ran for the presidency in 2012 as an Independent candidate and, as mentioned in Chapter 47, was almost alone in predicting – to within a couple of points – Donald Trump's convincing win in the Electoral College.

Jason Dasey is a good friend who is incorrectly described as an exciting young radio talent by Jim Nicholas in Chapter 37. Jase is an accomplished media performer who has worked successfully all around the world, including with CNN, ESPN, and the BBC.

I'm not Catholic – and am inclined more towards the thinking of Einstein in the final chapter – but have done my best to reflect, from a layman's perspective, the position of the Church. As of this date, Pope Francis is in poor health, but that was not the case in the months during which the book was being written. All the quotes attributed to him are accurate.

The twin aims of the book were to capture, in real-time, five months of history without the benefit of hindsight and to tell the story of two people I admire immensely. I hope you enjoyed the journey.

My sincerest thanks to Mike Patman for his ongoing support of my writing. He is a trusted friend and brilliant financial planner. I recommend him without reservation at: michael.patman@patmanplanning.com.au

You won't find Dan Shaw at the email address mentioned in the book, but I am always available at: gncary@gmail.com

I would be delighted to hear from you.

Greg

February 1
2025

www.ingramcontent.com/pod-product-compliance
Lightning Source LLC
Chambersburg PA
CBHW020543020726
47494CB00006B/1897